THE
TRUTH
PACT

THE
TRUTH
PACT

THE
Truth About Love
DUET
BOOK ONE

USA *TODAY* BESTSELLING AUTHOR
C.M. ALBERT

THE TRUTH PACT
The Truth About Love Duet, Book One

Genre: Contemporary Romance/Women's Fiction

Cover Design: Cover Me Darling, LLC
Editing: Dot and Dash, LLC
Proofreading: Denise McGhee
Paperback Formatting: Alt 19 Creative

FOREWORD

The Truth Pact is my first time writing a deeply romantic love story that reads more like women's fiction than my usual steamy romances. That's why I call it a contemporary romance/women's fiction hybrid. I hope you love Olivia and Ryan's world as much as I do. This book takes place in western New York. Though the exact town is not specifically named on purpose, I modeled a great deal of it loosely after my hometown of Oswego, New York—where sunsets reign supreme off the majestic surface of Lake Ontario. I remember being a little girl, skipping stones across the lake's surface with my family, throwing seaweed at my brother, and racing to see which one of us would be brave enough to jump first into the frigid water in April, after another freezing cold winter. As a kid, I could never understand why I couldn't see across the other side to Canada, since it was "just a lake." Unless you stand on this Great Lake's shores, you can't quite grasp how ocean-like it feels.

New York holds a special place in my heart, as do its people. That said, I specifically chose certain elements of Oswego and the surrounding area to highlight by factual name to honor my heritage, while most of their town I created myself and is entirely fictitious. So, please don't be upset with the vast liberties I've taken with the setting. It was intentionally done from a place of love, while also weaving in fictional elements I needed for my storyline.

The end result is the same, and I hope you feel it too—a deep love and appreciation for the beautiful, lush, green, historical land I called home for so many years. There is so much to love about New York, and even though I reside in the South now, the Empire State will always hold a huge part of my heart.

I also want to acknowledge the family and friends I still have "back home," who give me the best reason to visit every now and again. Especially my oldest and dearest friend, Jen Cooper, whom I've loved like a soul sister since we were about five years old. We Joan-Jetted our way through childhood, boy crazy, with belly laughs so hard we'd usually end up crying—or almost peeing our pants. No matter how many miles separate us, the second we're reunited, we still giggle like the kindergartners we once were. There are some people who ride with you for a lifetime, and "Jenny" is mine.

So, my awesome readers, no matter where you live in this great country, I hope you can find a little slice of home somewhere in these pages and feel like the extended *ohana* you are to me. May your best reading days be ahead of you!

XOXO!
Love, Colleen

DEDICATION

The Truth Pact is dedicated to my dear friend, Erin, and her beloved baby girl in heaven, Kailey. "Even those who never fully bloom still bring beauty into the world."

— UNKNOWN

THE TRUTH PACT
Playlist

These songs spoke to my heart while writing this emotionally difficult story. The ones bolded absolutely wreck me and speak the loudest of the complicated emotions between Olivia, Ryan, and Brighton. I hope when you hear them, you get all the feels, too.

"Backbone" – Anthony Callea

"Best Thing" – Anthem Lights

"Can't Help Falling in Love" – Emma Heesters

"Certain Things" – James Arthur

"Circles" – Jana Kramer

"Clarity" – Kurt Hugo Schneider & Sam Tsui

"Free Fallin'" – Tom Petty

"Here" – Stars Go Dim

"I Don't Want to Love You Anymore (Reimagined)" – Caitlyn Smith

"Little Do You Know" – Alex & Sierra

"Lonely as Love" – Rhys Lewis

"Paper Houses" – Niall Horan

"Stay" – Jasmine Thompson

"Stitches" – Shawn Mendes

"The Heart Wants What It Wants" – Ali Brustofski

"Time After Time" – Adam Ezra

"Total Eclipse of the Heart" – Westlife

"Toxic" – Kurt Hugo Schneider

"What's Love Got to Do with It?" – Britton Buchanan

"When I Look at You" – Miley Cyrus

THE TRUTH PACT

THE
Truth About Love
DUET
BOOK ONE

Ryan Wells

Olivia North was everything I always wanted. From the moment I laid eyes on her, I knew nothing would stop me from having her. Not even being her professor. *In the end, I got her.* Got the white picket fence and historic home, too. But nothing could replace the babies we lost before they were ever born, or the sleepless nights that followed.

We made a pact once, in those early days of grief. We would always put each other first and be honest about everything. Because the only way through our mourning would be together. *Until it wasn't.* When our last baby was stillborn, I was afraid I'd lose Olivia forever. The vibrant woman I'd married was slipping away under the weight of her unbearable pain. So, when Brighton Kerrington moves in next door to renovate his uncle's property, and I see light return to those haunted blue eyes, what do I do? *The one thing that could cost me my entire world.*

I'd do anything to see Liv happy again—even if it means ripping my own heart in two to sew hers back together again. But when pleasure replaces pain, the truth exposes more than we bargained for. What was meant to bind us together in love might be the very thing that tears us apart.

They say the truth shall set you free. They never tell you the cost.

"I *love* her

and that's the

beginning

and end

of *everything*."

—F. Scott Fitzgerald

PROLOGUE

Olivia

THEY SAY PAIN ebbs and flows over time, until one day, you find yourself accidentally living in joy again. Then each step from there is a little bit easier. The end goal? Being back to normal, I suppose. You know how the saying goes—maybe you aren't really buried in a pile of manure; you're really just waiting to bloom.

Here's what I say: SCREW THAT SHIT.

I mean, seriously. Maybe your life really *is* just a pile of manure. Has anyone ever thought about that?

These are the thoughts that race through my head at three in the morning. Or when I'm in the shower, the scalding water never hot enough to burn all the memories away. But when I'm in my therapist's office? Nothing. Not an ounce of my pain bleeds out. I pay Dr. Paul a hundred and fifty dollars an hour to sit in silence. Until one day, he tells me I either need to go on antidepressants to start coping with my grief in a healthier way, or I should probably find a new therapist—because obviously I didn't trust him enough to open up about my losses.

"And you chose to walk away again?" my husband Ryan asked, exasperated. He ran his hand through his wavy, dark brown hair. It was longer than normal, since it was summer break and he'd chosen to take the semester off—an unprecedented move for Professor Wells. I'd never seen him take a break in the eight years I've known him.

"I didn't choose to do anything, Ryan. I never wanted to see that dipwad to begin with. You did. But I'm done. No more therapists. No more interventions. Just let me work through this on my own!"

"Wow," he said, stepping away from the kitchen island to finish putting the groceries away. "Alone. That's what you want? How's that fair to me? We made a promise, remember? We don't do things alone. We tough it out together. We *fight*, damn it."

"I'm tired of fighting," I said, dropping to the floor. I rested my back against the kitchen island, noticing how ugly the beachy blue color was for the first time. "I want to paint the island farmhouse red."

"Really, Olivia? That's all you've got?"

He set a can of black beans down onto the counter, then stormed from the kitchen. I couldn't figure him out anymore, or what would trigger his anger. All I'd wanted was for him to hold me. To make this suffering go away. But I no longer remembered how to reach out to him. How to ask for the emotional intimacy I knew I needed to heal. Tears pooled at the corners of my eyes, threatening to spill over. I slammed my head back, trying anything to ease the pain. It was a stupid idea. Now my head just hurt.

I don't know how long I sat there, but eventually the light started fading, and I knew it was getting late. My therapist—*former* therapist as of today—suggested I start a new hobby or take on a project. Anything to give me purpose, something to look forward to instead of the endless, open, hopeless road I saw before me.

I pulled out my phone to scroll through Pinterest for the first time in months, looking for the exact shade of red I knew I wanted for the kitchen island. Maybe Dr. Paul was right for once. Maybe a nice little home improvement project would at least distract me for a few weeks.

Bad idea.

The first thing that popped up in my feed must've been the last thing I'd searched for: gender neutral nursery designs. I threw my phone across the room, hearing it shatter. I didn't care. The pain shattering my heart was far worse. It stabbed me over and over again, until my tears finally came.

Ryan ran into the kitchen, squatting down in front of me. "Aw hell, Livy," he said when he saw my tears. "Come here. I'm sorry."

He sat on the floor next to me and pulled me onto his lap. I inhaled deeply, still loving the fresh, clean scent of his aftershave. He must've showered because his hair was damp, and the small, curled ends dripped water down the back of his shirt.

"I'm sorry," I said between body-heaving sobs. "I'm sorry I'm so fucked up. I'm sorry I don't know how to feel whole again."

"You *will* get better, hon. It's just going to take time."

"It's never going to get better, Ryan. This is who I am now," I said, my tears breaking into hysterical laughter. I waved my hand in front of me, as if it were so obvious. "I'm more comfortable here on the kitchen floor than I've been all day. I'm fucking broken."

"Not broken, just bent," he said, offering me a small, sad smile with the tired cliché.

That's when I realized he would never really understand what it was like to carry a child inside your body, and then deliver it stillborn. Or to lose two others before that to miscarriage.

It had been seven months since we buried our daughter last November. She was a perfect six pounds, eleven ounces. Soft, brown hair like Ryan's. But I'd had to deliver her knowing she was already dead. There's nothing I could say that would make him understand the sharp pain I felt almost every single moment of every single day since coming home from the hospital without our baby.

Life just wasn't meant to nest in my body.

So, no. I wasn't bent. I was all the way broken.

CHAPTER ONE

Ryan

OLIVIA WAS MOST at peace when she slept. It's when her face was the softest and she most resembled the woman I'd fallen in love with eight years ago. Back when we were Liv and Ry against the world. I couldn't remember the last time she'd even called me that.

No—scratch that. I could.

It was the day she found out she was pregnant with our daughter. I was in the middle of a lecture when my phone buzzed in my pocket. I *never* answered a call during class. It's why I had it on Do Not Disturb. The fact that the call still came through let me know the person had tried calling more than once and it was most likely an emergency.

"Excuse me," I told my students as I stepped out of the lecture hall to answer Livy's call.

"What's wrong?" I asked, fear gripping my heart.

"Ry," she whispered, her voice tender and sweet, "we're pregnant."

"What?" I ran a hand over the new beard I was sporting. I was still getting used to it then, so it was an unconscious habit. "Are you sure?"

"Yes!" she squealed. "When do you get home?"

"Well, I was supposed to have dinner with the department, but I'll cancel. Of course, I'll cancel. Do you want to go out and celebrate?"

"No," she said, her voice lowering. "I want to *stay in* and celebrate."

Relief flooded my heart. Other than for baby-making purposes, our sex life had become a little stale lately. The last few years had been about nothing more than trying to get pregnant and stay pregnant. Two miscarriages were enough to make even the strongest couple go through a dry spell. I was afraid to let hope take root, but Olivia's excitement was contagious.

"I'm definitely cancelling dinner then," I chuckled. "Want me to pick anything up on the way home?"

"No," she said, breathily, the woman I'd first met here at the university finally coming back to me. "You're all I want for dinner. And breakfast. And lunch. Get your cute ass home so we can celebrate, Ry."

Maybe we lost the baby because of me. They say it's bad luck to tell anyone before week twelve. We'd been through two other losses, so you'd think I'd be a seasoned pro at this kind of protocol by now. But no. My excitement got the best of me. The entire class noticed my changed demeanor when I walked back in, floating on cloud nine.

"Everything okay, Wells?" one of my students called out from the front row.

It was the one thing I let them do that other tenured professors didn't. They all called me by my last name. I liked to keep my classes informal—I found students learned best when they weren't terrified of their teacher.

"More than okay," I said, beaming. "We're having a baby!"

I wish I could take those words back now. Swallow them whole. I'd never told Olivia about it, either. I don't know why exactly. I knew it wasn't the reason Laelynn died. But our little flower of hope was still gone, and that moment haunted me every day since. The last thing I needed was for my wife to have yet another reason to push me away.

There was no more Liv and Ry. Just two broken people trying their best to hold things together—though these days, I wondered if there really were *two* of us trying to do that. Somedays, I felt as if I was the only one trying to figure out how in the hell to not just survive each day, but to heal and move on.

To make our way back to Liv and Ry again.

I knew, as I now watched her resting, that there wasn't anything I wouldn't do to get us back to that place again. I ran my fingers over a long strand of her hair, brushing it out of her face. I sometimes wondered what she dreamed about, but we didn't talk about stuff like that anymore. Not for my lack of trying. I started to climb out of bed slowly, not wanting to wake her, when she grabbed my hand.

"Ryan?" She sat up, looking around like she'd forgotten where she was, and what her life was like these days. "I had the strangest dream," she said, sinking back against her pillows.

I lay down with her, taking any opening I could get. "What happened?"

She curled against my side and rested her head on my chest. I held my breath. It had been so long since she'd touched me on her own. I didn't want to jinx it or mess things up.

"I was being chased by an angry zebra across a field in the grasslands of Africa. The grass was growing taller and taller the closer he got, until I suddenly fell down a hole and through a long, dark tunnel. I couldn't see a thing. When I landed, I was curled up inside of an ostrich egg, and there was another fetus inside with me. We were bloody and wet, but I felt safe. Until my teeth started falling out. Which freaked me out. So, I started punching the walls of the egg, trying to escape, when I suddenly saw a crack. A guy's hand reached in and pulled me out. I thought it was you, but he didn't really have a face. He just felt comfortable, somehow. My faceless savior. Who knows? Maybe it was my dad, because the next thing I knew I was sitting at Bev's, eating an ice cream cone with my father, like I used to when I was younger. He picked up a smooth, flat stone and skipped it across the lake's surface.

"Then he turned to me and said, 'Livy, I don't trust children. They're here to replace us.' That's when I noticed he was really the Tin Man from the *Wizard of Oz*, and he was rusting on the bench right in front of me. There wasn't a damn thing I could do about it. So, I picked up a handful of stones and kept right on trying to skip them across the water. That's when I realized I was wearing Dorothy's checkered blue dress and sparkly red shoes—though they were really a pair of Converse high-tops I'd bedazzled. I heard something whimpering and looked around. There wasn't a soul in sight except for my fossilized father on the bench. But there was a basket sitting next to him, so I leaned over and peeked inside."

"Do I even dare ask what you saw? I'm a little terrified at this point that a T. rex might've climbed out and eaten you or something."

She actually giggled. My heart relaxed for the first time in months.

"No. It was the cutest puppy I'd ever seen. I think it was a terrier of some sort."

"Let me guess? We're going to look for puppies today?"

She sat up, using her elbow for support as she looked at me. There was the faintest sparkle of light in her pale blue eyes. That's all I ever wanted. I would genetically engineer the perfect puppy and sit with the embryo until I'd Frankensteined the little bastard to life if that's what it took to make Liv smile again.

"You mean it?"

I tugged at a strand of her warm, honey blond hair. "Would it make you happy?"

Her brows furrowed, and I worried I'd screwed up the moment once again. But her smile returned, and she nodded. "I really think it might help."

"Then puppy shopping it is," I said, ready to hop out of bed and shower.

She grabbed my hand again. This time, something old and familiar sparkled back at me from within her eyes. I didn't dare hope I was reading her mood right. But she pulled me back into bed with her, and for the next hour, she finally let me in.

CHAPTER TWO
Olivia

RY WAS ALWAYS so patient with me. Even in the early days—he was the holy, I was the wild. How we'd grown so distant over the past few years, I had no idea. I mean—I knew why, but I didn't know *how*. Not when he'd been the air I breathed in the morning, the succulent breaks I'd taken in the afternoons, and the peace I drifted off to sleep with each evening.

Now, I couldn't eat. I couldn't sleep. I couldn't *breathe*, for god's sake. But somewhere along the way, *our* grief had become *my* grief. Maybe it was the day he asked me if we could just move on. Slowly, surely, it was as if the hinges on my heart started to swing closed. Until one day, I couldn't feel anymore. I didn't want to get out of bed. I didn't want to be Liv, much less Liv and Ry.

No one tells you that when you become pregnant everything changes. Not only your body and your home as you prepare for the baby's arrival, but your heart. Your very soul.

It expands in a way you can't imagine is possible. I mean, you are literally growing another human being inside your body. It only lives because you live. So, what happens when it dies?

Exactly. A part of me died, too.

After two miscarriages, I was beginning to doubt I would ever have a pregnancy that stuck. We were about to give up trying all together when our miracle baby, Laelynn, came along. Her pregnancy was different. I felt great the whole time. She was growing and hitting every milestone. We'd even decorated her nursery.

One day she was kicking inside of me, strong as can be. Then, slowly, the kicks grew less frequent, causing me to worry. I'll never forget the day I realized I couldn't remember the last time she'd kicked. That, suddenly, she wasn't anymore.

Nothing has been right ever since.

And no matter how great Ryan is, he can never understand what it felt like to have to push her tiny, lifeless form from mine, knowing my body failed her. Of course I wanted to die, too.

I suffocated under the weight of an unspeakable grief the moment we got home and faced her empty nursery. I couldn't even help Ryan as he disassembled her room, putting every-thing into storage so I didn't have to be reminded that instead of coming home with us, we would have to bury her.

Soon, my grief morphed into self-loathing every time I looked in the mirror. I couldn't pass by one without seeing the curve of my belly where she'd lived. Without feeling the hollow emptiness that was there now, or the full weight of my breasts that would never feed her. I felt like a complete and utter failure—blaming my body on my inability to give her the life she was meant to have.

Ryan still held hope that "maybe someday" we could try again. I wasn't quite so sure. I'd gone on birth control so my body could take a break. I wasn't sure if I could live with myself if we lost one more baby. There were some days I wish we'd never started trying. It was *so* good when it was just Liv and Ry. What I called "the before."

But on my darkest days, there is the small, guilty wish that maybe if I hadn't taken Ryan's class, I never would've met him to begin with, which would've led me down a whole different path in life—maybe one without so much heartache.

So, when Ryan asked if I wanted to get a puppy—like the one I saw in my dream—something in me stirred. If I couldn't give a human life, maybe I'd be better off with the four-legged variety. My stupid therapist *had* suggested the same thing a few weeks ago—said something about how animals help us heal. Well, I wasn't getting a puppy to heal. I was getting a puppy to have something to *do*. To keep my mind off the fact that I would probably be introducing Laelynn to solids right now. Or how she would be crawling, so we'd have needed to install safety locks and baby gates. The *Parents* magazine email I'd gotten just yesterday was a stark reminder of the milestones we were missing with our daughter. Each time something like that was delivered to me, it felt like a knife to my chest. A constant reminder of our loss.

So, for the first time in weeks, I showered, dried my long hair, and then took the time to style it with my hot rollers. I even put on a little lip gloss and mascara. Instead of my usual yoga pants, I pulled on a pair of dark jeans, sandals, and a cute boho tank top.

"Whoa," Ryan said, hearing me come down the stairs. We lived in a historic home in the city, so everything creaked in this house. I loved it.

"Liv, you look ..." He stood, shoving his hands in the pockets of his jeans. "You look like Liv again."

I knew what he meant. I felt like that woman again, just the tiniest bit. But a part of me wished he would've just let it go. Not said anything. I was tired of talking about everything all the time. Of making everything about *that*. Even if it was. The thing I didn't want to examine too closely was the fact that outside of our loss, we didn't have much to say these days. We didn't have much to celebrate either. Or plan. Or dream about. It was just two lonely, broken people in a large, creaky historic home that Ryan bought me because it once seemed like the perfect family home. For our perfect family.

The myth of perfection was a bitch.

INSTEAD OF GOING to the shelter as I thought we would, Ryan surprised me when he drove out to the country instead. I didn't ask questions because that required energy. Ryan was listening to NPR, so I opened my Kindle and browsed my selections. It had been too long since I'd read, even though it had once been my favorite pastime. The only problem is I wasn't exactly in the mood for one of the rom-coms I'd normally read. I think I'd throw my fist through the car window if I had to read about some stupid chick's "meet-cute" with the hunky barista who happened to live across the hall in her new apartment building. Gag.

The only thing that caught my eye was a dark romance that was based on a true story. Even if Ryan and I weren't having much sex these days, it didn't mean I didn't think about it. Hell, that was one of the things that first drew us together like rabbits in heat.

"Whatcha reading?" he asked, glancing over at my Kindle.

I turned the device so he couldn't see. "Nothing that interesting."

He pulled off onto yet another country road. "Well, we're almost there."

"Where exactly is 'there'?"

"It's a surprise I really think you're going to like," he said, winking.

That wink had once done unspeakable things to my insides. Heck, it did something to *all* his students' insides. I wasn't stupid. He was a legend on campus—by far the hottest professor any of us had ever had. The youngest, too. There were only nine years between us, which seemed like nothing now. But when I was a twenty-three-year-old MBA student, and he was my thirty-two-year-old teacher, it had been quite the coup. Of course, we had to wait until I graduated before anyone could know we were officially dating. Even then, we acted as if we'd met outside of school. But everyone seemed to know it was a nudge (wink wink) story.

I glanced over at Ryan as he drove. Even at forty, he was still the most handsome man I'd ever laid eyes on. He had boyish good looks with dimples for days, dark brown hair, and a closely trimmed beard. On the rare occasions when he still wore his glasses, it was game over. He caught me looking at him, and his eyes warmed as they held mine.

The moment passed quickly, though, when we pulled onto a never-ending driveway in the middle of nowhere. "What are we doing here?"

"Patience, Livy."

When we got out of the car, we were met with an enthusiastic greeting from a small, curly dog.

"Sandie!" a woman shouted from a small building behind the yellow farmhouse where we parked. "Come here, you silly girl."

The dog did a couple circles, as if chasing her own tail, then darted back to her owner, a plump, older woman with brown, tight curls, much like her pet.

It was hard not to smile. The dog looked like a miniature dust mop. She was the sweetest toffee color, and her fur looked so soft, almost as if she were a stuffed animal of an actual dog. I glanced up at Ryan and he grinned, taking my hand as we made our way to a small barn.

"I'm Regina," the woman said as we followed her through the double doors, "and these are Miss Sandie's puppies."

The woman moved aside to let Ryan and me see over the small enclosure, and my heart nearly melted. In the corner of the pen was a mountain of puppies, their fat tummies rising and falling as they slept. They were all different shades of tan, brown, or brown and white, so it was hard to tell where one puppy stopped and another started.

"I'll leave you to look at them. Just give me a holler if you want to take one home."

"We're really here to get one?" I asked, looking up at my husband with hope.

"Well, if you make a connection with one, absolutely. Regina's daughter works at the university, and she sent an email around to faculty a couple weeks ago, asking if anyone wanted a Cavapoo from her mom's new litter. I was thinking about getting you one as a surprise, but when you dreamed about it last night—well, I took that as a sign," Ryan said. "Go on, get in there."

I stepped over the small barrier and sat in the center of the ringed enclosure. A couple of the puppies yawned and stretched, shaking their bodies of sleep. One puppy stayed where it was, even as others got up and started jumping on my legs and trying to chew the beads on my sandals. I reached over to pet the sleeping one and found its fur incredibly soft. Something about the lone puppy tugged at my heart.

It finally did a full-body stretch, its arms and legs going out like Superman, with the most adorable yawn. Its perky ears lifted, and the puppy finally noticed me. I bent over, lifting it with both hands and bringing it to my chest. That's when I noticed it was a boy dog, and he had an adorable patch of white fur running from his belly all the way up to his chin. Instead of acting crazy and jumping out of my arms or licking my face, he snuggled deeper against my chest, burying his head under my armpit and making me laugh.

I looked up at Ryan, my eyes full of love.

"Regina!" Ryan called out. "I think we found the one we want."

The elderly woman joined us inside the barn again and clucked with approval. "Good choice! Stitch is the runt of the litter, so he's a little quieter than the rest. But he's the sweetest of the bunch if you ask me."

"Why'd you name him Stitch?" I asked, running my fingers along his head and down his back. It was such a soothing gesture. I could see why dogs might be good, natural therapy.

"When he was first born, he was really tiny—and ugly," she said. She held up two hands in surrender. "Sorry, but it's true."

I looked down at the beautiful, plump puppy and couldn't imagine anyone ever thinking he was ugly. I kissed the top of his head and closed my eyes, inhaling his sweet puppy smell.

"Ever watch the Disney movie *Lilo & Stitch*?" she asked. When I shook my head no, she continued. "Hawaiian girl named Lilo adopts what she thinks is a small, ugly dog, but it turns out to be a genetic experiment from an alien planet that was made to cause chaos and destruction. Trust me—it gets better," she said, laughing when she saw my horrified face.

"In Hawaii, there's a concept called *ohana*, which means family. Because Lilo's heart is so open, she teaches Stitch to care about others through her own acts of faith, love, and this idea of ohana. She understood that sometimes your family may not look the way you planned, or be the one you were born into, but it's even better, because it's the one you create. Stitch was our reminder that even the littlest runt is an important part of our ohana."

"Well, shit," I said, tears dripping from the corner of my eyes and onto my cheeks. Stitch chose that moment to stand on his hind legs and place the soft pads of his paws right onto my face. Then he licked the tears, and my nose, and my mouth until I was laughing and had to pull him away. When our eyes met, I knew. Yeah, he most definitely wasn't the family I imagined, but maybe he was the one I *needed* right now.

"So, what'dya think?" Regina asked.

I would never say it to anyone else, but what I was really thinking was that maybe the little fur ball would be the one to finally stitch my broken heart back together again. I smiled, looking up at Ryan when I answered her.

"You had me at ohana."

CHAPTER THREE

Ryan

WHEN WE PULLED into our driveway, it was well past dinnertime. Olivia attached a leash onto the body harness Regina gave us and took Stitch to the backyard to do his business. Luckily, our corner lot had a white picket fence (yeah, I know) surrounding the backyard, and I could already see Liv and Stitch spending hours there together. I had a feeling the little runt might be just the thing we needed to pull Liv out of her funk.

I was shutting the trunk of my Jeep Grand Cherokee when I looked up, noticing a couple of work trucks in the driveway next door at the Kerrington property again. "Huh," I said, lifting the small box of dog supplies Regina had gifted us with.

A young guy came bounding down the front steps of the historic property, no shirt on, his T-shirt slung casually over his extremely sculpted shoulders. He nodded his head toward me.

"Hey, man. This your house?" he asked.

"Yeah," I said, setting the box onto the hood of my SUV and making my way across the yard. I extended my hand to say hello.

The guy was a lot bigger up close, and not quite as young as I'd first thought. He shook my hand firmly.

"Brighton," he said, his jaw a little too sharp and square for my liking, but his eyes were kind enough, saving him from the whole douchey asshole vibe.

"Ryan," I said, squeezing his hand back just as firmly. "You doing some work over there?"

"Oh, yeah. It was my uncle's place. The family's doing some renovations this summer. Probably putting it on the market in the fall," he said. "Thing sat here empty for way too long."

"We were wondering if anyone was gonna fix the place up," I said, glad to hear the dilapidated property was getting restored to its former glory. That was one of the reasons why Liv and I loved ours so much. There's character in an older home. "Always wondered what it looked like in there after being vacant so long."

"Wanna come take a look?" the guy asked, using his shirt to wipe his brow.

"We'd love to sometime," I said. "But you look like you've put in a long day. And we just got back home with a new puppy, so I should probably go give my wife a hand."

"Nice," the guy said, looking over my shoulder. Liv was standing in the backyard, holding onto a small rope toy and teasing the puppy as it jumped to capture it with his mouth. Liv's face was flush with pleasure for the first time in almost a year. She was breathtaking with her long, blond hair falling in waves down her back. The smile I'd missed so much brought out the dimples on each side of her full mouth, giving her the quintessential girl-next-door vibe, even though she was every inch a woman. From the look in Brighton's eyes, he hadn't missed how captivating she was either.

"What a cute dog" was all he said. But a man's not stupid. He can tell when another guy is checking out his wife.

I drank in her energy, unsure when I would see it again. It was almost like having the old Liv back. I could hardly blame the guy.

"It's gonna take some getting used to," I said. I ran my hand over the back of my neck and turned my attention back to the neighbor's nephew. "Just swing by sometime when you have a free minute to show us around. We'd love to hear your plans. We got lucky when we moved in here. The whole place had been restored immaculately. We didn't have to do a thing to it—thank god."

Brighton laughed. "That's what I'm hoping your new neighbors will say someday."

"You're welcome to come check out our place if you want. Whoever renovated it paid an insane amount of attention to the littlest details. It's what made Liv fall in love with it."

"Liv?"

"My wife," I said, not sure why I didn't like the way her name sounded coming from his lips. Truth be told, he was probably closer to her age. I doubted he was even thirty yet.

"Yeah," he said, glancing back at her one last time. "Well, I better head out. It's been a long day and I could use a beer about now."

"Nice meeting you," I said. "Good luck with the reno."

"Thanks," he said, yanking the gray shirt from his shoulder and shrugging into it before climbing into an older-model, white Silverado. He unrolled the window and cranked some

Tom Petty as I gathered up the small box and headed down the stone walkway to our front porch.

Brighton waved at me from his truck before making a right at the corner of our house, driving past Liv on his way out of the neighborhood.

"I MET MR. Kerrington's nephew today," I told Olivia later.

We were in the study, sitting on the carpet and playing with the puppy. Between this and going to get Stitch together earlier, it was the longest I'd spent with my wife in months.

She looked up, only vaguely interested in what I was saying. "Oh, that's nice. I didn't think Mr. Kerrington was still alive."

"He's not," I said, patting the floor and grinning when Stitch pounced my hand. "The family's renovating and selling."

She lifted her head, finally intrigued.

Olivia was a designer—well, she'd *been* a designer, before our lives imploded. She owned her own interior design firm, Live Well Interiors. We thought it was cute because who didn't want to live well? And it was especially clever since it was so close to Olivia's real name—Liv Wells. Though the business was still technically operating, Liv hadn't done much paid work over the last few years. It fluctuated between each pregnancy and each loss. This last stretch of time off had been her longest yet.

"Would you like a tour of the house? I know you've always been curious what the inside looked like."

"You really think he'd let us?" she asked, trying not to sound too excited.

"Already talked to the guy about it today. Name's Brighton."

"Brighton?" she asked, scrunching her nose. "Brighton Kerrington? That sounds pretentious."

I thought about the man who'd shaken my hand, with his tan, ripped chest, messy blond hair, and pale green eyes. His biceps were sculpted from an honest day's work, and the two tattoos he sported said anything but pretentious.

"He was nice enough," I said, shrugging. "I hope you don't mind, but I told him he could pop over here sometime to check out our place, too."

She chewed the corner of her mouth, less excited now. I knew that would be a stretch for her, having someone else inside our house. It was her safe place, her sanctuary. Even more so after we lost Laelynn. She'd spent far too much time in it over the last seven months.

"I can make something up, maybe say it's not a good time," I said, not wanting to upset her.

"I'll think about it." She picked up Stitch, then stood, cradling the puppy to her chest. "I hope you don't mind, but today took a lot out of me. I'm taking him out to go potty, then I may sleep in the guest room down here. That way I can let him out at night without having to wake you."

"Liv—"

"It's not permanent. Maybe just a few nights. Till Stitch can make it through the night in his crate without peeing."

I bit back my frustration. Today had been a good day, and I didn't want to set her back. But this was not going to fly for long. We'd spent too many nights apart already after Laelynn died. One excuse had led to another before she just gave up and started sleeping alone downstairs and shutting me out even more.

It had taken a lot of work to get her back into our bedroom. I wasn't letting a puppy come between us—no matter how cute he was.

"Truth?" I asked, knowing she'd never break our pact to be honest at all costs, no matter how much it hurt the other person.

"Truth."

I breathed a sigh of relief, then wrapped my arms around her. "I love you," I said, kissing her forehead goodnight. "I think Stitch is going to be a nice distraction for us."

She tensed in my arms, and I knew instantly it was the wrong thing to say.

"I don't need a distraction, Ry. I need Laelynn, and that's not an option. Everything else is just second best."

As she walked out of the study with Stitch in her arms, I wondered if she felt that way about me, too.

CHAPTER FOUR

Olivia

LOVED STITCH. I really did. But a dark wave of sadness washed over me ever since we brought him home. I'd taken to sleeping in the guest bedroom so I could take him out of his crate at night to go to the bathroom. Like clockwork, every night at 2:00 a.m., I put him on the leash and walked him down our long driveway and back up again on autopilot. Maybe it was the interrupted sleep. Maybe it was the grief I couldn't escape no matter what I tried. Either way, I spent the next week lying in bed crying again, like I had right after the funeral.

Having a puppy should've helped, but all it did was remind me of the daughter we'd never get to raise. It wasn't fair that Laelynn would never meet Stitch or get to play with him in our fenced-in yard.

Ryan tried. Lord knew the man was a saint. But my heart ached so badly I could hardly breathe most days. I had nothing to get up for. No job. No daughter. No joy. Just a big, empty void that not even the new addition to our ohana could fill.

A couple of times, I caught Ryan over in the neighbor's yard, talking to some guy—though I never got a good look at him from my bedroom window. Ryan was spending more and more time next door and often came back sweaty and smiling. A few times, he even went to have a beer with Brighton, coming home late and affectionate.

He popped his head in the guest room today to say hi and see how my night was. I wanted to say: *It was like shit. That's how it was. Just like the other night. And the night before that.*

But the hopeful look in his warm brown eyes stopped me. I was dead inside, but I wasn't cruel. The reason I fell in love with Ryan, other than our earth-shattering chemistry, was because of his compassion for others, and the way he could easily put himself in someone else's shoes. I'd seen him do it time and time again for other students, and then one day, I'd needed his compassion, too. The day I'd found out that my adoptive parents had died in a freak boating accident. I was shaking when I went to his office to explain why I wasn't going to be in class the following week.

The lines between professor and student evaporated in that moment as he gathered me into his arms to comfort me. He later told me he didn't treat other students with *that* kind of compassion but was often a sympathetic ear for them.

Me? I was different. I was the one who finally captured Professor Wells's attention for good. We both knew it the instant he touched me. We didn't say anything—especially since I was consumed by the grief of losing my parents—but the look that passed unspoken between us transcended time and space. It was a silent knowing. An acknowledgment passed between us that whatever it was we were feeling, it would eventually need to be explored.

That exact moment is when I started to believe that Ryan could be my soulmate.

"What are you thinking about?" he asked, coming into the room. He sat on the edge of the bed and stroked Stitch's back. Even though the puppy now slept on the bed more than he did in the crate, it wasn't a lie. I took him out religiously every night at 2:00 a.m.

"I miss you," I said, surprising myself. "I was just remembering how you treated me after my parents died, when you hardly knew me."

"There was always something special about you," he said, squeezing my leg through the blanket.

Even though his hand was over the thick, waffled fabric, it still shocked me how much I responded to his touch. We hadn't had sex more than a handful of times over the last seven months. We'd tried too soon after Laelynn's death, but it's not exactly sexy when your wife is crying while you're trying to get her to orgasm. That put an end to that. I just hadn't been ready to let him inside me. I couldn't explain it—and he wouldn't have understood. But my body was still a shrine to the memory of our daughter, not a safe port for my husband. It felt like a betrayal, as if our making love would wash away the memory of how she felt being inside of me.

Not that Ryan wasn't willing to keep trying. He initiated intimacy often—no matter how many times I rejected him. It wasn't because I didn't love him, or that I wasn't attracted to him. I just felt disassociated, if that makes sense. My body is there, but my heart and soul are usually somewhere else. Maybe in a little field somewhere, with a stream, and flowers.

And Laelynn, crawling through the grass on chubby, dimpled hands and knees.

But I was rarely in our house on West Liberty Street where my heart and soul belonged.

So, it surprised me that I was feeling something again so soon after making love to Ryan only a few days ago. Or had it been a week? I couldn't remember. Time meant little to me now. But there was something different about him—though I couldn't put my finger on what it was exactly. He seemed more like the man I'd fallen head over heels in love with all those years ago. His spirit felt lighter somehow, almost playful.

"Liv, you know I'll always protect you and be here for you, right?" he said, his eyes as intense, passionate, and steady as the day I met him. "I only want to make you happy. It's all I've ever wanted."

"I know," I said quietly, pulling him down for a kiss. I could tell he was as surprised as I was, but Ryan never turned away an opportunity to connect. He once told me he physically craved everything about me. And as he worshipped my body for the next hour, he proved that no matter how shitty I've been to him, that hasn't changed.

I just wished I could say the same.

Sometimes, I could hardly remember who I was anymore. I'd been prepared to be someone's mother, before that dream was snatched away from me. Now, I was just an empty vessel. No matter how many times I made love to Ryan, he would never be able to fill the void that Laelynn left behind.

ON FRIDAY, I finally got to meet the infamous Brighton Kerrington. Apparently, while I'd been spending my days curled under a blanket in the dark, Ryan had been bro-ing it up with the neighbor's nephew. I didn't know what to expect when we crossed the yard so I could finally see inside their family home. The rest of the crew had sloughed off for the day, but Brighton stuck around to give me a private tour of their work in progress.

What I never saw coming was the godlike man leaning back on the front steps, with his T-shirt off and slung casually over his broad shoulders. His eyes were closed as he worshiped the last rays of the day's sun. Everything about him was hard, raw, sexual power. My mouth ran dry as my eyes traveled down his perfectly sculpted chest, over washboard abs, and finally to a V so prominent and mouthwatering, I nearly lost my footing on the uneven terrain.

Ryan was holding my hand as we neared, and I was glad. Otherwise, I wasn't sure my legs would support me. I'd only ever had this kind of reaction to a man once before, and it was the day I stepped into Lecture Hall 303A. I'd been early because I was nervous and getting there first would give me time to calm my nerves and get situated before the other students arrived. I didn't deal well with change, so this was par for the course each new semester.

The classroom was small and intimate, configured with semicircular, stadium-style seating. With no one else in the room, there was no escaping the devastating brown eyes that connected with mine. Or the dimples that quickly flashed when his mouth curled into a grin that nearly decimated me.

Ryan had waved his hand, suggesting I take a front row seat. I wanted the floor to open and swallow me whole.

"Professor Wells," he'd said, extending his hand. He didn't look like my other professors in either my undergrad or graduate courses. His demeanor and presence were physically disarming. The man oozed sexuality and confidence.

I set my books down where Ryan had pointed and reached out to take his hand. It sounds corny, even now, but when he cupped my hand warmly and shook, I felt a spark so intense and real it was alarming. He was my *professor*. I quickly let go, running my hand over my hair, which I'd taken a painstaking amount of time perfecting for my first day of classes.

I licked my lips, any coherent reply escaping me.

"And you are?" he'd asked, smiling.

He was sitting on the tabletop near my seat, his sports coat hanging over the back of the lecture chair, his sleeves rolled up his muscled forearms. Worst of all? He was wearing dark-framed glasses, and I literally couldn't focus on anything beyond those and the kind brown eyes staring back at me, amused.

"Olivia," I finally said, laughing at my own delayed response. "Olivia North."

"North," he repeated as if etching my name into a permanent database inside his brain. "That certainly won't be hard to remember."

"Why is that?"

"It's a cardinal direction," he said, as if that answered everything. "The polar stars are permanently visible in the night sky, so many people believe the north is god's celestial dwelling. It represents permanence. Eternity."

If we'd been in a bar, I would've thought he was using a cheesy pickup line to get in my pants, but the man knew his stuff. And there was nothing humorous about the way he traced my lips with his eyes or held my gaze for what felt like an eternity.

It was the beginning of my obsession with Ryan Wells.

As I stood with my husband now under the bright, late-day sun—once again unable to formulate a coherent sentence—the familiar, unsettling feeling of my heart slipping somewhere beyond my control washed over me.

That was the moment I knew my obsession with Brighton Kerrington began.

CHAPTER FIVE

Ryan

SOME MOMENTS BURN themselves in your psyche so deeply you know it will irrevocably change your life as you know it. Olivia meeting Brighton was one of those moments, and I wished immediately I could take it back. As their eyes locked, and my new friend reached out his hand to shake Liv's, I knew the damage was done.

I wanted to vomit.

She was looking at him the *same exact way* she'd looked at me the first time we met. Not everyone believes in love at first sight, and I probably would've called it hogwash before meeting Olivia, too. But after I met her, I knew Liv was the one. My heart literally held up its white surrender flag and called the game the minute she walked into my classroom. And while I couldn't say the same today, our love story had once been a textbook fairy tale come true. But as I stood there watching Olivia and Brighton introduce themselves, it felt as if the pages of our romance were curling, darkness threatening to burn everything we'd worked so hard to build.

And yet, there was something breathtaking about seeing the light return to her eyes. She turned to me, excitement bubbling over. She was saying something, but I hadn't heard a word she'd spoken. I focused on her lips—the ones I'd memorized over the years. The ones that fit my own as if they were made specifically for me.

"Sorry. I spaced out for a minute. What's that?"

She laughed, and the musical tone cascaded over my chest and slammed into my heart, capturing the rare, elusive sound.

"Brighton was telling me he's interviewing interior designers, and he'd love to see my portfolio!"

"That's great," I said. Work of any kind would be therapeutic for Olivia and help her get out of the house, where she seemed to dwell too deeply in her grief lately. "Maybe you want to check the place out first though? It would be a big job."

Her bright blue eyes glowed as she looked back to Brighton and started talking design elements and vision again. I had to look away. I focused instead on the front of the historic home. It was large and square, with two dormer windows at the top and a large, open-air front porch that ran the length of the house. Semicircular steps led up to the porch, and a circular portico supported by colonial columns capped off the stately entrance. I couldn't help but notice the chipping, sage green paint and wondered what color the Kerringtons would paint the house.

That's where my mind went, because every cell in my body couldn't handle what was happening right in front of me as I followed them the rest of the way up the front steps.

I didn't know if I could join them inside and bear witness to whatever the hell was happening. Was it all in my mind? I mean, just because Olivia was looking at Brighton the way she'd looked at me once didn't mean anything. She'd just met the man, for god's sake. But something Brighton said made her laugh again, and I found myself balling my fingers into fists when she placed her hand on Brighton's upper arm, as if it were so funny she almost fell over laughing.

When his gaze slid back to mine, and he saw the way I was watching them, the cocky smile I'd never minded before vanished. He grabbed his T-shirt—white this time—and slid it down over his fifty pack or whatever the heck he had.

While Brighton had noticed my reaction, Olivia hadn't.

I stood there feeling helpless, engulfed in the heat pulsating off the porch's floor from a day of absorbing the sunlight, bearing witness to the heat now radiating from every pore of my wife's tantalizing body. She'd worn torn jean shorts today, the kind where the pockets peeked from the bottom of the frayed hemline. At five-six, Liv was all legs. Tan, muscular legs built from years of tennis, kickboxing, and jogging. And even though it hadn't been that long since Liv delivered Laelynn, her body had bounced right back, the extra curves making her only that much more desirable.

Her breasts were still a little rounder too, and I could see the outline of her padded bra beneath the thin material of her white tank top. She'd thrown on some loose sea-green wrap, though the material was silky and transparent, and the cream-colored fringe only drew my attention back to her thighs where the length fell. It did nothing to really cover her, and I hated my desire to hide her, as if she were the problem and not me.

"You coming?" Brighton asked, moving aside so Olivia could go in first.

I shook my head. "We're actually grilling out tonight. I've already seen the place a dozen times. Why don't you guys go ahead? I'll go light the Egg."

Liv peeked her head back out the front door and looked concerned as she glanced between me and Brighton. "You're not coming?"

I shook my head. "Nah. You're in good hands. I have a feeling I'll get bored anyway, listening to all the design talk. I'd rather chill with Stitch by the grill with an ice-cold beer."

I couldn't help but notice the longing in Brighton's eyes at the mention of burgers and beer. I sighed, wondering if my decision would be the straw that broke the camel's back—or whatever the stupid saying was.

"Why don't you join us for dinner? We can finally show you the place—and maybe Liv could grab her portfolio," I suggested.

It was a Friday night, so I assumed someone as young and good looking as Brighton would have better things to do than to hang with an old married couple. So, when a grin broke out across his face, and his chest puffed out, I knew I'd made a mistake.

"You sure you don't mind me crashing your dinner?" he asked, looking at Liv now. Even I could see the electricity pulsating between them.

My wife licked her lips, and for a moment, I thought she was about to have a panic attack at the thought of having someone inside our home—her sanctuary. But she shrugged her shoulders as if it were no big deal. Like we did this every Friday night.

"Sure, why not? It sounds like fun," she said, looking up into Brighton's green eyes. I couldn't help but notice the way they matched her summer wrap. "Besides, Ryan makes the best burgers. You're probably starving after working so hard all day."

"Awesome. I'll show Olivia around, then take a quick shower. Trust me when I say you won't want me over otherwise."

I nodded, backing my way down the porch steps. It was hard to believe that I felt on steadier ground walking backward down a cement staircase than I did right now about the future of my marriage.

I'd wanted the light to come back to Liv's eyes for months. I just never anticipated that it would be because of anyone other than me.

CHAPTER SIX

Olivia

THE HOUSE HAD so much potential. For the first time in months, I was able to focus on something other than my pain. The idea of putting storyboards together for each room had me excited again, and I hoped the feeling would last. As we walked from room to room, I couldn't stop the design visions from flooding my head and my heart.

Brighton started up the grand staircase to the second floor, but then paused, looking down at me. He looked like a Greek god standing there so tall. The last rays of sunlight saturated the foyer, streaming in from the back windows upstairs, casting a halo around his warm blond hair.

"You can see it, can't you?" he asked, quietly. He looked around the house, his eyes full of hope. "This place is something special, isn't she?"

I'd never heard someone else use a gender for a house like I did. But houses had energy, and this one was distinctly feminine. I couldn't help but grin, appreciating that he was the type of man to notice something like that.

"She is."

"Come on," he said, taking the stairs two at a time. "The best part is up here."

The house was already spectacular enough, even if she was currently stripped down to her bare bones. I couldn't imagine what he was so excited to show me. He led me down the hallway to where a set of ornate doors sat closed. The original cherry wood could still be seen under the flaking blue paint someone had covered them with long ago. I cringed, causing Brighton to laugh.

"Sorry," I said. "But who would do something so horrendous?"

"That would be my uncle, Isaiah. He did a lot of crazy things in the end. Which is one of the reasons the repair work has been so extensive. However, this was his sanctuary. It's the one room he didn't touch, so it's still mostly in its original glory. Here," he said, putting his hand over my eyes.

I drew in a deep lungful of air, my heartrate accelerating. I knew it was wrong for my body to be responding like this to a stranger. But the feel of his large, strong fingers next to my skin sent goose bumps down my arms.

He led me through the doors and stopped, his body closer to mine than I'm sure it would've been if Ryan joined us on the tour. Brighton's hand slid from my eyes, resting on my upper arm from behind.

"Open," he said, his breath warm on my neck.

I stood there, breathing deeply, almost afraid to look. Afraid to see something so beautiful my heart would stop. I needed every beat it had left just to get through the day.

"It's okay, Olivia," he said. "You can trust me. I promise, you'll love it."

I slowly opened my eyes, adjusting to the much darker room.

"Are you kidding me?" I spun around to get a better look at the spectacular library.

It was more masculine than the rest of the house, with richly saturated, dark-wood bookcases covering nearly every square inch of two floors. A small balcony circled the upper level, and I itched to get up there and run my hands along the bookshelves. The tray ceiling was painted white, a giant gold-leaf medallion showcasing an enormous chandelier that spanned both floors.

"It's breathtaking!" I murmured in awe.

"The ceiling is the only thing not original to the house," he said. "It originally had a tin ceiling. I have an old photograph of it, and we're trying to decide whether or not to recreate it."

"Are you able to find period tiles similar to the ones the house had?" I asked, my eyes soaking in the massive fireplace. I'd done tin ceilings before and could get him in touch with someone if he hadn't had any luck yet.

"We actually have all of the original tiles," Brighton said, grinning. He stuffed his hands in his pockets while he looked around the room, as if trying to see it through my eyes.

"Get out!" I said, clapping my hands together. "That's amazing! You have to!"

His eyes were fixated on mine, but I couldn't read what he was thinking.

"I have to now," he said.

I tried not to sound as breathless as I felt. "How come?"

He cleared his throat, looking away. "Because if it makes you this happy, imagine how excited buyers will be."

"She deserves it," I said, referring to the house.

"Yes, she does."

The air was thicker than it had any business being. I needed to keep moving. I was starting to think he might be flirting with me. How stupid was that?

"How do you get upstairs?" I asked, ready to finish our tour and get back outside, where I could breathe easier.

"That's the fun part," he said, taking my hand. I wondered if he'd done the same with Ryan when he was giving him the tour. I giggled, not able to imagine something like that. Still, I clasped his hand back and let him drag me across the room to one of the many bookcases.

"So, we're scaling them, then?" I asked, quirking my brow as I looked up at the tall shelves.

He laughed, drawing my eyes to his Adam's apple as the warm, rich sound slid somewhere deep inside me—as if tucked into a hidden pocket so I could pull it out later to examine it closer.

"Nope," he said, pressing a tiny button behind a book he moved. The bookshelf pivoted, swinging open to reveal a small room lined with more books, a narrow staircase leading up to the second floor.

"No way," I said, my eyes wide as I turned to look at him. "Did you show Ryan this? He would flip."

"We never made it up here," he said honestly. "He's mostly helping with some things downstairs, and since I wasn't counting on renovating this room, I hadn't thought to show him yet. I just knew you'd appreciate it from a design perspective."

"Thank you. It's incredible," I said. "I didn't realize Ryan was helping you. I mean, I know he's been hanging out over here more, but I didn't know he was doing actual work."

"Yeah, he stopped by one afternoon to look around, and I found out he's good with a sander. You can imagine the amount of woodworking projects we have with all this molding. Suckered him in to coming by a few times."

It had been at least a year since I'd seen Ryan in his workshop in our detached two-car garage. Now suddenly he was over here, volunteering his time to restore someone else's house. Why would he do that?

"It's a huge project," I said. "I imagine you'd appreciate all the help you can get."

"Absolutely," he said, his easy smile disarming.

It had been a long time since I looked at another man and noticed his good looks. But Brighton made it impossible not to.

"I can't wait to see your design work," he said.

"I think it'll be a good fit and help sell it even faster," I said, trying to focus less on his full lips and more on the reason why we were here. "Though, with a secret gem like this, I'm sure you'll have buyers lined up."

"Ready to go see it?"

"We can go all the way up?"

"That's why I opened the magic door," he said, winking at me.

I bit my lip, trying not to notice his square jaw, or piercing, pale green eyes—more aqua than seafoam, like I'd first thought. I skipped up the stairs to get some distance, curiosity steering my heart for the first time in months.

The top floor was every bit as magnificent, and maybe even more so. The small walkway circled the room below, just big enough for one person to browse through the floor-to-ceiling bookcases. The library was massive, and every shelf was still filled with classics and god only knew what else. I couldn't imagine how long it took to curate so many books.

I walked the perimeter in awe, admiring the original wood-work while scanning the shelves at eye level. When I got halfway around, I glanced over to the door, realizing Brighton hadn't followed me. Instead, he was leaning against the door-frame, looking devilishly handsome, his eyes trained on me.

Something passed between us, something that felt like an understanding. I knew he found me attractive, and I suspected he knew I felt the same. I would never act on it, of course, but even acknowledging an attraction toward another man felt like a betrayal to Ryan. So much can be said and read with just the eyes—no words ever needed to tell the whole story. Ryan and I had a lot of experience with that from our early years, when our affair was secret. The eyes held feelings one couldn't speak from the heart.

As I held Brighton's heated gaze across the room, I suspected he was reading more from my heart than I meant to share. He seemed to drink in my pain, and my loneliness. But I knew he also saw me as a desirable woman—not the broken one Ryan knew these days. If things were different, if I wasn't a married woman, I would've given Brighton even more in that glance between us.

But I was, so I looked back to the books and finished my lap around the room as quickly as I could. "I should get going. Let you shower."

"There's still the whole top floor to show you."

"Ryan's waiting for me," I said, making myself clear.

Brighton nodded, moving out of my way so I could head down. He walked me all the way to the front door, but when

I started to open it, he put his hand over mine. I didn't move, but I could feel the heat from his body he was so close.

"Tell me you still want me to come over for dinner, Liv," he said, calling me by Ryan's pet name.

I almost whimpered, tears threatening to rise to the surface. What had I done? I had no business looking at a man with the longing and desire I accidentally bared to Brighton. Maybe if he saw how happy Ryan and I were together, he would forget it ever happened.

I took a deep breath, steeling myself as I glanced over my shoulder at him. The man had confidence etched into his very DNA. His gaze softened as he backed up, dropping his arm from the door.

"I know Ryan would love to have you join us," I said. "See you in fifteen?"

"Sure."

As I darted across the yard to our house, I realized Brighton wasn't the only one who would need to forget it ever happened.

CHAPTER SEVEN

Ryan

I WATCHED LIV CUT across the yards, though she hadn't seen me out by the grill yet. What she missed, since she was so busy fleeing the Kerrington estate, was how Brighton watched her from the big picture window until she made it safely inside. I saw it though.

I took a swig of my beer, sliding our burgers onto the grate of Big Green Egg. Even if it was just for Brighton, it was kind of nice grilling out with a friend again. Ever since the funeral, we'd slowly lost touch with our friend group. It wasn't that they didn't try, but the pain of being around their kids was just too hard for Liv. After dozens of excuses, they finally stopped inviting us over, giving us the space we needed to heal. Our efforts to safeguard our privacy worked a little too well, though, because this was the first time since Laelynn died that we had a guest over to the house. I just hoped Olivia could make it through the entire dinner.

Fifteen minutes later, Brighton popped the latch on our white picket fence and made his way across the yard to me. Stitch ran over to greet him.

The guy was hard to hate. He bent down and scratched between the puppy's ears. Stitch immediately rolled over on his back for Brighton, and I couldn't help but hope my wife didn't respond to our handsome neighbor the same way. Hell, even I seemed to be under Brighton's spell, enjoying the developing friendship between us.

"What a great dog," he said. "Wish I could have one."

I realized how little I really knew about him, other than the fact that he was flipping his uncle's estate. "Why can't you?"

"Just not home enough. That wouldn't be fair to a pet."

"Do you flip houses for a living?"

"Not really. I usually build homes, not restore them."

"You a carpenter then?"

"Guess you could say that. That's where it all starts, right?"

"I wouldn't know. I mean, I have a workshop, and I love getting my hands dirty. But I'm a professor."

Brighton looked up. "Here? At the university?"

"Yep. Just taking the summer off for once."

"Nice. Anything fun planned?"

You mean, other than watching my wife disappear further and further into herself?

"Nah. Just a lazy summer."

"I hear ya. I'd take one of those, too, if I could."

"Man, where are my manners?" I grabbed a beer from the cooler and popped the top off before handing the cold bottle to Brighton. "How do you like your burger?"

"Medium," he said, "but I'll eat about anything right now."

Liv took that moment to come out the back door, a large goblet of red wine in her hand and a platter of appetizers in the other. Her hair looked freshened up, and I noticed she applied a light dusting of makeup. I wanted to punch a hole in the stupid green egg as I stood there flipping our burgers. She looked like a breath of fresh air the way her soft, blond hair framed her face like a living angel. Her lips were rosier now than they'd been before, and I saw her sneak a peek at Brighton before she sidled up to me and wrapped her arms around my waist. I'd waited seven months for affection like this from Olivia.

One day with Brighton and she was all over me. *Great.*

We chatted while I pulled the burgers off the grill, then made our way to the back porch. We had an open-air seating area under the second-floor patio, with massive stone columns anchoring the whole thing. Large, palm-bladed fans kept us cool, and the fairy lights Liv had installed soon after she found out she was pregnant with Laelynn added a laid-back ambiance to the evening. Surprisingly enough, conversation with Brighton was easy; he was smarter than I judged him for. We fell into easy banter and most of the conversation wound its way back to decorating, but Liv looked happy, so I didn't mind.

"So, what's it like being a new dog mommy?" Brighton asked, having no idea the landmine he'd just stepped in.

I held my breath, waiting for Olivia to set her napkin down and excuse herself. But she didn't. She took a big sip of wine and smiled. I could tell it wasn't a real Livy smile, but it was executed smoothly enough to fool Brighton.

"We love it. Don't we, honey?"

Honey?

I nodded, practically speechless. "Mostly. Except for the 2:00 a.m. bathroom breaks. Luckily, Liv's been taking one for the team and covering those."

"How'd you manage that?" Brighton asked, laughing.

"He takes care of me in other ways," she said, glancing at me from under her thick lashes. "The least I can do is let him sleep through the night."

I felt like I was in the *Twilight Zone*. Had Brighton secretly replaced my real wife with a Stepford wife during his tour of the house?

We all shared an after-dinner drink, then Brighton asked about Olivia's portfolio. "Mind if I show him, Ry?" she asked, her eyes bright.

My heart soared seeing the excitement there; but it was also a knife to my heart, knowing it wasn't me who caused it. But the truth was, I'd do anything to see her keep smiling like this.

She walked by my chair, and I reached my hand out, catching hers. She glanced down at me, and I saw the real Liv in there again. Not the Liv buried in pain. Not the Liv who was unfunctional on the best of days. But the strong, capable woman I'd fallen in love with. The one who had started her own business and built a lucrative career from nothing. The one who stole my heart from the first moment I laid eyes on her.

Her hand slipped from mine, and I watched as Brighton followed my wife into my home.

AFTER OUR NEIGHBOR left for the evening, Liv and I fell into a comfortable silence while I washed the dishes and she dried them. She was humming as she wiped the towel over the platter we'd served appetizers on. There was a spring in her step as she stood on her tiptoes to put it away on the top shelf.

When she turned and found me staring at her, she grinned.

"What?" she asked, self-conscious as she tucked a strand of hair behind her ear. Then she thought better of it, pulling a rubber band from around her wrist and securing all those long blond waves into a messy bun high on her head. "Why are you looking at me like that?"

"Because you're beautiful. Because it's been a long time since I've seen you this happy—and it looks amazing on you."

She blushed. "I think maybe you were right."

I set down the pan that I was washing and dried my hands.

"About what?" I asked, walking over and wrapping her in my arms. I put my chin on her head as she snuggled against my chest. I never wanted to let her go, wishing I could bubble up this moment and keep us safe forever.

"I'm spending too much time inside the house. I need to have something to do—to keep my mind busy. To fill all the silence," she whispered.

That's exactly what she needed, and also what terrified me.

"You thinking of taking the job with Kerrington?"

"Maybe. Would you be okay with that?"

"Yeah," I said, though my heart was kicking my ass inside, yelling at me to say no. To stop her from spending more time with him. "Why wouldn't I be?"

"Well, you took the summer off to be with me. To help me get back on my feet—so we could work on us. I don't want you to think that's any less important if I do this."

This.

What would *this* turn into? She didn't need my permission. I wasn't her keeper. Still, I closed my eyes, holding on tight. I knew our balance hung on what came next. But I couldn't clip her wings. She needed whatever she needed to heal . . . and I had to trust her. I knew she loved me more than anything on this planet. Just because her heart had been decimated when we lost Laelynn, it didn't mean she wouldn't come back fully to me.

I still believed in Liv and Ry.

"I know, babe," I said, kissing her forehead. "I think getting out of the house and using your creativity will be good for you."

"Brighton told me you've been helping over there, too," she said, grinning. "Sounds like it's been good for you. Who knew the secret to our therapy might've been right next door this whole time?"

Indeed.

CHAPTER EIGHT

Olivia

N O MATTER HOW much I tried, I couldn't fall asleep. I lay in bed, looking up at the tin ceiling in our guest bedroom. It had once been the dining room, adjacent to the sunroom off the side of our house. We'd considered making it our master suite, but we didn't want to reconfigure the bathrooms down here when the previous owners had done so much work on the house already. It ended up being perfect for Stitch because it let me take him out through the sunroom and into the side yard easily, never disturbing Ryan. Maybe I should ask him to install a doggy door for when Stitch gets a little older, so he can make these nighttime trips on his own.

As I tossed and turned, I couldn't help but think about the past two years with Ryan. The tide felt like it was turning when I got pregnant with Laelynn. The years we'd suffered before seemed to disappear, as if our miracle baby could magically erase all the damage we'd done to one another after our miscarriages. Ryan had taken the first one the hardest. That's when his anger started to surface—feelings he didn't know what to do with. He spent months getting mad for no reason whatsoever. It's how we ended up with a hole in the garage wall. Back then, I hadn't known how to soothe it. Or how to get him to talk to someone about his feelings—especially when I was so devastated myself, I couldn't be there for him the way he needed. Eventually, he bottled it all up inside and capped it off, going back to work as if nothing had happened.

Meanwhile, I was trying to hold us both together, and failing miserably. So, when I found out I was pregnant again only a few months after the first baby, I was elated. Ryan? Not so much. The pain I held from the night I told him still haunted me. I'd taken him to his favorite steakhouse on the lake, eager to tell him the good news. Had it been too soon? Probably. But I'd taken it as a sign. God wouldn't have given us a baby if it weren't meant to be, right?

Ryan, however, hadn't shared the same sentiment. That conversation was what played on repeat in my head tonight— though I didn't know why. I remembered the way he'd coolly set his fork onto the table, wiping his mouth with the starched white napkin sitting on his lap. He took a sip of his red wine, looking over the beveled edge of the goblet at me as I waited for him to say something. Anything.

"It's too soon."

"Obviously not," I said, upset at his reaction. "I thought you'd be happy."

"We just lost our baby three months ago, Liv. Your body hasn't had time to heal, and neither have our hearts. I'm not done loving the last baby. I can't do this."

"*You* can't do this?" I hissed, looking at him incredulously. "You should've thought about that when you wanted unprotected sex last month, then. It's a little too late for regrets."

"It's not though. Your body needs a rest. Even your obstetrician said that."

"Right. But again, *we* messed up. That doesn't mean this baby isn't meant to be."

"It's not meant to be, Liv. It's too soon."

"What are you saying?" I asked, my hands shaking.

"I think we should—"

"No!" I said loudly, pushing my chair back and standing. People were looking at the scene I was making, but I didn't care. "I won't."

"Sit down now, Olivia. You're embarrassing me."

"And you're breaking my heart." I threw my napkin on the chair and walked away, knowing Ryan would think I was headed to the restroom to cool off.

He picked up his wine and signaled calmly to the waiter.

Instead of making my way to the bathroom, though, I walked out the front door and kept going. I headed along the lake's walkway and got almost all the way into town before the bright sting of headlights shone from behind.

Ryan's car slowed down beside me, the window rolled down. "Get in."

"No," I said, continuing to walk home.

"Liv, get in the fucking car. It's late."

I stopped, with my fists balled at my side. "Do not tell me what to do," I said. "I am the only one who can decide what to do with *my* body. Not you."

"I'm sorry I upset you, hon."

"But you're not sorry about what you were about to say, are you?"

Ryan looked down at his hands on the steering wheel. "All I was going to say is I think we should talk about our options. I wasn't saying that's what we should do."

"There's nothing to talk about when it comes to having this baby," I spat. I turned my back to him and walked the long, lonely road home alone.

Well, I wasn't completely alone. Ryan turned off his lights and followed me all the way back to the house at a respectable distance. When he pulled in the driveway, I was already inside, stripping my clothes off to shower.

"We need to talk about this," he said from the doorway. "You're being childish."

I spun on him, not caring that I was naked. I'd already bared my entire soul to this man. There wasn't an inch of my body that wasn't already his. "Look at my body, Ryan," I challenged him. "This body—the one you want to *fuck* so badly all the time—it has a baby inside it again. *Your* baby, you asshole."

I turned toward the shower, not leaving an inch of room for him to try to convince me of something I would never do. Especially when all we'd ever wanted was a family.

He grabbed my arm before I could get in. "I'm sorry, Livy. I'm so sorry." I looked into the warm, brown eyes I'd fallen in love with and realized that he was terrified. "I'm so scared to lose you."

I shook my arm free and stepped under the hot, soothing spray, washing the anger off my skin. Then I pulled Ryan into the shower with me. We worked our anger and fear out on one another that night. Punishing each other for things that were never our fault. We bridged the space between us, holding on to the shred of hope we'd been given.

The next morning, I miscarried.

I FINALLY GAVE up the idea of sleep. I glanced at the clock. It was 1:55. "Come on, Stitch," I said, lifting the snuggly puppy from the end of the bed. Ryan would kill me when he learned I'd foregone the crate. I inhaled the puppy's sweet smell before sliding on my tan Oran sandals and following him into the backyard.

We didn't see too many stars being in the city, but the moon was bright white, in its third-quarter phase. I was about to sit down when I saw a movement from the corner of my eye and Stitch growled, giving me a low warning.

"Easy," Brighton said from the shadows.

Stitch ran to the fence, jumping up and down excitedly after recognizing the man who had scratched his tummy all evening. Even in the dark, I could tell when Brighton's face broke out into a smile, his straight white teeth drawing my attention to his full lips and sensual mouth.

"Sorry, didn't mean to startle you."

"It's okay. I couldn't sleep anyway. And it was time for Stitch's bathroom break."

"I couldn't sleep either, which is why I gave up and went for a jog. Mind if I join you?"

"Sure," I said, waving him over. I sat on one of the chaise lounges, leaning back and resting my head on my hands. "It's the witching hour."

Brighton laughed. "I'll say. The neighborhood's nice and quiet, though, at this time of night. Not a car in sight on my run."

"That's because most normal people are asleep right now," I scoffed.

"No sleep for the wicked," he said, sitting onto the lounge chair beside me. "What keeps you up at night, Liv?"

Stitch jumped onto Brighton's lap and snuggled into the crotch of his shorts. He immediately turned so our neighbor could scratch his belly. Traitor.

"You don't want to know," I said, feeling haunted by an onslaught of memories tonight.

The hardest part in remembering wasn't looking back. It was the realization of what we'd never have in the future now that our babies were gone. All the milestones we'd miss. The holidays that we'd never get to have with them. Those made me ache the most. Usually when someone important in your life dies, you at least have the memories of a lifetime to look back on. You miss what was. But when you have a stillborn—the ache is never ending because all you can think about is a future you'll never have.

"Maybe I do," he said, pulling me back to the present.

"How old are you, Brighton?"

"What does that have to do with anything?"

"Just curious."

"Twenty-nine. How old are you?"

"Thirty-one," I answered. "But I've been through things you can't even imagine. It ages you."

His eyes swept over my body, and I realized that my thin cotton nightgown probably left little to the imagination. I hadn't been expecting a nighttime visitor when I'd slipped outside with Stitch.

"You don't look old to me."

"What ages us usually hits the heart more than the body," I said.

"What's hurt your heart, Liv?"

"I don't know you well enough to share the scars of my heart with you," I said sadly. "And you need to stop calling me Liv."

"How come? It suits you."

"That it does. But it's Ryan's nickname for me, and I'm fairly certain my husband won't like hearing our hunky neighbor calling me by his pet name."

"Hunky, huh?"

I shot Brighton a side eye, noticing his playful grin. There was something so masculine about his hard, square jawline and intense green eyes. "That wasn't the takeaway from all of this."

"Fine, *Olivia*."

"Thank you."

"So, back to your heart—"

"No. Just no."

Brighton shrugged. "One day, I'll get your secrets from you," he teased.

If he only knew the things that lay buried in this broken heart.

"I better get back inside. The morning's going to come soon enough, and I'd like to get started on some mood boards tomorrow."

"Relax, Li—Olivia," he said, catching himself. "We've got all summer."

"It's something I enjoy doing. Plus, I could really use the focus right now. I need to keep busy."

"You're really running from something in there, aren't you?" he asked quietly, surprising me.

"How'd you know?"

"You're not the only one with buried pain."

He got up, stretching long, hairy legs that for some reason did things to my insides. He was fair-haired, and the curls looked soft and inviting from beneath his running shorts. My hands had no right to reach over and find out, though. And my head seriously needed to be examined.

It was after four by the time I fell asleep. And all I could dream about was what pain Brighton was hiding.

CHAPTER NINE
Brighton

'D HAD NO right stopping at Olivia and Ryan's as I did
last night after my run. It was true that I couldn't sleep, and
that running was my stress reliever and sleep inducer. For
some reason, seeing Olivia and Ryan together reminded me
of all I'd lost, the weight crushing down so heavily on me I
had to run to escape it. So, I'd laced up and jogged a couple
of miles until I finally burned through those heavy feelings
enough to call it a night.

That said, it hadn't escaped me when Ryan mentioned
Stitch's 2:00 a.m. bathroom breaks, and I might've done my
best to time my run to coincide with a chance of bumping
into Olivia. I knew I was a bastard, but the woman was
seriously the most beautiful creature I'd ever laid my eyes
on. She wasn't mine to have—and she never would be. But
I couldn't stop myself from finding ways to catch a glimpse
of her, ever since that first day I'd met Ryan.

And I hated myself for that because Ryan was one of the good guys.

But seeing Olivia lying there against the lounge chair last night under the moonlight in nothing more than her thin cotton nightgown . . . let's just say it drove me to a cold shower and a restless night as my mind went in directions it had no business going with another man's wife.

I finally pulled myself out of bed at seven. It was the weekend, so the work crew wouldn't be joining me. But Ryan would. He'd offered to come help sand the formal staircase and replace the broken spindles.

I hadn't been planning on staying at an active worksite with the type of renovations we had going on, but I lived almost two hours away, and the drive was getting to be too much to do twice a day. So, for now, a king-sized air mattress in one of the guest rooms would have to do. Eventually, I'd finish the room I was sleeping in and buy a real bed so I wouldn't need to spend the first thirty minutes of my day having to stretch out the kinks.

I heard a knock at the front door and padded over, opening it in nothing but my shorts. Olivia was standing on the other side of the door, three coffees in a drink holder. She looked adorable in some sort of soft, camouflage, overall shorts and a white tank top underneath. The bib cut off right at her breast line, and when I looked closer, I realized I could see through the sides of her overalls. The tank top didn't quite go all the way down under the outfit's stringed waistline, and I could see the bare skin of her hip bone. I already had a morning woody, and seeing Olivia all freshly showered, smelling like flowers, and standing there with coffee for me wasn't helping.

"Wasn't expecting you this morning," I said, my voice scratchy from sleep.

Her eyes dropped to my cotton sleep shorts and I knew what she was seeing, but I couldn't do a damn thing about it. "You brought coffee?"

"I—"

Ryan came up behind Olivia, putting his hand on her back. "Morning, Kerrington," he said. "Go on in, Liv."

When she hesitantly walked forward, and Ryan came in beside her, he saw the issue. "Damn, Brighton, go take a cold shower or something. Looks like we came over a little too early and woke someone up."

Glad Ryan thought it was so funny.

I grabbed one of the coffees from Olivia's outstretched hand, then bolted to the downstairs guest bathroom. I locked the door, leaning my head back against the cold tile of the shower as freezing cold water washed over the long, hard planes of my body. Did I mention "hard"?

There was only one way to fix this, and the quicker I did the better. I closed my eyes, seeing a tumble of long, blond hair, aviators resting on top of Olivia's head. And those long, athletic legs that weren't mine to fantasize about. I was surely going to burn in hell. But right now, under the freezing cold spray, I'd have willingly traded my soul for a chance to switch places with Ryan for just one night.

THIRTY MINUTES LATER, I was clean shaven and relaxed, a smile on my face as I went out to the kitchen. The familiar sound of a sander filled the hallway as I made myself some eggs. I popped my head around the corner, surprised to see Olivia sitting on the front porch with a sketch pad, her hair piled on top of her head in some sort of messy updo that left little tendrils of her hair escaping wildly, and her long, lean neck bare.

Ryan was one lucky SOB.

I glanced over to where Ryan was sanding the stairs and saw him look away. *Shit.* It wasn't the first time he'd caught me checking Olivia out. I really needed to be more careful.

He turned the sander off, setting it down on the step he was working on. He wiped his brow with his forearm. "See you've worked things out."

"Sorry about that," I said, sheepishly. "Can't help a strong morning salute."

Ryan chuckled, lifting his coffee to his lips. "No harm, no foul."

"Thanks for helping with the stairs today."

"Yeah, no problem," Ryan said. "Keeps my mind off things."

"Thought you were taking the summer off?"

"I am," he said, his eyes darkening. "Between you and me, things have been kind of tough between Liv and me lately."

"Sorry to hear that," I said sincerely. I never would have guessed; they seemed so solid.

"It'll be okay. We've just had a hard few years. We lost a baby last November," Ryan admitted, causing my eyes to snap up and meet his.

"Dude, I had no idea. I'm sorry to hear that."

"Thanks," Ryan said, glancing out at his wife, who was sketching away on her jumbo-sized drawing pad. "I appreciate you letting Liv show you some ideas for the house. She's amazing at what she does, and I know she can already see a vision for this place. Once something gets in her blood, there's a fire inside her that can't be tempered until it burns its course. It's one of the reasons I fell in love with her."

I looked at Olivia in a whole new light, her nighttime confession of buried secrets suddenly making so much more sense.

"I haven't seen this fire burning inside her for a long time," he murmured.

"Glad I could help," I said roughly.

Ryan looked at me, and I froze. Did he suspect the attraction I felt toward his wife? I mean, I'd never act on it, whether we were friends or not. But it was hard not to be taken by Olivia. The minute his dark brown eyes pegged mine, I knew.

"I'd do anything to make that woman happy again," he said, pulling his goggles back over his eyes and turning on the sander again.

I watched as Ryan took his frustrations out on the stairs, wondering what in the world I'd gotten myself into with these two.

CHAPTER TEN

Ryan

I MOSTLY STUCK TO the stairs all day, but my eyes followed Brighton and Liv around all afternoon as they hashed out her plans. At one point I glanced over and saw them huddled over the kitchen island, their heads nearly touching. I noticed the way her body unconsciously leaned into his. The way he looked at her like she hung the moon when she laughed.

It felt like a knife lodging into my heart, but I'd push the damn thing in even farther if it made Liv this happy.

I wasn't stupid. Kerrington was a good-looking guy. Whether she realized it or not, Olivia was attracted to him. I knew she'd never act on it—I wasn't worried about that. But a small part of me wondered if it would help. If it would wake her up from the sleepwalking she'd been doing over the last few years since our first miscarriage.

She thought she was okay after that, trying to stay positive about the baby we'd have together one day. But the next miscarriage changed something in Liv. It's what started the fault line in our marriage, too. The irony was, that baby, our second baby, had been created out of our deepest love for one another.

Our commitment to stand with each other no matter what.

It was only a couple of months after our first loss that Olivia woke screaming in the middle of the night. It was the start of her long journey with night terrors. I'd cradled her against my chest, our bodies naked in sleep as they always were back in the beginning of our marriage. Her whole body shook against mine as she released torrents of tears she'd kept buried inside. We spent the whole night comforting and soothing one another.

It was that night, while I was buried deep inside of her, that we made our pact.

"I need you to be honest with me, Liv. No matter what. The only way we're going to get through this is with complete and utter honesty. I'll do whatever I can to support you, but I have to know what you're feeling if I'm going to help you."

She nodded, her mouth finding mine and mingling the salty trace of tears with our kisses.

"No matter what," she breathed out as I rolled my hips slowly, pressing so deep inside of her she shuddered. "It's always you and me, Ryan. No matter what happens with our family, I'm not okay unless *we're* okay."

I thrust deep, causing her to cry out as she held on tightly, wrapping her body completely around mine. "There's nothing that will ever come first before you, Olivia."

"I won't hold anything back again," she promised.

"One hundred percent complete honesty. I mean it," I growled, sucking on her throat.

Her body arched against mine. "Truth," she gasped.

"Truth," I said, letting her swallow the words on my lips as I came inside her.

I meant to pull out, but we were so overcome by our renewed closeness, and the truth pact we'd committed to. I knew in that moment that we were indestructible. That the pain we'd gone through with losing our first baby was the worse we'd ever face. If we could get through that, we could get through anything.

I was so naïve.

CHAPTER ELEVEN

Olivia

RYAN WAS ACTING strange all day, but when I asked him about it, he just wrapped his arm around my waist and kissed the tip of my nose, sending butterflies to my tummy. We took a much-needed break when Brighton had sub sandwiches delivered to the house. We decided to eat them at our place since there was so much dust, thanks to Ryan's progress on the stairs over the last few days. The air was so thick we'd all had to cover our mouths and noses. So, when we stepped into the bright sunlight, removing our sweaty masks, it was easy to smile with gratitude, taking in a deep lungful of clean, afternoon air. I hadn't felt this carefree in a long time.

"You know what we ought to do?" I said with a sudden burst of excitement as we crossed the yard.

"What's that, babe?"

"We should take Brighton to the Hole," I said, grinning. There was a fun energy in the air today, and I didn't know how long it would last. I wanted to hold onto it with both hands.

"Would that make you happy?"

I had to be careful because the man would do anything to put a smile on my face. I bit my lip and nodded.

"Let's do it then," he said.

He looked over at Brighton, who was following us over to the house to eat. "You have swim shorts in that duffle bag of yours at the house?"

"Yeah, why?" he answered, taking a sip of his Coke.

"Got a surprise if you're game to play hooky for a couple of hours. Get some of the sweat of the workday off us."

Brighton cocked his head, looking back and forth between us. "We could use a break."

I jumped up and down, excitement flooding through me. I couldn't remember the last time in seven months that I looked forward to going out and doing something. I ran the rest of the way to the house and opened the back door for Stitch to come outside while we ate lunch. The puppy ran around manically at first, trying to say hello to each of us equally while also having to pee. His bladder came first, and he trotted off to the side yard, sniffing the grass to find the perfect spot.

We sat on the same lounge chairs as we had the other night, Ryan leaning back against mine on the ground between Brighton and me. His head was resting against my thigh, and I ran my fingers through his hair as we all ate our subs and talked, getting to know each other even better.

"Where do you live when you're not here?" Ryan asked him.

"Watertown. I was doing the commute every day, but it got to be too much. I was losing too many work hours, and when there was a problem on site, I just couldn't respond the way I needed to. Like the time the guys hit that gas line."

"Yeah, that was fun." I rolled my eyes, remembering the incident a few weeks ago.

"That's why I prefer doing most of the work myself," he said, chuckling.

"You seem to have a lot of knowledge about renovating for someone who doesn't do it too often," Ryan observed.

"I know my way around," he said.

Though it was a playful, offhand comment about something so benign, it did things to me. I thought of the way he looked at me from across the landing in the library and imagined he did know his way around.

"You staying next door for the rest of the reno, then?" Ryan asked casually.

"Yeah. It sucks being on a blow-up mattress, but it makes more sense than commuting. Once I get that back bedroom finished, I'll move a real bed in there. Anything's better than an air mattress," he said, laughing. "I haven't slept on anything that bad since college."

I didn't know why it surprised me that he'd gone to college. I didn't know much about him yet.

"Where'd you go to school?" Ryan asked, taking the words from my mouth.

"Duke," he said, biting into his sub.

I gaped at him. "You went to Duke?"

He shrugged. "Yeah, so?"

"What'd you study?" I pressed.

"Mechanical engineering."

"And you're not using your degree in that because . . . ?" It was none of my business, but I couldn't imagine why he'd move away and go to such a prestigious university just to return home and throw his degree away being a handyman.

"I'd rather be happy."

Oh.

We talked some more about lighter subjects, then went our separate ways to change into swimsuits, meeting back at the car when we were all packed up for our little adventure. Instead of taking Ryan's SUV, we drove my Wrangler, roof off. I sat in the back so the guys could talk, resting my head against the seat and closing my eyes.

The sun whipped through my hair, and I thought about Brighton and how easy he made it all seem.

I'd rather be happy, too.

CHAPTER TWELVE
Brighton

THE HOLE ENDED up being a small hike up a trail off the side of the road a few hours from home. The car ride had flown by, and Ryan and I found we had more in common than we originally thought. Once he knew I'd gone to such a good school, his academic came out, and we spent a lot of time talking about the SUNY system vs. private institutions. That and college basketball, of course.

By the time we fully ascended the trail, I realized we were at the top of a quarry, which seemed an awfully long way down. Ryan and Olivia tossed their things onto the ground and went to a large tree at the ledge. That's when I noticed a rope tied back to a huge metal peg sticking out from the bark. Ryan undid the rope and got a good grip with both hands, then took a dozen steps back and grinned.

"Watch and learn," he said.

I watched as he ran forward, howling as he hurled himself from the side of the cliff. When he was out far enough, he let go, his body disappearing.

I ran to the ledge to stand next to Olivia, seeing the large, circular rings where Ryan had splashed into the water far below. He didn't immediately pop back up, but Olivia didn't seem concerned. She grabbed the rope when it swung back and held it out for me.

Ryan finally popped out of the water and yelled, "Get your sweet ass in here!"

I leaned over and cupped my hands to my mouth. "You must be talking to me!"

Ryan laughed, shaking out his wet hair. "Heck yeah, Kerrington. Get that sweet ass down here!"

I glanced at Olivia, who was wearing a huge smile, the light mood obviously contagious. "Go on," she said.

I took the rope from her hand, stepping back as far as it would let me. "You sure this is safe?"

"Of course," she said, laughing. "You saw it held Ryan."

I looked at her, then glanced down at my bare chest, my pecs solid slabs of muscle. "Just saying."

"You're awful," she said. "Go! You aren't scared of heights, are you?"

"No," I scoffed. "Just feels like you should go first."

She grabbed the rope from me, bumping me playfully with her hip. "Move over, sweet cheeks."

Speaking of sweet cheeks . . . I watched as Olivia pulled the rope back, the navy-blue one-piece doing little to cover her backside. She looked over her shoulder and grinned at me—my heart catching in my throat.

"As soon as I let go, you have to catch the rope on its way back so you can go next, okay?"

I nodded, unable to get my mind off the soft curve of her bottom, or how her bathing suit set off the blue in her eyes.

Before I could reply properly, Olivia ran, throwing herself over the cliff as the rope swung out. She turned right as she dropped, and I made eye contact with her. It felt like a kick in the gut, and I was suddenly terrified. I ran to the ledge, holding my breath until Olivia broke the surface, laughing out loud, her hair in long, wet tendrils around her.

"Grab the rope!" she shouted.

Crap! I just barely caught it on its next swing back. I wasn't sure who would get it after me, but that wasn't my problem. I took a deep breath, my knuckles white as I gripped the thick cord. Then I ran, throwing all my faith to the wind as I jumped off the side of the quarry's cliff, suspended in the air for what felt like forever.

"Let go!" Olivia shouted from below.

I released my hands, my stomach dropping as I free-fell, hitting the water hard as my feet entered. It felt like I was submerged forever, but eventually I broke the surface, hollering out with adrenaline as Ryan had done. I looked around the small swimming hole, finally seeing Olivia. She was treading nearby, alone.

"Where's Ryan?" I asked, looking around.

"He hiked back up so he could grab the rope," she said, swimming closer.

"Ready to get out?" I asked, my eyes fixated on hers. They were full of mischief.

"Yep," she said. "After I do this!"

She laughed, plunging my head beneath the water and catching me off guard. I grabbed her wet body, grappling as we broke the surface, laughing.

"Oh, no you didn't," I growled.

She giggled, and the sound went straight to my shorts. I couldn't help it. She must've seen the look in my eye and mistook it for something playful, revengeful. But it wasn't anything like that. It was a burning deep inside that lit something primal within me. I wanted nothing more in that moment than to bury myself deep inside Olivia Wells.

I grabbed her hand as she was swimming away, eliciting a shriek from her as she splashed me. I dunked her as she had me and gasped when she grabbed my legs, pulling me even deeper with her. I opened my eyes, trying to find her, and saw her right in front of me, looking back through the water.

Then she grabbed on to my biceps, her legs intertwined with mine. I swear she was about to kiss me under the water. Instead, she used my body to shove off against me, propelling herself to the surface and leaving me in the murky depths below.

When I surfaced, she was swimming back to shore, using a stroke only serious swimmers could execute. Her body sliced through the water as I watched her go, my dick too hard in my board shorts to get out anytime soon. I was treading water, not sure what had just happened, when I looked up and saw Ryan staring down at me.

THE DRIVE BACK was more subdued, and it was nearly dark by the time we pulled into the Wells's driveway. Olivia grabbed her tote bag and bolted into the house before I could say goodnight.

"Sorry about that," Ryan said.

I wasn't sure what he was talking about, so I didn't say anything back. How much had he seen of us frolicking in the water today?

"She gets like this sometimes," he said quietly. "You've only seen her on her good days, but they're few and far between. I never know when something's going to set her off. When I'm going to set her off."

"No worries," I said, making light of it. "Thanks for the fun time today. I needed a break from that dusty old house."

"About that," Ryan said. "Why don't you stay here? We have four spare bedrooms, and you won't have to break your back on that damn air mattress. It just seems silly with all the space we have, and we're right next door anyway."

Was he for real?

"I couldn't impose on you like that. The last thing you and Liv need is me hanging around, especially if things are already rocky. The stress of having a stranger staying with you might not be the best thing for her."

"Or it could be exactly what she needs," Ryan said. His eyes darkened, as if he were battling some hidden demons. "Let me run it by *Liv* tomorrow. See what she says."

Oh man. I'd screwed up royally, realizing my mistake.

"Ryan—" I started, but what could I say without giving away that I knew how much the pet name meant between them. "I appreciate the offer. I'll think about it."

He nodded, climbing from the Wrangler and slamming the door. He'd just invited me to move in with them, then slammed the door in my face.

Yeah, I'm thinking this would be a huge mistake.

CHAPTER THIRTEEN

Olivia

"**Y**OU ASKED HIM to do what?" I asked in disbelief early the next morning. We were having coffee in the sunroom, watching as Stitch explored the fenced-in yard.

"It was a spur of the moment offer," Ryan said, lifting his English muffin to his mouth. I watched the way his lips closed over the soft bread and swallowed, my body responding. Only I didn't know if it was responding to my husband's mouth or the idea of having Brighton under our roof for the summer. It seemed like a *very* dangerous idea.

"Why would you do that?"

"I don't know. He's a nice guy. He's busting his ass to turn his family's home around. And why wouldn't we? He's right next door all summer anyway, and we have four extra guestrooms. It's not like we don't have the space."

"Three," I reminded him. "I'm still using one."

"Right. But it shouldn't be for much longer. I've done some research, and Stitch should be getting closer to being able to stay all night in his crate without soiling himself."

"About that," I said.

"Liv . . ."

"I couldn't help it! He whimpers every time we get back from going outside. It's easier to put him at the end of the bed so I can at least get some sleep."

"You promised you would keep him in the damn crate!" he snapped.

"Well, sorry!" I said, standing. I knew he was frustrated because the longer Stitch was out of the crate, the longer it would be before I went back to our bed. I couldn't explain why, exactly—but I just wasn't ready to do that.

"Where are you going?" he asked, reaching out for my hand.

I yanked it from his grasp. "I need some time alone today. The week's taken a toll on me."

"What about Kerrington?"

"What about him?"

"Do you want him to stay here with us?" he pressed.

"He can stay wherever you want him to," I said, exasperated.

"I didn't mean to snap, Olivia."

"You never do," I said, walking from the sunroom. I couldn't even curl up in the guest bed because that would mean Ryan would walk by me on his way out. And I really needed some alone time. The last thing I wanted was for him to see me curled up on the bed, crying again.

On our drive home yesterday, the joyful mood I'd felt all day suddenly started to fade, and I shut down. It wasn't anything either of them said or did. It was just hard to have fun for long these days. One minute I was smiling and laughing along with the guys. The next, my pulse was racing as I thought of Laelynn and how she'd never get to do these kinds of things with us.

I ran upstairs and pulled on some workout clothes, deciding to go for a run. Somedays, I needed to cry the anger out. Today I needed to sweat it out. I needed room to breathe, and the house felt like it was closing in on me. I needed to do something with all these feelings crashing down on me. I had to exorcise them from my body because all I could think about as I grabbed the armband for my phone and a set of wireless earbuds was how to stop the pain.

I slammed out the front door, avoiding Ryan. I ran from our house with no destination in mind, the burn in my lungs a welcome sensation as I pushed myself hard. After the first three miles, my legs finally warmed up, and my pace settled into something more comfortable. I was lost in my music, not paying attention to where I was going, when I heard screeching brakes. The car slammed into my hip, sending me flying over the hood before landing on the grass along the roadside.

The last thing I remembered seeing before I blacked out was Brighton Kerrington panicking above me, yelling for an ambulance. He gripped my hand, and I slid peacefully into darkness.

A FAINT BEEP was really annoying me. I kept swatting at it, trying to make it go away. I tried opening my eyes, a blinding light causing me to wince. My mouth was parched, and I couldn't remember where I was.

Ryan's face swam into view.

"Ry?"

"I'm here, baby," he said, his warm hand covering mine. "You're okay."

"What happened?"

"Don't you remember going for a run?"

I closed my eyes, vaguely remembering my jog along the lakeside road, my legs and lungs burning. "I was on my way to our park," I said, licking my lips. "I think a car hit me."

"It did," I heard from off to the side, another deep voice.

I turned my head, seeing Brighton standing there like a golden angel, his body framed by the bright sun pouring through the hospital room window.

"You were there," I said, as he moved toward my bedside. His eyes were full of relief as they swept over me. "What happened?"

"I was on a run, too, heading down the opposite side of the street. I saw you and waved, but you didn't see me. That's when I realized your eyes were glazed over, like you'd been crying. I called out your name, screamed it actually, but you didn't hear me, so I knew your music was too loud."

I nodded, the memory coming back slowly. "Then the car hit me, didn't it?"

He nodded, and I glanced over at Ryan, grimacing.

"I'm sorry," I said quietly to my husband. I didn't know what I was apologizing for, but I could see the toll of years of pain reflected back at me. "I—"

"Shh," he said. "It wasn't your fault. The guy wasn't paying attention, veered too far over into the shoulder and hit you. If Kerrington hadn't happened to be there, we wouldn't have known who hit you, or gotten you an ambulance so fast. The asshole panicked and drove off. He was just going to leave you there."

Ryan leaned over, kissing the side of my head as my eyes locked on Brighton's. "Thank you," I mouthed to him.

He nodded, then started toward the door. He clapped Ryan on the back before heading out of the hospital room and giving us some privacy.

My heart was overwhelmed with emotions when I glanced back up at Ryan. "I'm sorry I got so frustrated and left angry. I must not have been paying attention. That was so careless of me."

"None of this is your fault. I'm just glad Kerrington was there for you. I'm sorry I wasn't."

He brushed his lips against mine, letting me drift back to sleep, with two very different men on my mind and in my heart.

CHAPTER FOURTEEN

Brighton

A FEW DAYS LATER, I watched as Ryan walked Olivia from his Jeep to the house. She was leaning on him, nestled under his arm where she belonged. So why did it hurt to see her there? The truth shamed me. It was because I was jealous of her own husband. Because I wished it were me she was leaning against. Me who could bring her home and slide her into bed and hold her all day, loving her back to good health.

The honesty of that slammed into my chest, nearly taking my breath away. I didn't know how I'd let her in so quickly, but I knew I had to let her go—it was foolish to invest any feelings into the couple next door. I was finishing a job, and nothing else. Then I'd walk away from here forever. And Olivia would still be here, in her perfect house on the corner, with the white picket fence and her stable, nice-guy husband.

My friend, no less.

I went back into the house, not understanding the emotions flooding over me like a tidal wave threatening to pull me under some very dark waters, with a bitch of a current. I picked up a sledgehammer, eyeing the wall between the dining room and the formal front sitting room. Taking it down was one of the few concessions for modern living that I was making, to give buyers the open floorplan they seemed to love these days.

No time like the present.

I lifted the safety goggles in place and slammed the wall over and over again until my arms ached and I could hardly lift the sledgehammer anymore. Drywall was everywhere, but I could now see through the unfortunately placed wall. The rest of it had to come down. I called my foreman, putting him on speaker phone. I currently had him out on other projects but realized quickly I needed his help with this beast.

"Hey, boss," he said. "How's the house coming along?"

"Good, good. It's a passion project, for sure," I said, thinking of Olivia next door.

"Still on schedule?"

"Yep," I answered. "Have some cyclical crew coming in and out when I need help, and the neighbors next door are pitching in too."

"Oh no. Weekend warriors?"

"Nah, man. The husband's a god with a sander and has a steady hand with wood carving. And his wife's an interior designer. I'm hiring her to help with the design end of the flip. To install some permanent fixtures and drapes. Help pick out the hardware. Staging. That kind of stuff."

"That was a lucky break," Rob said.

"You're not kidding. They've been a godsend."

"Which design firm does she work for?"

"She owns it, actually. Live Well Interiors."

"You hired Olivia Wells?"

"You know who she is?"

"Smoking hot blonde? Great ass?"

Why did I suddenly want to punch my foreman? "She's a client, Rob, not a girl I met out at the clubs."

"Sorry, man, that was unprofessional. She's worked on houses I've built before, and I've crossed paths with her a few times. It's hard not to remember a woman as pretty as Olivia Wells."

Wasn't that the truth? "That's her, then, I guess."

"Good for you. It'll sell in no time," Rob assured me. "So, what can I do ya for?"

"Can you come down tomorrow to relocate some plumbing and HVAC lines?"

"I'll be there."

"Appreciate it, man. See you in the morning."

I hung up the phone, wondering what to do now. I turned toward the kitchen, so I could look through the exterior paint samples again, when I noticed Ryan standing by the front door, waiting for me. I lifted a hand in greeting.

"How's Olivia doing?"

Ryan nodded his head, his arms crossed over his chest. I couldn't get a read on him, so I waited. He finally ran a hand over his face, looking tired. "She's as good as can be expected. Still pretty bruised up. She was exhausted from the last few days, said she wanted to nap."

"Oh, good. That should help her. Want to come back for a beer?" I asked. "I'm going through some paint colors. I want to narrow them down before showing Olivia."

Ryan followed me back to the kitchen, taking one of the chairs and flipping it around, sitting down. He accepted the long neck gratefully, taking a pull from the cold pilsner. "I don't even know how to thank you."

I turned and got a better look at him. He seemed on the verge of a breakdown. "Aw, shit," I said, sitting down across from him, crossing my ankle over my knee. "What happened?"

"Nothing, I just—I don't know what I would've done if I'd lost her. If you hadn't been there for us."

"No worries. I was in the right place at the right time."

"Livy wants you to come stay with us," Ryan said, his eyes rimmed red.

"Huh?" Well, that was eloquent.

"I told you I'd ask her about you staying at our place since we have the room. You're doing more demo now. The air's not good to sleep in over here. She said yes. She's fine with you coming to stay at our place."

I nodded, taking a long pull from my beer. Ryan was gauging my reaction.

"All right, cool. It'll be nice not to breathe this crap in all night."

"One thing, though, Kerrington?" he said, standing to leave. "Don't mess around with her under my roof."

I nearly spit my mouthful of beer onto the floor but tried to remain calm. "Dude. Why would you even say that? I'm not that kind of guy."

He set his empty beer onto the countertop, then trained his brown eyes on mine. "Right, but you didn't say you didn't want to, did you?"

"Look, Ryan, I consider us friends. I would never do that to you."

"Again, you never said you didn't *want* to," he pointed out, heading to the door. "She's my everything, Brighton. You won't know what that's like until you're married someday. There's not a single thing in this world that I wouldn't do to make her happy, even if it meant sharing her. I'm not stupid. I see the war in her eyes when she looks at you."

"Yeah, but she's *your* wife, Ryan. I'm not stupid either."

"No, you're not, *boss*. Maybe a little more than a carpenter, eh?"

I shrugged. "So? It's still at the heart of what I do."

"And what exactly do you do, Mr. Kerrington?"

"Well, for starters, I built Brighton Estates, a gated waterside community in Watertown," I said, assessing his reaction. He could do a Google search on me easily enough, so there was no point hiding the rest. "I'm the CEO of Brighton Design and Build. And I have a line of furniture with Erickson's called Bright and Classic."

Ryan ran his hand through his hair but didn't say a word. "Why not just lead with that?" he finally said, laughing. "Christ. You're what? Thirty? And you're a fucking CEO? I'd be flexing with that from the first handshake."

"Twenty-nine," I said, relaxing for the first time since he'd shown up. "Sometimes it's better to just be the guy next door renovating his uncle's estate, Ryan."

He nodded. "Just do me a favor, okay?"

"Anything."

"Seriously, don't mess with Liv behind my back. It's the one thing I ask, man to man."

He was dead serious.

"You have my word."

CHAPTER FIFTEEN

Olivia

WATCHED FROM THE sunroom as Ryan crossed the yard, coming back home to me. He entered the French doors and waved, taking his shoes off.

"Hey, babe," he said, leaning over to kiss me. "I didn't know you were up."

I was sitting on the rustic, oversized swing that was more daybed than bench swing. Ever since I'd gotten home from the hospital, I'd felt off-kilter. Before that, I'd just started to feel like myself again—well, that wasn't exactly true. I'd felt like myself, but different. I was more hopeful than I'd been in a long time. Something about the new energy of working on a project together with Ryan had invigorated me. And it was hard to deny that Brighton was an unexpectedly bright addition to my life. As a friend, of course. After Laelynn died, I didn't know how to be around the friends I'd known practically my whole life. There was no hiding with them. I couldn't just be Olivia. I was now Olivia, grieving mother.

And it was like they didn't know how to be around me without that heavy weight anymore.

It was easier with Brighton. With him, I was just Olivia Wells, interior designer. Even though we were still getting to know one another, I felt as if he could see the real me. The me before all the trauma. It wasn't like I wanted to forget about it, but it was a refreshing change for once—even if it was only a temporary feeling.

"I've been up for a while," I said to Ryan, patting the swing beside me. I was curled up, reading another dark romance, my heart still not ready for rom-com. "Where were you?"

"I went to see Kerrington."

"Is he still comfortable staying here?"

"He is," Ryan said, rubbing my thigh.

"Good. Hopefully, he'll feel better about not having to be over there every night with all that construction dust."

"Yeah," Ryan said, distracted.

"Hey, are you okay?" I asked, putting my hand over Ryan's. He seemed deep in thought, trying to process something he was grappling with.

He nodded, squeezing my hand. "Yeah, I'm all right. I just . . ." He took a deep breath, dragging his eyes up to meet mine. "Liv, have you ever thought about having an affair?"

I gasped, confusion flooding over me. "No! Why would you even ask that?"

He picked at the threads of the blanket spread across my lap. "I just want you happy," he said in way of explanation. "I feel like we need some help."

I didn't know what he was talking about. "Ry, we're doing better now, aren't we? We're starting to be intimate again. I feel closer, don't you? You know I'm not unsatisfied in that arena."

He smiled sadly. "Sometimes sex isn't about the sex, though. Is it, Liv?"

"What does that even mean?"

"We've never had a problem with our connection, hon. But lately, I can't help but notice you don't light up the same way around me as you used to—like I was the only one in the world who could make you feel that way. I can't seem to pull you from the darkness you descend into sometimes, either. I just thought, maybe instead of acting like it doesn't exist, maybe we just walk through it together."

"What are you suggesting?"

He ran a hand through his thick, dark hair. "I don't know. I'm just trying to make things better. And I feel like I'm failing at every turn."

"Ry," I said, moving closer, "I don't need anyone else. It's Liv and Ry forever, right?"

"It'll always be Liv and Ry. But what if something could help bridge us back to ourselves quicker? I feel like nothing else has worked. I don't know. I just wonder what it might be like to spice things up a bit."

Ryan ran his hand farther up my thigh, whatever he was considering clearly turning him on. "I would do anything to be the one to put that light back in your eyes again. But I'm not. At least, not alone."

"I don't know where this is coming from, Ryan. But you're completely enough."

"Damn it, Liv!" he said, cupping my face in his hands. "Don't you get it? I've seen the way you look at him. I've seen the way your body craves closeness when you're around him!"

I pulled back, my eyes wide with shock. "I don't even know what you're talking about, Ryan!"

"Don't you?" he asked, running his hand over my hair.

"No, I don't. You're talking crazy."

"Truth?" he asked quietly.

"Truth," I said softly, knowing I had nothing to hide.

"Are you attracted to Brighton?"

I swallowed. So that's where this was going. If I told him the truth, I worried I would break him. But we didn't lie to one another. Especially not after making our sacred pact during our first round of grief. We both took that as seriously as our wedding vows. It was a hard line we'd never break in our marriage, and the one thing that had gotten us this far in our healing—if that's what you could call this damage we were now sitting in.

"He's a good-looking guy, Ryan. It's not hard to see that."

"It's not at all. Hell, even I know how handsome he is. But I'm not asking you to acknowledge his inherent good looks. I'm asking—are you, Olivia, sexually attracted to Brighton Kerrington? Truth."

I bit the inside of my cheek, feeling like my whole world was about to shatter into a million pieces. I didn't want to do this.

"Truth, Liv," he ground out.

"Yes," I said, closing my eyes. "But I would never, *ever* act on it. It's not like I want to have an affair with him or anything."

"But you feel a sexual pull with him. I'm not stupid."

What could I say? I *had* felt certain ways around Brighton, but Ryan was my life. Our neighbor was certainly no threat to our marriage.

"I don't know what to say, Ryan. I'm not ever going to step out on you."

"What if I asked you to?"

"Why would you do that?" I nearly shouted. "I don't get what you're trying to do. Are you trying to tear us apart?"

"No. I'm trying to stitch us back together again," he said sadly.

"I want the same thing. I just don't think whatever it is you're suggesting is a healthy way to solve our problems."

"Do you still love me?"

"Of course. More than I've ever loved anyone."

"Then let me do this my way," Ryan pleaded. "You want to stitch us back together? We do it my way. What we've been doing hasn't worked. You know it as well as I do."

I didn't know what he was trying to say, but I couldn't see anything positive coming from any of this. Yet the pain in his eyes told me he was breaking, and I was the one causing it. All I'd tried to do the last few years was pick myself up, piece by piece, so I could return to Ryan whole again.

The entire time I'd missed how broken he was, too.

CHAPTER SIXTEEN

Brighton

I DIDN'T SEE OLIVIA again for a couple of days—Ryan said she was having a hard week and was laying low. So, it was Ryan who set me up in their bonus room, on the same floor as the kitchen. It gave me access to the backdoor and allowed me to come and go without worrying about waking them. I ate at my place though, refusing to impose any more than I already was.

Ryan came over to help a couple more times alone. We started playing basketball at the park together on cooler evenings or grabbing a quick bite to eat at the pub around the corner after a long day of hard work. He showed me his technique with a spokeshave, and I showed him how to drywall a room. The sooner I got the bedroom done, the sooner I could get back over to my uncle's place. As much as I enjoyed Ryan's friendship, it was still a little weird being in their home after what he'd said to me . . . after what he'd made me promise.

Besides, Olivia's design aesthetic and heart were in every square inch of their house. Even on days when I wasn't bumping into her, I had to see little reminders of their love all over the place. Like the painting Ryan told me they got in Peru on their honeymoon. Or the accent wall in the living room where Olivia had hung custom-made wallpaper created from blown-up images of their personalized wedding vows. Or, best yet, when I constantly walked by the giant picture of Olivia in her wedding dress on my way to my bedroom—looking like a sun-kissed, free-spirited gypsy goddess in white lace and bare feet. They were all constant reminders that she was not, and never would be, mine.

It was starting to become a sick form of torture that I couldn't walk away from—and would gladly endure to be so close to her every day.

We were making progress on the house, and a new work crew came in during the week to swap out all the bathroom fixtures with new environmentally friendly toilets, claw-footed tubs, and high-end vanities that Liv picked out. Then my tile guys laid all the walk-in showers and bathroom floors, leaving them to dry overnight. I was grateful to be crashing next door with all the fumes in the house.

When I made my way across the yard after a long day's work, I saw Liv and Ryan through the window, laughing together as they ate their pizza. I didn't want to intrude, and I was almost tempted to hop in my truck and drive back to Watertown for the weekend. But I couldn't afford to give up two days of work—especially with all the time I was spending with them.

I opened the back door leading to the mudroom and took off my work boots before quietly making my way to my room.

"Kerrington!" Ryan called out. "That you? We got enough pizza for an army!"

"Yeah, get out here, sweet cheeks," Olivia said, laughing.

I cautiously made my way to the kitchen where they were sitting, their clothes covered with splatters of red paint. Liv was in a pair of running shorts and an oversized blue T-shirt that said "Totally Koalafied." She looked adorable in the ridiculously large shirt, her hair fastened in two little buns on top of her head like Miley Cyrus or Princess Leia, and those long, smooth legs crisscrossed under her on the kitchen chair.

I regretted joining them instantly.

"How'd it go today?" Ryan asked, handing me a beer. Olivia piled a couple slices of veggie pizza onto a plate and handed it to me.

"They'll be over there well into the night getting all the tilework laid," I said. I glanced at Olivia. "The vanities you selected are spot on, by the way. They're gorgeous against the new floors."

"I knew they'd look great together," she said, beaming.

Even though she'd only been back over to the house a handful of times to work alongside me, she sent all her plans and purchase requests to me online for approval. I found myself looking forward to the times when Olivia joined me more and more. The house always seemed more alive when she joined Ryan and me on site.

I snuck a glance at the newly painted kitchen island. "Looks like I've walked from one active construction zone into another."

Liv threw her head back and laughed. "My former therapist said I should start a new project, so here we are." She waved to the island, which was now painted with its first coat.

"Farmhouse red?" I observed. "Great choice."

"See!" Olivia said to Ryan, sticking out her tongue at him. It was hands down the most relaxed and laid-back I'd seen her since—well, ever.

"Don't encourage her, Kerrington."

"But she's so fun when she's feisty," I said, laughing.

We sat and talked some more over pizza, then I decided to crash early for the night, despite Ryan offering another round of beers out by the firepit. It had been a long week of hard labor, and I hadn't been sleeping very well, despite the more comfortable bed. So, I took a pass. This elicited a response of *"Booo!"* from the two wise guys sitting across from me. I lifted my hands, asking for mercy.

"I've been working on the house for over a month now," I said, "but this was by far the most labor-intensive week. I think my body just needs to unwind and catch up on some much-needed sleep."

"I know just what you need!" Liv said, jumping up from her seat.

Ryan chuckled, giving me a sympathy shrug. "Think you're about to get Liv-a-fied."

"What you need is a hot bath in our soaker tub with a bath bomb and some Epsom salts, followed by a quick neck massage. It'll knock you out cold."

"Come again?" I looked to Ryan for help. "Okay, a beer doesn't sound so bad after all."

Olivia rolled her eyes. "Trust me! I'm an expert on self-care. I promise you'll feel like a new man afterward."

"I haven't taken a bath since I was a kid."

"Then you don't know what you're missing!"

"How often do you take baths, Ryan?" I asked, snickering.

His face was completely blank as he sipped his beer.

"Exactly!" I said, as if it proved my point. But somehow, I let Olivia cajole me into a bath in the giant soaker tub in the other spare bedroom downstairs—because it was nearly impossible for me to say no to her. I couldn't help but notice there were some of her things scattered around the room, though I didn't say anything.

After she started running the hot water, she poured half a bag of Epsom salt into the bathtub and swore it would work miracles on my sore muscles. Then she let me smell a variety of bath bombs, but I drew the line at those. She set a fluffy bath towel on the floating shelf by the tub and lit a couple candles before leaving me on my own.

I felt like the biggest idiot climbing naked into a bathtub at twenty-nine. But it only took about five minutes for me to see Liv's wisdom. I closed my eyes and nearly fell asleep as my muscles melted under her magic elixir. After about twenty-five minutes, I washed the day off my body with some fancy liquid body soap, then hoisted myself out. I wrapped the large blue bath towel around my waist, though my hair was still dripping wet. That's when I realized I either needed to put my dirty clothes back on, or sneak to the other side of the house with nothing but a towel wrapped around my waist. I peeked my head out of the bathroom door, and not seeing Liv anywhere around, I made my way to my bedroom.

I wasn't sure who was more embarrassed at my half-naked sneak—Ryan or me. He was washing dishes and glanced up as I casually walked by.

"No face mask and fuzzy slippers tonight?"

"Screw you," I said, laughing. "I'm gonna sic Olivia on you next."

"Do your best."

I was still grinning when I walked into my bedroom, stopping dead in my tracks when I saw Liv waiting there. Her eyes widened in surprised as they slid down my naked torso, the cinched towel leaving little to the imagination.

She quickly turned away, covering her eyes with her hand. "God, Brighton. I'm so sorry. Here, let me give you some privacy."

"Thought I was getting a back rub," I joked.

"A neck massage," she clarified, her voice hoarse. "I didn't think about you needing clean clothes first. Why don't you get dressed and come out when you're done?"

"I can get dressed with you here," I said, grabbing some athletic shorts. I quickly slid them up my legs and over my backside, letting the towel drop to the floor. When she turned and saw I was still shirtless I noticed the faintest pulse skip in her throat.

"Where do you want me?"

She looked around at our limited options. "Why don't we go out to the kitchen?"

I thought of Ryan standing there doing the dishes and knew there was no way I was going to make this even more awkward.

"Or I could sit right here," I said, pointing to a small reclining chair next to the fireplace. That looked comfy.

"I won't be able to get to your neck that way. Just lie down across the bottom of the bed."

I closed my eyes and breathed in deeply. I could do this. I could. I was a grown-ass man who had a ton of self-control.

I sat on the edge of the bed, flopping over onto my stomach. I thought I was prepared for the feel of Olivia's hands on my bare skin, but I wasn't. Nothing could've prepared me. They were soft and gentle but applied a firm pressure as they started working my tired muscles. I groaned as the pain began leaving and all that was left was the seductive roll of Liv's hands over my skin.

I wanted nothing more than to roll over and pull her down on top of me, so I forced myself to close my eyes and think of anything other than Liv leaning over me, her breasts occasionally brushing my back as she worked the kinks from my neck. If she'd ever once given Ryan a massage, I was having a hard time believing he would ever let his wife give someone else one. She was almost done when she ran her hand up the back of my neck and into my wet hair, massaging my scalp and causing my entire body to break out in goose bumps.

"We're done," I growled.

"That didn't feel good?" she asked, genuinely surprised. "Everyone in college always said I gave the best massages."

I rolled over, lifting myself onto my elbows. My gym shorts were now tented, and I did nothing to hide it. "It felt just fine," I said. "But I think maybe you need to go find Ryan and let me get some rest."

Liv bit her lower lip as she allowed herself the briefest glance down the length of my body. She put her hand over her mouth and started giggling when she saw my shorts.

"Glad this is so amusing for you," I said, standing. I towered over her but didn't dare move a muscle. One wrong brush by either of us, and I'd lose any ounce of self-control I had. "Goodnight."

I turned Olivia around by the shoulders and marched her out of my room, her laughter warming my insides even as I closed the doors and turned out the lights. I threw my arm over my eyes, trying to get comfortable. When it was clear I wasn't going to fall asleep unless I took care of my situation, I dropped my hand under the covers and began stroking myself. Much to my shame, it was the memory of Olivia in her navy-blue bathing suit, pulling herself up my body under the water at the quarry that finally did me in. I hadn't broken my word to Ryan, but as I fell into a fitful sleep, it was his wife who was in my dreams making me wish I had.

I knew I was walking a razor's edge, but this was one path that would lead me anywhere but to my salvation.

SOMETHING WOKE ME from a dead sleep, and I groaned, rolling over and grabbing my phone from the nightstand. Two in the morning. It must've been Olivia taking Stitch out.

I knew the right thing to do was rollover and go back to sleep. But I never said I was perfect. I pulled on a T-shirt and slipped quietly into the backyard. The moon wasn't as bright as it had been the first night I'd joined her outside this late, but it was easy to spot her. Tonight, she'd laid a large lap blanket onto the perfectly manicured grass and was laying on her back, looking up at the night sky. Stitch was happily stalking a bug by the fence and barely looked up as I made my way to join her.

"Couldn't sleep either?" I asked, my eyes tracing over her long, sleek, catlike body. She was wearing a matching baby blue sleep set that consisted of a silky pair of shorts and a camisole. Lace edged both, and I swear I'd never look at blue lace the same way again.

"No," she said quietly, patting the blanket beside her. "Care to join the Insomniacs Club?"

"Are you the founding member?"

"The one and only," she said, laughing. "But we're taking new member applications."

I lay down next to her, crossing my arms behind my head, too. The grass tickled my calves since I was longer than Liv and was hanging off the edge of the blanket. We relaxed in companionable silence, both of us feeling the weight of one another without the need for words.

Liv was the first to fold. "Do you ever wonder if there's more to life than this?"

"I know there is."

"How?" she asked.

"Because I have faith that there's life beyond this body that we're living in. Our soul has to go somewhere when we die, and I believe it comes back one day—to get a second chance or maybe right a wrong."

"I hope so," she said quietly.

Liv hadn't told me about the baby they'd lost yet, Ryan had. So, I didn't want to ask if that was why she was asking. Instead, I said, "Have you ever lost someone?"

She searched my eyes, as if trying to decide what to disclose of her heart and whether she could finally trust me. "Other than Ryan, I've lost every single person I've ever loved."

"I'm so sorry," I said. I wanted so badly to reach over and draw her into my arms, but I didn't. She wasn't mine to love the pain away, and it would've crossed the line of our growing friendship.

She turned her attention back to the few faint stars that were visible. "I met Ryan when I was getting my MBA. He was my professor—shocking, huh? When my adoptive parents died during my final year, he was the one to catch me, preventing me from spiraling all the way down. We started dating soon after that—obviously on the DL," she said, grinning.

"Obviously."

"We got married when I was twenty-five, and our first baby was due when I was twenty-six, but I had a late-term miscarriage. They think she developed a heart defect, and we lost her at twenty-two weeks," she said quietly.

Well, shit. Ryan only told me about their most recent loss. I hadn't realized there were others. No wonder he was so protective; the last few years had probably been hell on her.

"God, Liv—"

"It gets worse," she said, biting her lip. "Three months later, we accidentally got pregnant again. I was over the moon, but Ryan was worried it was too soon. He had reason because I was still experiencing low-grade depression at the time, after losing our first child. But our 'oops baby' was never an accident to me. I think maybe because I was adopted, I was grateful my birth mother decided to have me, even though something obviously prevented her from keeping me. She carried me all that time, then gave me up so I could have a better life. I think that's the most selfless act of love imaginable."

"Have you ever met your real parents?"

"No," she said, growing quiet. "I decided long ago to leave that door closed. She gave me up for a reason."

I knew something was still bothering her by the way she closed her eyes, her body tensing.

"I think Ryan wanted me to have an abortion," she admitted. "I'm not against others making that choice for themselves, but it didn't feel like the right answer for us at the time. Even though it *was* too soon, we wanted a family so badly. I'm ashamed to admit that I refused to hear him out. We got into a huge fight about it, and I miscarried the next day."

I rolled onto my side so I could look at her. "You know that wasn't your fault, right? It was your body's way of agreeing with you that it was too soon."

She looked at me, surprised that I had such a strong opinion on the matter.

"I know in my heart you're right. My doctor said the same thing. And Ryan tried telling me, too. But I was so mad at him. It felt like a betrayal for him to *not* want our baby. To even consider any other option than having it."

"It didn't mean he didn't want the baby. He was probably just scared. That's how guys get."

"How do you know? You don't have any kids."

"I almost did though," I admitted.

A long silence stretched between us. Maybe I shouldn't have said anything. This was about her, not me.

"Do you want to talk about what happened?" she finally asked.

"Would it help you if I did?"

She nodded. "I think so."

"It was with my college girlfriend. She was on the pill, so we weren't always as careful as we should've been. In our senior year, she got pregnant. It was definitely an oops baby—I mean, we were only twenty-one. We were both really freaked out at first, to say the least. She knew right away that she wanted to have an abortion, but I didn't want her to."

I didn't know if I could tell the rest of this story—not even for Olivia.

"You don't have to tell me, Brighton."

I glanced back over at her stunning blue eyes, and suddenly, I wanted to let her read me like an open book. She was the first woman since Caroline who would *know* what I'd gone through. Hell . . . maybe it would help us both.

"I knew it was her body, and her choice. But I begged Caroline to consider keeping the baby. I even told her if she didn't want it, I would take him. I had all these fantasies about having a boy and teaching him how to play baseball and ride a bike." I closed my eyes, too many memories rushing back at once. I rolled onto my back, putting my arm over my eyes so I could say the rest without seeing the sympathy I knew would flood Olivia's eyes.

It would be my undoing in the worst possible way.

"I haven't told anyone this story in eight years," I admitted. "You're the only woman I've ever told other than family."

"Anything you say is safe with me. I promise."

"I know," I said, sighing. "Against her better judgment, she decided to have the baby. We even found out it was the boy I'd been hoping for. We hadn't worked out the details yet about who would raise him or if we'd try doing it together. But at least she was giving him a chance."

It felt as if an entire crater fell from the heavens and landed on my chest. I could hardly breathe. I dropped my arms to my sides and opened my eyes, looking for some otherworldly courage to say what happened next.

That's when Olivia slid her hand across the blanket. She looped her fingers through mine and held on tight, giving me the courage to finish.

"Somehow, between her last doctor's appointment and when she went into labor, our son flipped his position and became breech. The umbilical cord got wrapped around him and was pinched while she was in labor," I said, steeling my jaw so I wouldn't lose it in front of Olivia. "He lost too much oxygen. Never stood a fucking chance."

A tear slid from the corner of my eye and down my cheek in the dark. "I know I was a lot younger than Ryan when I lost my son, but men get scared shitless, too. Even if we're too stubborn to admit it. And I can tell you this . . ."

Liv squeezed my hand.

"If you were my wife and got pregnant again too soon—I'd be way more worried about your life than the baby's. I don't mean to be a prick, Olivia. But I'm sure Ryan felt the same way."

"Thank you," she whispered. "I never considered that his reaction might've solely been because of how protective he was of me."

"If you were my wife, I'd move heaven and earth to protect you," I said, my voice thick with emotion, knowing she would never be.

All I was doing was living vicariously through another man, longing for the wife I'd never have.

CHAPTER SEVENTEEN

Ryan

IKE CLOCKWORK, I heard Olivia gently close the backdoor and watched as she laid a picnic blanket over the dew-covered grass. Stitch roamed the yard happily, and Olivia stretched out on her back under the stars, just like we always used to do together. I wanted to go down there, take her in my arms, and remind her how much life we still had worth living. Be the safe place I knew she needed.

Then I saw him.

Kerrington cut across the yard from the mudroom door, making his way toward Olivia—not in the least bit surprised to see her there. Had they planned this?

I dropped my forehead to the glass windowpane of our second-story bedroom. It felt so empty lately with Liv sleeping downstairs again. I woke up every night, as if my heart were tethered directly to hers. When she was restless, I was restless. Instead of turning toward each other like we used to, she now turned away, finding her solace in almost every answer other than me.

It felt as if my heart was slowly being strangled to death as I stood there staring at them. Brighton stretched out beside my wife, his arms comfortably supporting his head as he gazed at the stars. It wasn't long before their heads fell together as if they were sharing secrets in the dark—and that gutted me more than anything else. It was one thing to be attracted to someone else. It was another thing altogether to give that person any part of your heart.

It should be me down there with Liv. Not Kerrington.

I couldn't take it anymore. I needed to *do* something. Something had to give with us.

Before I turned away and went back to bed, I glanced down one last time. Liv traced her hand slowly across the blanket and wrapped it around Brighton's fingers. It was like the oxygen was vacuumed from the room. I couldn't breathe, I couldn't see straight.

Tears slid down my cheeks as I retreated into the darkness of our room. I turned on the shower and stepped under the scalding hot spray, giving myself fifteen minutes to let my grief swallow me. I would never give into it like Olivia had.

I slammed my fist against the travertine tile, and the searing pain took hold of my body, shooting straight up my arm. It felt amazing, even as my hand tingled. I felt more alive than I had in a long time. So, I hit the wall again, not caring if I broke a tile or my fist. I did neither, so I took my anger, my fear, and my pain out on the only thing I could—until the water ran pink with my blood, surprising me.

I turned off the water, in shock, as I looked down at my bloody knuckles.

"Ryan?"

I glanced up, finding Olivia staring back at me with confusion in her eyes. She quickly rushed into the bathroom. She grabbed a hand towel and wrapped it around my fist before I could formulate any words that would possibly make sense.

"What are you doing?" she moaned, shaking her head.

I hated seeing the fresh pain I brought to her eyes. She had enough to deal with; she didn't need me to add even more.

I ran my other hand through my wet hair, water rivulets running down my naked body. She was so close. I could smell the night on her. The freshly cut grass.

And Brighton.

I pulled her in close, pressing her against my wet body. "Why do you smell like our neighbor, Liv?"

She jerked back, shaking her head. "Ry—"

"Don't deny it. I saw you outside with him. I saw the way you reached for him. You want him, don't you? It's more than just being attracted, isn't it? Do you want to sleep with him?" I choked out.

"What? No. It's not like that!"

"But it would be if you had no strings to hold you back. Wouldn't it? If I wasn't here."

"Ryan, stop!" she begged. "I didn't do anything. We just talked."

"Then why can I smell him on you? I know what my wife smells like, and that's not it."

I lifted a strand of her hair and inhaled, smelling the shampoo we had in the downstairs guest bathroom—the one he used. "Truth, Olivia?"

"Don't, Ryan. Please," she said, tears nearly spilling over onto her cheeks. "It's been a long day. I'm exhausted. You need to let me help you clean those cuts."

I didn't care that blood was now dripping onto the bright white tile of our bathroom floor. That's exactly how my heart felt. It was open, gaping, bleeding. There was only one way to put it back together.

And all the answers started and ended with Olivia.

"Truth," I growled.

She bit her bottom lip. "Truth," she agreed. Tears were running down her face, and I knew this would be something I could never take back, but I had to know.

"If I wasn't in the picture, would you want to fuck Kerrington?"

"Ryan!"

"I need the truth, Olivia!" I said, grabbing my boxers from the bathroom counter and sliding them on. I yanked open the top drawer where we kept a stash of bandages. I looked down at my knuckles, really seeing the damage I'd done. *Fuck*. That was stupid of me.

I squeezed on some ointment and grabbed a roll of wrapping gauze, choosing that over the ridiculous number of Band-Aids I'd need.

"Let me help," she said, taking the gauze from my hand. I sat on the chair near her vanity and let her wrap my knuckles while she stalled for time.

When she was done, she turned off the bathroom light and led me back to our bedroom. Stitch was lying at the foot of our bed fast asleep, as if he did that every night. He was a good puppy. I had to give him that.

Liv surprised me when she climbed into bed and turned on her side to face me. "Get in, Ryan. We'll talk in bed."

I climbed in, sliding close to Olivia. Despite the pain in my heart, desire pooled in my belly. Smelling Kerrington on her didn't help either. It confused me how that could possibly turn me on so damn much.

"Would you fuck him, Livy? If he asked? If I wasn't a factor?"

"That's not a fair question, Ryan. You'll always be a factor. The *only* factor."

"I just need the truth."

She slid closer to me until her body was just inches from mine, her head sharing the same pillow. She raised her gaze, and I knew in an instant what the answer was. A mixture of sadness, guilt, and longing were at war in the gorgeous blue eyes staring back at me.

"Yes," she finally breathed out. "Is that what you wanted to hear?"

I pulled her against me, and she nestled her head against my chest, my chin resting on the top of her crown. It was everything I needed to know.

At least now there was hope.

CHAPTER EIGHTEEN

Brighton

"KERRINGTON!" I HEARD over the sound of the table saw. I turned it off, lifting my goggles to see Ryan standing in the doorway of the kitchen. He was dressed casually, but not grungy enough to be offering his help today.

"Hey, man," I said, nodding his way. That's when I noticed the gauze wrapped around his knuckles, my brows furrowing. "Everything okay?"

He better not've touched Olivia.

Ryan looked embarrassed as he glanced down at his bandaged fist. "Just a little testosterone overflow. Think I'm gonna buy a punching bag for the garage," he joked.

"You all right?"

He shoved his hands in the pockets of his shorts, then finally looked up at me. "Nah, not really. Think you could grab some lunch? I have something I'd like to run by you."

Ryan's dark eyes were fighting a battle, growing even darker with whatever was eating away at him.

"Sure, I could use a break," I said as I took my goggles off. "This thing is going to be the death of me."

Ryan glanced over at my handiwork, where I had several lengths of wood clamped together. I was cutting the last piece for the butcher block island. It would be the kitchen's showstopper centerpiece when it was all finished. The bamboo wood was a rich, warm honey brown—and its natural grains would be darkened to perfection.

"She sure is beautiful though," Ryan said appreciatively.

Except when he said it, all I could think about was Olivia.

The short drive to the Crown and Feather was fast. We found ourselves talking about college basketball again—a safe and easy topic. Ryan was a die-hard SU fan—keeping it local—while I was a Blue Devil, through and through. I was proud of the 9–6 lead we had over SU out of the fifteen times we'd battled it out. Ryan was confident they'd bridge the gap this year though, with the new recruits who were coming in. I agreed to disagree.

By the time we kicked back in a dark-wood booth with a Great Adirondack Whiteface Stout in hand, I was genuinely curious what was going through Ryan's mind and why he'd dragged me away for lunch. Not that I minded. The fridge at my uncle Isaiah's house was getting sparse, but I hated to waste time shopping when I could be working.

"What's going on?" I asked, taking a pull of my beer.

"I need a favor."

"What kind?" I grabbed a fried zucchini slice from the complimentary basket the waiter left before we ordered. These things were quickly becoming a favorite of mine.

"Look—I don't want to beat around the bush. I know you and Liv have a connection. I've seen the way you guys interact, and it's not just you. Liv has been happier since you showed up than I've seen her in almost two years."

"Ryan—"

"Hear me out. Please."

I nodded, moving my beer so the waiter could set our burgers onto the table.

"Liv and I have never had problems—in or out of the bedroom. It's always been easy with us . . . until it wasn't. We wanted a family so bad. We would've done almost anything to make it happen. We've lost three babies, Kerrington. Three. You can't imagine what that does to you."

"I'm so sorry, man," I said. Then I shared a condensed version of the same story I'd told Olivia the night before while he ate his lunch. I thought maybe it would help to know he wasn't alone in his grief. It was one thing to show your vulnerability to your wife, and another to share it with a bro. I considered Ryan a true friend now, so hopefully me sharing my deepest, darkest suckfest would make whatever he needed to get out a little bit easier.

"You do know, then," he said quietly. "I wish you didn't. No one should have to go through something like that. After our first loss, we rallied together, held each other up, even though Olivia was pretty shaken from miscarrying the baby so late. The miscarriage that followed was brutal, too. Especially because it was too soon after our first loss. Liv thought I didn't want it. But that wasn't the case. I just needed to talk through it with her because I was scared shitless."

He took a pull from his beer to finish it and signaled the waiter for another.

"It was the first fissure in our 'perfect' marriage," he said, using his fingers to make air quotes. "We were so close to just giving up after that. It hurt so fucking bad each time, but I know it hurt Olivia even worse to have those babies inside her, and then not. She says I can't understand what it's like, and I know I can't—but I've seen the way it's wrecked her. Changed her. It's been brutal."

Tears were pooling in Ryan's eyes, and he didn't try to hide them. Instead, he looked dead at me. "The last pregnancy was our miracle baby—it happened without us even trying. We'd finally gotten it in our heads that maybe it just wasn't meant to be for us. Then out of nowhere, she got pregnant again. It was like a gift from heaven. We let ourselves celebrate. Decorated the nursery. Picked out a goddamn name," he said, choking back his anguish.

The waiter dropped the check and beer off, but took one look at Ryan and muttered, "No rush." I grabbed it before Ryan could object, setting my black card under the receipt.

"Laelynn. That was her name. We buried her eight months ago now, and almost every day since then has been a struggle." He shook his head. "Some days, I can't tell if we're getting better, or if Livy's really broken like she says she is."

"What about you?" I asked quietly. "It wasn't just Olivia who lost a daughter."

"No, it wasn't." He pursed his lips, biting back the tears. "It's been hell for me. I grieve when I think too much about who our babies would be right now. What our family would look like if even one of them had lived. The happiness Liv would have if just one thing was different."

"Nothing's guaranteed. I think you're putting too much pressure on yourself to make her happy."

"No, I'm not," he insisted, shaking his head. "Olivia's my soulmate. There's not a single thing I wouldn't do to make her happy. To crack that pain wide open and see her soar again like she was meant to. This pain is changing her. I'm scared if I don't get her back soon, she'll be gone to me forever."

"And you think I can help somehow?"

Ryan nodded. "This may not make sense to you, but just hear me out, okay?"

I nodded, curious where this could possibly be going.

"I want you to share a night with Livy and me."

Whoa. That was so *not* what I was expecting him to say. "Come again?"

"You heard me. I want you to join us—intimately."

"Like—a threesome?" I asked, my brows furrowing in disbelief.

He nodded, his eyes clear and sharp. "Exactly like that."

I cleared my throat and chuckled. The man had lost his goddamn mind. Luckily, the waiter came back with my card and the receipt. I signed it, grateful for the momentary distraction. When he left, I turned my focus back to Ryan.

"Why in god's name would you share her with me, Ryan? How is that supposed to help?"

"She's intrigued by you. She lights up when you're around. I think if she can completely let go of any inhibition and be vulnerable again with someone, it may open her heart back up for good. With me, she's open, but her heart is still so fragile. She's told me she can't help but see Laelynn whenever we're together. It's not that she doesn't love me. But she can't seem to separate me from the pain she's experiencing.

"With you, she'd have to set it all aside to really let go—to explore her actual feelings again. She's so disconnected these days from what she's really feeling. It would be nice, for just once, to see the *real* Liv again—to have her be present in her body, with all her wide-open feelings. To see passion running through her veins again. You think she's gorgeous now, wait till you see her when she feels aligned. There is nothing I wouldn't do to see *that* Liv again. Nothing."

"Including sharing her," I marveled, starting to feel what he was throwing my way.

"Exactly."

"Why the three of us? Why not just Liv and me?"

"Because she's still my wife," he growled, as if I needed the reminder. "If anyone else is touching her, I will be, too. This isn't about me being a cuckhold. This is about me—and hopefully you—waking Olivia back up. Bringing her back to *me*."

"So, I'm nothing more to you than a basic stud horse," I said, grunting in disbelief. He really thought I could taste Olivia and walk away? Was he insane?

"It's not like that."

"What's it like then, Ryan? Enlighten me," I said, shaking my head.

"It's not just what I need. Olivia needs you, too."

"What are you talking about?"

"She's already told me she wanted to be with you."

"She what?" I sputtered in complete shock. "She's never hinted at anything like that with me. I swear to you."

"I know," he said. "We have a truth pact we made years ago. We keep *nothing* from each other, no matter how badly it might hurt to say. No matter how broken she's become, that pact is sacred to us. She would never admit that to me unless she means it. I asked her point blank, and she admitted she wants you, *like that*. As much as I hate it, there's nothing I can do to change it. So, I figured it was better to lean into her desire with her, rather than taking away one more thing that would bring her joy. She's lost enough already."

Shit. What could I say to that? I took a long pull from my beer, meeting Ryan's eyes. Everything he was feeling was mirrored in those dark pools of pain. It was either the most noble thing I'd ever heard, or the stupidest.

Ryan wasn't a stupid man, but he was a complete fool to think there would be no casualties from this. Even I knew better.

And yet . . .

The pull of having Olivia—even for just one night—was too strong to ignore. I'd be a liar if I said I didn't want it. If I hadn't fantasized about this very thing before.

"All right. I'm in," I finally said. "But I want our own truth pact, man to man."

He nodded. "You got it."

"If this goes south—and I'm fairly sure it will—you don't blame me. This was your decision. I never asked to sleep with your wife. Don't you ever forget that."

I leveled him with my gaze. "Our friendship comes first. I need you to be upfront with me, a hundred percent. If it gets weird—well, weirder than this already is—or if you change your mind, it stops. If I need to move out of your house, you tell me. And if anything changes for me, if I start feeling anything other than something physical, this stops. I respect you, Ryan, and consider you a good friend now—hell, you're probably one of my closest. And I like Olivia, too. But the last thing I need is a broken heart. I won't help you fix Olivia at my own expense."

Ryan was quiet, as if he'd never considered me in all this. That was exactly what I was afraid of.

He met my eyes and nodded, sealing our fates.

What in the world had I just agreed to?

CHAPTER NINETEEN

Olivia

"EXCUSE ME, WHAT?" I was flabbergasted in a way I've never been in our entire marriage. Ryan had taken my breath away on more than one occasion, but never like this. "You aren't serious, are you?" I asked shakily.

I went back to cutting the stems off the summer bouquet Ryan brought home for me. Pale blush-pink peonies, so light they looked like a watercolor version of themselves. They were stunning in the silver square vase Ryan's sister gave us as a wedding gift.

"Liv, stop fiddling with the flowers and look at me," Ryan said, dragging my hips around until I faced him, nestled between his thighs. He sat on one of the barstools at the island. We'd finished the paint job and the new swivel stools, with their black wrought-iron legs, looked amazing against the farmhouse red.

"Baby," he said low, stirring something deep and hidden inside me like he did in the early days. I swear the man used to get me so hot and bothered, just the thought of him made my heart spin in circles like I did when I was as a kid—arms stretched wide open, twirling too fast until I got dizzy, falling over in the grass, and laughing with delight. That's what being with Ryan felt like. Carefree freedom, an open heart, and laughter.

I wanted that back so badly I could cry.

"Listen to me . . . I promise we'll be okay. We can do this, just once. One time, that's all I ask."

"Why? Don't you believe me when I tell you I'm happy with you?" I ran my hands over his broad shoulders and down his arms.

"I do. But sometimes, relationships need something else. I never thought ours would. I swear to god, this was never more than a secret fantasy. Never thought I'd be asking you to do something like this—or that I would ever consider it without ripping someone's face off."

He squeezed my hip. "I don't want to share you, Livy, but I will. And I think we need this. We've been broken for too long."

"And you really think having sex with someone else will solve everything?" I asked, raising my eyebrow.

"It couldn't hurt to try," he said sheepishly. "We've done everything else. I just want to see you happy again. I want to see something light you up and bring back that energy I fell in love with."

"Ryan, that girl doesn't exist anymore," I said sadly.

"No, but the one before me does. And we have a lifetime of happiness to still live together. But we can't do that if we don't start *really* living again. You used to look at me the way you look at Brighton. And don't try to deny it—I've *seen* the way your eyes follow him around. When you look at me, all I see is pain in your eyes. I know you still see Laelynn when you look at me. You've said as much."

"Ry—"

"It's okay, Liv. I get it. Kind of. But I don't want you to just think about what we lost when you look at me. I want you to see me as your partner. As someone who excites you and brings you pleasure. The way I used to."

"You still do. I don't know how to make you believe me."

"By doing this for me. By *showing* me that you can see beyond what we lost. That we have something more than just pain to build our future on. Consider this our relationship's defibrillator. Just once, Livy. If you never want to again—we don't have to. I just need you to trust me."

I nestled my head into his shoulder, breathing in his familiar scent. I wrapped my fists around the collar of his shirt. "I'm scared, Ryan. What if this changes things?"

He calmly brushed my hair from my face and tucked it behind my ear. "That's exactly what I'm hoping will happen. That we'll get a new spark—an adrenaline rush like we had in the beginning, when we chased the thrill of doing something that we knew was taboo. When I was sneaking around with my student. You with your professor. Remember that one time—"

"Oh my god! At the awards ceremony?"

Ryan growled, yanking me closer to make sure I knew exactly how exciting he found the memory. "You were so freaking hot, Liv. You still are. This will bring back all those fun memories, back when we were carefree and walked a little on the wild side."

"I don't know," I said, shaking my head. "It just doesn't feel like the safe way to go about this. I don't want Brighton, babe. I want you. I want myself back."

He nuzzled the side of my face with his own, nudging till he found my lips. He nipped the bottom one, sucking it in. "This will bring the old Liv back, trust me. Or maybe an even more adventurous version. We used to joke around about wanting to have a threesome, don't you remember?"

I groaned, pressing my hips against his thighs as I revisited the numerous times Ryan and I would talk dirty to each other in bed, sharing our deepest, darkest fantasies. Somehow, I'd always imagined a threesome as more about Ryan—which would mean another woman sharing our bed. Never in my wildest dreams would I have imagined him pleading with me to let another man join us. I just couldn't wrap my mind around it.

Still. The thought of being with both Ryan *and* Brighton together . . . what woman in her right mind would turn down an offer like this? When it was her husband's idea, no less. I hadn't ever let myself fantasize about really being with Brighton because I never would have done that to Ryan. But the thought of getting to touch him, to open to him fully . . . it was almost too much to comprehend.

The scariest part? Now that Ryan suggested it, I wanted it. Badly.

"When?" I whispered, running my tongue over his lips with delicate, sensual kisses as the idea took root.

"Really?" He pulled back and looked at me with so much hope in his eyes. How could I say no to anything he asked after all I'd put him through?

I nodded, biting my lower lip. Because as much as I convinced myself I was doing this for Ryan, heat was already pooling in my lower belly at the thought of getting to know Brighton Kerrington in a whole new light.

"Just promise me something, Ry?" I asked, looking up into my husband's familiar brown eyes.

"Anything, baby."

"Truth?"

"Truth," he said.

"Whatever happens, or however this goes . . . we'll get through this together. Honesty all the way. Because I didn't ask for this. You did. And I never want you to think that this will change the way I feel about you. You're my whole heart, and I can't live without you. I couldn't bear for this to change *us*."

"I promise it won't."

I nodded, giving him a quick kiss before I returned to finish arranging my flowers. "So, when does this whole thing go down?" I asked, my voice giving away my nerves.

Ryan stood, following me to the kitchen island. He put his arms on both sides of me, the hard lines of his body pressed against my back. He breathed warm against the sensitive skin of my neck as he trailed kisses toward my ear. Goose bumps raced over my arms, and I had to set the kitchen scissors down I was so distracted.

"Tonight," he said, flicking my earlobe with his tongue.

"Tonight?" I squeaked out, trying to turn in his arms. He wouldn't let me, scooping my hair to the side, and drawing my skin in between his lips. He sucked hungrily, setting off a chain reaction of sparks that fled south.

"Yes, Liv. Before we change our minds. Now go take a shower. Relax however you need. Then meet us outside on the back patio in an hour. I've arranged to have some appetizers and wine delivered from Colloca's. I even got a couple bottles of your favorite Cabernet Sauvignon."

"You were awfully confident," I said. He reached around to cup my breasts, kneading the soft flesh until my nipples responded.

"This is going to be incredible, baby," he murmured. "Go get ready for us."

Us.

Oh my god. What did I just agree to?

CHAPTER TWENTY
Brighton

WHAT DID ONE bring to his first threesome? I felt ridiculous, stopping by the store after I was done with a sweaty day of work, but I was nervous, and this gave me something to focus on other than the fact that I was about to sleep with my good friend's wife. I grabbed some sunflowers, hoping Ryan wouldn't get upset. I didn't know what Olivia's favorite flower was, but these always made me happy. Besides, my mother would've skinned me if I showed up to a get together without something for the hostess. Then again, I was pretty certain there was nothing in Emily Post's etiquette book about threesomes.

When I got back to the house, the light was on in the master bedroom, and I couldn't stop myself from imagining her up there getting ready. I swallowed, dropping my dirty work clothes to the floor and stepping into the shower to wash off the day. I took extra time scrubbing under my fingernails and trimming them, too. I hadn't had sex in almost six months. The truth was, I was getting tired of the whole pickup scene. I wasn't into online dating either. And since most of my days were spent with a houseful of dudes, I was resigned to meeting my future wife the old-fashioned way— probably through a friend.

I just never expected the next person in my bed would be my friend's wife—*and* my friend. I shook my head, gripping the shower wall. Could I really do this?

Then I thought of Olivia's cornflower blue eyes, and the way she made me feel appreciated when she looked up at me and laughed. Or the way her fingers kneaded the stress from my shoulders, and how they slid across the blanket to offer me comfort.

I wrapped my hand around myself and closed my eyes, taking the edge off so I'd have more to give Olivia later. I wanted to make sure I could give her everything she needed from this experience, and I couldn't do that if I exploded like a schoolboy the first time she touched me.

Fifteen minutes later, I was clean and more relaxed than I'd been since talking to Ryan at the pub. I threw on a pair of khaki shorts and a tight-fitting navy dress shirt with a simple pattern of small white dots of different sizes. I rolled the sleeves up high, checking myself out in the mirror. Then I undid a couple buttons, feeling much more relaxed and causal. I ran a hand through my shaggy blond hair with some gel before heading out to the back patio, where Ryan was already waiting. He'd turned on the fairy lights above the seating area; they ran between the ivy, making it look serene, yet magical. I made a mental note to ask Olivia about doing something similar over at my uncle's place.

"Hey, man," I said, grabbing Ryan's attention.

He turned, his eyes trailing over my outfit. He lifted his glass of red wine. "Can I get you one?"

"Please," I said gratefully.

I had to laugh. Ryan wasn't dressed much differently than I was. He had on a pair of dark blue dress shorts and a white dress shirt, also opened low at the collar. His sleeves were rolled up but sat lower on his forearms. Unlike me, he had dark brown hair at the opening of his shirt, and his short, well-groomed beard game was strong.

But we couldn't be more different, Ryan and me. At least if I had to see a dude naked, it was this friend. I'd seen him in his swim trunks at the Hole, and the guy was almost as ripped as I was. For someone with a desk job, it was impressive.

"Cheers," he said, his eyebrows raised.

"Cheers," I offered back. I took a large sip of wine, not knowing where to look or what to do. "Well, this is awkward."

He laughed. "We'll be fine. We need to be, for Liv."

I nodded. "You sure she's okay with this? Knows what she's getting herself into?"

"I don't think any of us really know what we're getting ourselves into," he answered honestly.

"True," I said, watching as he continued setting the table, moving some flowers to the center. *Crap!* I'd left the bouquet I bought for Olivia in my room. I glanced at Ryan's delicate peonies and thought of my big, gauche sunflowers. Guess they were staying where they were.

"Can I ask you a question?"

"Sure," he said. "Transparency, right?"

I nodded. "You guys aren't really swingers, are you? I mean, this is truly the one and only time you've ever done something like this?"

Ryan burst out laughing, easing the tension in the air. "Don't be an ass, Kerrington. You know we're not swingers. Jeez."

Before I could banter back with something clever, the backdoor swung open. We both turned, and my heart took a beating as I dragged my eyes over Olivia.

Hugging her body was a long white sundress with flowers resembling her peonies, sage green petals nestling them. The skirt was slit up the front, revealing a pair of caramel-colored cowboy boots I wasn't expecting. The dress was opened low in a V at the neckline, and I could see a sheer, white lacy bra beneath when she moved just the right way—as she did when she sauntered across the patio to us.

Her large silver necklace looked Native American, holding a few small beads that matched the colors of the flowers on her dress. Something about the way the carved medallion rested on the flat plain just above her breasts stirred something inside me. She accepted the goblet of wine Ryan handed to her and leaned forward, kissing him lightly.

"Liv," I said when she lifted the blood red wine to her full, nude lips, "you look stunning."

"Thank you," she replied, her cheeks pinking from the compliment.

She had to know how gorgeous she was. A woman didn't come out like that, her long, blond hair tousled like already sexed-up bedhead, ready to greet two lovers, without knowing she was the shit.

The three of us stood there awkwardly for a moment, until Liv finally broke the silence. "Let's just get it out in the open, shall we? Because I feel like Ryan's talked to you, and he's talked to me, too. But you and I haven't had a chance to talk about any of this—to make sure we're on the same page."

"We're on the same page," I answered gruffly.

Warm laughter parted her lips, and I wanted nothing more than to possess them. "So, you're truly okay with this?" she asked.

"I wouldn't be here if I wasn't."

"All righty, then." She nodded, biting those soft, pillowy lips of hers. She looked toward Ryan. "I don't know how to do this. This was your idea. Should we have some appetizers first, or jump straight to dessert?"

Ryan stepped toward her, his hand snaking up to her hair and holding her head captive. Olivia's eyes were full and bright, like the shiniest, wildest moon the northern hemisphere had ever seen. The heat that radiated from her as she looked at her husband's mouth was the biggest turn-on I ever could've imagined. I never thought of myself as someone who'd get off on watching someone else be intimate; but suddenly, I knew everything I'd assumed about this evening would be shattered—expectations exploding into a million little pieces and rearranging themselves into something far bigger than any one of us alone could've seen coming.

Something I may never recover from.

I watched as Liv's chest rose when Ryan leaned forward, whispering something in his wife's ear. She glanced over at me, biting her lower lip. Something silent was communicated between us in that moment, and it terrified me.

Because that single, heart-stopping look told me this was more than just Ryan talking Liv into going along with some crazy scheme. The fierce desire aimed straight at me was enough to confirm I wouldn't be recovering anytime soon once I got a taste of Olivia Wells. She *wanted* this. She wanted *me*.

The moons in her eyes disappeared as she closed her lids, her body purring as Ryan kissed along her long, graceful neck. He glanced up at me, our eyes meeting. He was marking his territory before we started. I nodded, letting him know I understood and wouldn't forget who her heart belonged to. I also knew, though—before I ever touched her—that my heart would never be able to let go of Olivia once I gave myself to her.

When she opened her eyes again, they were half full of lust and aimed straight at me. I knew one thing for certain in that moment. Ryan may be her husband and own her heart, but before the night was through, I would brand Olivia forever, making sure she never forgot having me between her thighs.

CHAPTER TWENTY-ONE

Ryan

I KNEW I WOULD have to be the one to break the ice. We'd had a couple glasses of Liv's favorite wine already by the fire pit. It wasn't enough to make any of us drunk—just took the edge off as we relaxed over appetizers and good conversation. I saw Olivia glance at Brighton a few times from the corner of her eyes when she thought I wasn't looking. I knew I should probably be jealous, but the truth was, Olivia North Wells would always be mine, even if she was intrigued by our neighbor. Brighton may be sharing her with me tonight, but when all was said and done, I knew I was her home.

That was the sexiest part of all of this.

"Come here, baby," I finally said, looking at my wife across the flames. We were sitting in the oversized Adirondack chairs Livy had had custom made for us.

It was time. I could tell by the sweet, lazy look in her eyes. She was *feeling* things. She held my gaze as she stood, her hips swaying as she made her way around the fire pit. She brushed Brighton's legs on her way over to me, and I couldn't help but notice his hand reach out, making brief contact with Livy's fingers as she passed by him.

Olivia set her wine onto the ledge of the fire pit before climbing onto my lap, facing me. Her dress was slit up the front, making it easy to part as she planted her bottom against me. I groaned when she dipped her head, cupping my face in one of the softest, most open kisses I'd received from her in a good, long while. *This.* This was the feeling I was chasing, I realized. Olivia—wide open and free. Without the weight of death hanging over her.

This carefree, uninhibited woman on my lap was the Liv I'd fallen in love with all those years ago. The one who loved me back just as fiercely as I did her. I would've given anything to take her right there under the moonlight if it guaranteed everything would be magically woven back together again, healed and better than before. To hell with Brighton Kerrington.

I could feel his eyes on us as I wrapped my arms around her waist, then slid them up her back, holding her possessively against my chest one last time while she was still only ever mine.

I stood with Olivia still on my lap, her legs wrapping around my waist as I lifted her up. She looked over her shoulder at Kerrington, and the look of longing that passed between them reminded me why we were doing this in the first place. Thanks to me, the fire between them had been lit, allowed to breathe in oxygen as the flames flickered to life. I knew Olivia, and she wouldn't be able to let go of the passion now pulling them together like an invisible thread until she burned him completely from her system.

I'd keep my word—for all our sakes. Give us this one night to lose ourselves, so we could find ourselves again. After hearing Kerrington's story, maybe we all needed the healing it would bring.

My eyes landed on his when she pressed her warm, soft lips to my neck. Something special was brewing between the three of us, and I couldn't explain it any more than I could fight what I'd started. It was time. I nodded for him to come join us. He walked over, then carefully moved Olivia's hair off her neck while running his other hand slowly over her shoulder and down her arm. Liv's breath hitched, and I could feel her walls start to crumble the moment she relaxed, moaning into my kiss as she shuddered under another man's touch.

She closed her eyes and rolled her head to the side, giving him the access he was searching for. I watched as he leaned forward, his mouth finding her collarbone as he tasted her flesh for the first time. Livy's lips parted in surprise as he slowly, gently traced my wife's skin with his lips—from her shoulder to her jaw. Then he lifted her hair so he could kiss the small, intimate space on the back of her neck, just below her hairline. I found myself aroused by the sensual gesture, even as I was at war with the desire to pummel him.

It was Olivia's moan that brought me back to my senses. This wasn't about me. It was all about her. The sooner I let go of any remaining jealously, the better this would be for all of us.

I gripped her jaw, dragging her dreamy gaze back to mine. "I love you, Livy," I reminded her, crashing my lips to her mouth. She kissed me back hungrily, matching the intensity I was suddenly feeling.

"Ryan," she said softly when we parted.

I watched the pulse in her throat flutter as Kerrington sucked the delicate skin on the back of her neck. I palmed her breast, running my fingers along her pebbled nipple underneath too much fabric. An audible moan escaped her throat, and there was nothing I could do to stop what would happen next—thanks to the wheels I'd set in motion.

No matter how hard it was for me to watch Kerrington's mouth on my wife's skin, I'd give anything to watch her unfold—to bloom again as we peeled back layers of her grief, petal by petal.

Olivia dropped her legs, sliding them down my body so she could stand, my arms steadying her.

"You ready?" I asked, searching her silky blue eyes.

Liv nodded, quietly taking my hand in hers, even while reaching back for Kerrington. "Let's go inside."

CHAPTER TWENTY-TWO

Olivia

HAVING A THREESOME wasn't how I imagined it would be, or anything like I'd read in my romance novels. It was sensual, confusing, awkward, and earth shattering all at once. Ryan didn't just sit back and watch—he was an active partner, often choreographing the beautiful dance our bodies were engaged in. There were many times I lost track of where my body ended and theirs began. The one constant was that Ryan and Brighton never once touched one another intimately—all their focus was on pleasuring me. The feeling of two sets of hands, and two sets of lips, worshipping every inch of my body as if I were the most precious treasure on earth was more intoxicating and all-consuming than I ever could have dreamed. Nothing else mattered that night—except the giving and receiving of pleasure, acknowledging the deeply rooted passion that had been building to a crescendo over the last month, no matter how badly we all wanted to deny it.

I closed my eyes the moment we made our way into the guest bedroom where Brighton was staying, letting my husband take the lead. Ryan was a sensual man by nature, but tonight, his primal side emerged—handing over every last part of his heart, his body, and his soul in the most vulnerable and loving way—by making room for Brighton in the equation.

As much as Ryan took and gave, Brighton was there, too, loving my body with an equal force and skill all his own. There was no comparing them; they were like the endless, all-consuming beauty found in both the night and day. Where Ryan was more tender from our years of shared intimacy, Brighton was untamed, demanding. Where Brighton's passion was endless, Ryan met my heart at the depth I needed to see this through, never once making me feel ashamed for the pleasure I was feeling with another man. In fact, he let me know exactly what turned him on, bringing about a new wave of desire that tumbled the three of us back together long into the night. I didn't know what time it was when we finally burned through our desire enough to succumb to sleep; but the three of us tumbled into dreamland together, in Brighton's bed, with our arms and legs entwined in an intimacy only the three of us would ever understand. It took a limitless well of strength and confidence for Ryan to share me the way he had—knowing even if it hurt him, it may very well be the spark we needed to crack my grief wide open.

Our grief, I reminded myself.

That night, I fell into a deep, dreamless sleep for the first time since we lost Laelynn—my body and heart satiated and full in a way that left little room for anything else. When I woke, the sun was casting a pinkish-orange glow from behind the breezy curtains, warming Brighton's room. Ryan was still spooned around me, and my arm was wrapped around Brighton's waist, my head nestled on his firm chest. There was no graceful way to untangle myself and get up for my morning coffee without waking them. I started to shift slowly, when Ryan pulled me closer, nuzzling my neck.

"Mmm," he said. "Morning, Liv."

I was so worried it would be awkward with him. That he would regret what we'd done. If anything, it was just the opposite. He pressed against me, his hands reaching up to cup my breasts. In doing so, he accidentally brushed against Brighton's chest too, causing him to stir.

My eyes were the first thing he sought as he opened his lazily, adjusting to the bright morning light. They gleamed with mischief when he looked down and saw Ryan gently brushing his fingertips over my nipples, giving Brighton tacit permission to be with me one last time.

"Morning," Brighton said. He shifted onto his side so he could face me. Then he ran his fingers down the side of my face as he leaned forward, brushing his lips lightly over mine.

"I didn't mean to wake you. I was just going to get up and make some coffee and pancakes."

Ryan perked up, lifting his head off his pillow. "Did I hear pancakes?"

"Yes! If you stop trying to tempt me from getting out of bed."

"Is that an option?" he asked, grinning over at Brighton. "You awake, Kerrington?"

"Never more so," he said, running his hand down the front of my body with reverence. His hand slid over my bare hip, then found its way between my thighs, pressing them open.

Ryan's lips brushed my collarbone, his tongue tracing hot, wet circles up my throat until he found my mouth. I wasn't expecting it to feel so natural with them—especially after everything we'd done the night before. There are some things best left under the veil of darkness. The guys didn't seem to get that memo, though.

"I guess pancakes could wait," I said, my laughter quickly dying when Brighton's fingers pressed deep inside me.

For the next hour, pancakes were the last thing on my mind. We found a natural rhythm together again, as we had the night before. Ryan already knew the things I liked, but Brighton was learning my body—and let's just say he was a quick study. Where Ryan was gentler and more commanding with me, Brighton was unapologetically hot and dirty. He wasn't afraid to tell me what he liked, and to give into any desire my body begged for. The combination made Ryan even hotter, both of us pushing boundaries we'd only fantasized about together. With the three of us, there were no walls in the bedroom. It was the freest I'd felt in a long time. Maybe ever.

Because, for once, I wasn't in my head. I was in my body, living sensation to sensation, feeding off the next kiss, the next touch. I never wanted to leave the bedroom. I was afraid that once the safety of our bubble was broken, it would all disappear, and I would crash into darkness once again. This wasn't a permanent fix, after all. It was a catalyst.

I already felt different in my body, though, so maybe Ryan had been right. I guess only time would tell. All I knew as I stretched lazily between them, under the rays of the bright morning sun, was that my heart and my body were finally satiated as one.

Finally, the three of us rose together. Ryan was the first to leave, padding naked from Brighton's room as he headed upstairs to our shower. Brighton slid his boxers on as I stood, searching for my clothes. I slid my underwear up my sore legs, my body well-loved many times over.

"I'll grab the rest of my clothes and wash them after we all shower," I said, making my way toward the door. Brighton stopped me before I could leave, his hand gripping my wrist and spinning me back toward him.

My breath hitched as I met his stormy green eyes, one of his arms now wrapped around my waist.

"Brighton," I said, trying to find the right words. Without Ryan in the room, I couldn't be as free with him, and that hurt my heart after giving him my entire being only moments ago. These were going to be tricky waters to navigate, and we hadn't discussed any "after-the-fact" ground rules.

"Olivia," he drawled as he grinned at me, "I just want to say a couple things before I lose the nerve. I'm not asking for anything."

I relaxed against his chest and looked up at him. "Okay, go ahead."

"First of all, I want you to know that you're the single most beautiful woman I've ever met. But I never would've crossed a line with you, no matter how attracted I am to you. Even though neither of us intended for something like this to happen, I'm so freaking glad Ryan initiated it so I could be with you. Even if it was just this one night, I regret nothing, Olivia. It's important to me that you know that."

"Thank you," I said quietly, under the intensity of his gaze.

"I've never wanted someone as badly as I do you," he admitted, brushing a hair from my face, and tucking it behind my ear. "I know it's wrong—you belong to Ryan. But even if this breaks my heart in the long run, it'll be worth it. *You* are worth it, Olivia."

"Brighton," I started—but what could I really say?

There was no us. There was Ryan and me—and that didn't leave room for Brighton beyond last night. I didn't want to tell him how much it had meant to me, either. How he'd unlocked something buried so deep inside me. How I felt more alive and hopeful this morning than I had in years. I couldn't tell him everything that was racing through my heart because I didn't understand all my own feelings, and I needed time to process them. Most of all, none of that would be fair to him. Because at the end of the day, he was right. I *was* Ryan's, and I didn't want to hurt him any more than we probably already had.

"It's okay. You don't need to say anything. I just want you to know that if we were both single, I would never let you go," he said, his voice raspy. "You'd be my end game."

I choked back a cry, burying my head against his chest.

He soothed my heart as much as he could, giving me a long, soul-melding hug. I prayed it wasn't his way of saying goodbye. We both knew I could never be his, but I wasn't ready to not *see* him anymore. The truth was, I loved being around him—even if we had to go back to being just friends.

"Here," he said, breaking free from our embrace. He walked over to the writing desk and grabbed a bouquet of sunflowers I'd somehow missed last night—my mind preoccupied with other things. "These were for you. They make me happy, so I thought they might make you a little happier, too."

My heart hammered as I wrapped my fingers around the bouquet's stems. I looked up into his now familiar eyes, full of so many things left unsaid between us. The worst part? I wanted nothing more than to stand on my tiptoes and kiss him. To thank him properly for the gorgeous flowers. For the simple act of caring and making me a priority. He hadn't needed to do that, to get me into his bed last night with Ryan.

The fact that he had told me all I needed to know. And it was a dangerous game that had no winners. I took my flowers into the kitchen and set them on the counter before making my way upstairs, seeking comfort from my husband for the ache in my heart caused by another man.

CHAPTER TWENTY-THREE

Ryan

THE HOT WATER was a relief on my worn-out muscles. I was hurting in places I'd forgotten I had muscles. But last night was amazing—better than I ever could've dreamed it would go. The energy and chemistry between the three of us had been so electrifying it was almost scary. I was hard just thinking of the way Livy looked in Brighton's strong arms. I'd done it for her initially, but the truth was, it ended up being for me, too. I discovered there was nothing sexier than being pleasured by your wife while another man's face was buried between her thighs. It was something I'd use as fantasy fuel for years to come.

I don't know how long I stood under the hot spray, hard with longing for my wife. Like magic, she slipped into the shower behind me, wrapping her arms around my waist.

"God, Liv," I said, turning to face her. I dropped my mouth to hers, the water streaming over us as I took my fill tasting her. I couldn't wait, though. All the energy and momentum from the evening before came rushing over me, and I had to have her again. I hoisted her up, her legs wrapping around my waist on instinct as I buried myself deep inside of her. She gave herself over to me without hesitation, our bodies colliding until we both climaxed, my name tumbling from her lips. I held her against me in a chest-to-chest embrace until the aftershocks left our exhausted bodies.

I lowered her slowly, and Olivia chuckled when her trembling legs nearly gave out on her. "I think I need something to eat."

"I think *I* need something to eat," I said, grinning mischievously at her. "But let's get some food in you first."

She swatted my ass on her way out of the shower, and I loved seeing this side of her again. It had been almost two years since Olivia's playful side had come out, and it was everything.

She sauntered to her closet naked, a new spring in her step. When she came out, she was wearing one of my favorite summer outfits—a denim skirt, some cute brown ankle boots, and a white, bohemian-style shirt. The gold embroidery lining the V-neck of her shirt drove me to distraction, and all I could think about was tumbling back into bed.

I dressed, watching as she styled her long blond hair into a loose, sexy braid. She spritzed on something sweet smelling, then turned to give me a kiss.

"Meet you downstairs?" she asked, as if this was our normal routine again.

I couldn't remember the last time we'd gotten ready for our day like this together. I missed the hell out of it. I pulled her into my arms, burying my head in the crook of her shoulder so I could better smell the sweet floral notes of her perfume—something mixed with lemongrass and pineapple. I wanted to devour her, never leaving our room again. The problem with having every inch of Olivia again was that I wanted more. I wanted every bit she would give me before she closed back up. And I was scared it was only a matter of time—as all the other times had been.

"I love you," I told her. "You were so beautiful last night. We need to talk about it later."

"I know," she said, kissing me sweetly. "But not yet. Can we just have some breakfast first, maybe go to the farmer's market?"

"They got First Street closed again?" I asked.

She nodded. "They have some amazing goat milk candles I want to pick up. And the apples that I love from Ontario Orchard. I'd like to grab a basketful, maybe make an apple crisp for dessert tonight."

It was my favorite. She was trying, and the effort nearly undid me. It had been so long since she'd done something like this for me. Then a thought occurred to me, like a dark cloud hanging over my head.

"Did you invite Brighton to join us?"

"No. I thought we could make a day of it by ourselves. It's been a long time since we've gone out to do something."

I pulled her closer. "Like a date?" I asked, hopeful.

"Like a date," she breathed out. "But first, Brighton *is* waiting downstairs for the pancakes I promised you guys. And you both have to be starving after last night."

"You're right," I said, kissing her neck one last time.

Then she took my hand and we walked down to the kitchen—to make breakfast for the man I'd let sleep with my wife. The world didn't get any crazier than this.

BRIGHTON WASN'T IN the kitchen by the time we made our way down. I wish I could say I was disappointed, but it meant I got more of Liv to myself today. While she whipped up her homemade batter, I checked my emails. Even though I wasn't teaching this summer, I was planning my classes for the fall and keeping up with faculty news and issues.

I was about to set my phone down and help Liv set the table when I got a text from Kerrington.

Had an emergency at the worksite this morning. Had to rush to Watertown for some supplies and a new sink. Tell Olivia I'm sorry to miss out on her famous pancakes. Hope I can get a rain check. See you guys later.

Olivia smiled at me from the stove. "Everything okay at work?"

"Yeah," I said, standing. I ran a hand over the back of my neck, debating whether to pass his message along. I finally settled on the truth, as we always did. "Brighton had an issue at the house. He had to head home for the day to grab some parts."

"Oh. Okay. Well, it's no big deal since we're playing hooky anyway. I wasn't planning on going over there to work today, were you?"

I hooked my thumbs in her jean skirt, tugging her toward me. "Can't say I was. I have a date with a hot blond. She's kinda easy on the eyes. I was hoping I might get lucky later."

"Your forecast is looking promising," she said, laughing.

When I ran my hands up her thighs and under her skirt, she swatted me with the spatula. "*If* a certain sexy professor stops trying to cop a feel and gets busy setting the table, that is. These pancakes won't serve themselves."

We spent the rest of the day eating our breakfast, winding our way down the closed streets of the farmer's market, and then eating ice cream at Bev's on the lake. We'd brought Stitch with us, and he was excited to see the water for the first time, barking at the aggressive seagulls. It was the best day I could remember in a long time, and I never wanted it to end. We were exhausted by the time we got home, but not *too* tired. Like teenagers, we couldn't keep our hands off each other. We giggled like school kids as we slipped into the darkness of the backyard, letting Stitch relieve himself one last time.

While he was hunting for the perfect place to do his business, Liv surprised me, pressing me up against the back of the house for a deep and sensual kiss. Then she playfully tugged at my zipper and gave me *the* look. Could my day get any better?

"What are you doing?" I whispered.

Not that I didn't like where this was headed, but Brighton's pickup was in the driveway, which meant he was probably in our house somewhere, waiting for us to get home. And he was the last person I wanted to run into. I needed Olivia all to myself.

I groaned when she nipped at my lips, then dropped to her knees, freeing me from my shorts. "Liv," I growled, even as I fingered her soft, wavy hair, which was messy from the Jeep ride.

"Shh . . . you don't want Brighton to hear us, do you?"

It was the last thing I wanted. I closed my eyes, forgetting all about our neighbor as Liv wrapped her mouth around me, losing herself in the moment. "Jesus," I said, pressing my hips forward. That's when I heard a small noise and turned my head, just as Brighton rounded the corner, breathing heavy from his run. He stopped short when he realized what was going on, his jaw clenching. He didn't back away, though, so I didn't stop Livy from finishing.

"Fuck," I growled. My eyes were trained on Brighton's as I palmed Olivia's head, using my hips to help set the steady pace I needed. When I couldn't hold out any longer, I closed my eyes, surrendering as my body shook through its release. When I finally opened my eyes, Kerrington was nowhere to be found, making me wonder if he'd been a figment of my imagination.

Liv tucked me away and stood, kissing my lips and bringing me back to the moment. "My turn," she said, taking my hand and leading me inside.

It no longer mattered where Kerrington was, or what he was doing. All I knew was tonight, and every other night from now on, my wife was mine. I was finally, finally getting a part of Livy back, and I'd never risk losing it again.

CHAPTER TWENTY-FOUR
Brighton

COULDN'T GET THE image of Olivia and Ryan out of my head, no matter how hard I tried. Now that I knew the feel of her mouth wrapped around me, it was torture thinking of her and Ryan together alone. Without me.

I wished I could rewind time to right before we were together last night, so I could slow things down and better savor every second I'd been graced with to touch Olivia. She'd held nothing back when she was with us both, and Ryan never once stopped her from giving or receiving pleasure. It was the sexiest thing I'd ever seen, so I tried to focus on those memories instead. But my mind betrayed me, circling back to the scene I'd stumbled upon tonight.

Resigned to the truth that I'd get no sleep until I stroked one out, I hopped in the shower. I let the spray wash over me, imagining it was me Olivia had been kneeling in front of instead of Ryan. I slid my hand over myself, squeezing until I finally exorcized the frustration from my body. Still, nothing I did brought sleep after that. When I checked the time on my phone and saw that it was 1:55 a.m., I slid on my sneakers and went to the backyard. I felt compelled to see her, even if it were just for a few minutes. There was so much that was left unsaid.

Like clockwork, the sunroom door opened, but this time, it was Ryan standing there, waiting on Stitch to do his business. I slid back into the shadows, hoping he hadn't seen me.

"I know you're there, Kerrington," he said. "I heard you sneak out five minutes ago."

I stepped forward, walking over to Ryan. "Sorry, man. Just couldn't sleep."

"Did our peep show keep you up?" he asked, a little cocky.

"You're a lucky man" was all I said, shrugging. I kicked at the earth, unsure of what else to say.

"I hope this doesn't get weird between us now," Ryan said.

"Isn't it already?"

"Doesn't have to be."

I nodded. "Can I be honest about something?"

"Of course."

I crossed my arms over my chest, worried how this was going to come out. But we had promised to be straightforward, so I knew I just needed to say it. "I don't know how to share your wife, Ryan, and then act as if nothing ever happened. Do you have any idea how hard that is?"

Ryan shoved his hands in his pockets. "I knew the first time I slept with Olivia that I never wanted another woman in my bed. So, I imagine you're feeling something like that. She's special. I get it. But you made a promise, and I expect you to keep it."

I glared at him. "This isn't about me wanting to be with her without you, fuckhead. As a matter of fact, it was even hotter with the three of us. It's not something I ever thought I'd be doing with my life. But now that I have, I can't get you both out of my head. It's all I could think about today—which is what caused the freaking emergency earlier. I couldn't keep my head on straight and nearly broke my foot when I dropped a farmhouse sink on it."

"Oh, crap," Ryan said. But I could tell he was trying hard not to laugh.

"Yeah, real funny," I said. "I'm out seven hundred dollars, and you're over here getting blown. I can see this was a great bargain for me."

"Aw, come on," Ryan said. "Lighten up. Did you at least find a replacement sink?"

"Yeah," I said grudgingly. "I'm still pretty salty about the whole thing, though. I never even got my pancakes."

Ryan let out a full belly laugh, then whistled for Stitch. "How about I help you install it tomorrow? Make it up to you? Liv said she needed to show you some sketches anyway."

"Sounds good," I said, heading back toward the mud-room door.

"Hey, Kerrington?"

"Yeah?" I said, turning at the last minute.

"I'll make you some freaking pancakes in the morning, too."

CHAPTER TWENTY-FIVE

Olivia

WHILE WE WERE at the farmer's market, I'd found a couple of gifts for Brighton—to give the house some good mojo when he put it on the market. I didn't know why, but I was suddenly nervous to give them to him. It was just a housewarming gift, and I did the same thing for all my clients. So why was Brighton any different?

I groaned. He was different for a million and one reasons. What had we done?

The truth was intimacy was better than ever with Ryan. And I *was* feeling better in some regards, even though I still had my blue days, too. But I was excited to get over to the house today because, other than in passing, it had been a few days since I'd had a chance to really talk to Brighton. Today I was helping with the lighting delivery and installation in the rooms that were ready. They were about halfway done—and it made me want to vomit thinking of Brighton no longer being next door. Or in our home, for that matter. *That* was the problem. *That's* what made him different.

It's also what made him dangerous.

I felt like I was betraying Ryan when I found myself daydreaming about Brighton while I was sketching one afternoon. I hadn't even realized what I was doing, but I sketched him leaning over the kitchen island in his uncle's home, no shirt on, with sweat beading at his brow as he oiled the bamboo countertop. I'd never seen anything more beautiful. He was a mix between a superhero and a Greek god. And I suddenly had an urge to go to a toga party with him.

I was giggling, shading in his abs and finishing the sketch from my sunroom, when I heard Ryan coming in from the kitchen. I quickly shut my drawing pad.

"Whatcha working on today?" he asked.

"Nothing big really," I said. "Brighton's stuff."

"Have you been enjoying getting back into the flow of things with a new job?" he asked, looking at me cautiously. "I know in the past it was a little hit or miss after taking time off."

I couldn't blame him. I'd spent the last few years fluctuating between being deeply depressed, mildly ambivalent, and immobile on the worst of days. Sure, we'd had a few good days in there. But the truth was, I hadn't been willing to do the work. I hadn't wanted to move on because I was more comfortable in my grief than trying to find a way to live without my babies. There was a quote I read once that said something like: "I will never forget the day your heart stopped and mine kept beating."

Unless you live through something like that, you can't know what that's like. It's the opposite of every maternal instinct—and there were still days when I prayed to god to let me trade places with my babies. Asking why he hadn't given them breath, and let me go instead? There were days I gladly would've let myself close my eyes and slip under a heavy blanket of despair, suffocating until I joined them. But something in me fought—despite not being able to imagine going on even one more day when my heart was still beating, and theirs had stopped.

"I have to admit, you were right," I said, sighing. "When Brighton moved in, it was kind of like a catalyst. I saw it open something new inside you, too. You were happier, even when I couldn't be. You developed an amazing bond with him—a guy friendship I haven't seen you nurture in years. It made me realize you've been hurting too. And I didn't allow myself to see that because I was too lost in my own unbearable pain. If I saw it, I would've had to set mine aside to be there for you. And I'm ashamed to say I haven't been ready to do that yet, before now. But seeing you open back up and live again—that inspired me, Ryan. And meeting Brighton—"

I paused. I didn't know how to say what needed to be spoken. I just knew the man had changed my life in ways I probably couldn't even tell yet.

"It's okay, Liv. I like to call it the Brighton Effect. There's just something about the guy, isn't there?"

I chuckled. "I like that. Does he know about your coined phrase?"

"Nah. I don't want our bromance to go to his head," Ryan said, leaning against the doorframe and grinning.

He looked like he had eight years ago when I first met him—full of swagger and confidence. Only, now, he had a new light in his eyes. It was sexier than anything we'd done with Brighton the other night. And yet . . . I couldn't get our neighbor out of my head or heart either. And I couldn't hide that from Ryan.

I wouldn't.

"Meeting Brighton changed me, Ry. But maybe not in the way you're thinking. His project gave me hope again. Sure, there are days when I can't face going over there. When I start to, and something hits me like a ton of bricks and reminds me of Laelynn until I break under the weight of it. But he has so much vitality and strength in him—the way he's tackling this labor of love for his family. He pours so much passion and work ethic into everything he does. Just being on a worksite around that again—smelling the fresh sawdust, seeing the walls come down to the studs, picking out paint colors and fixtures—it gave me a purpose again, outside of myself."

"Are you saying your therapist might've been right?" he teased.

I bit my lip. Dr. Paul had been right on several things so far. He was a decent man; I'd just never given him a real chance to help.

"I thought he wasn't the right person for me, Ryan. You know I've had a hard time opening up to therapists in the past. But I found out about a Moms in Mourning support group from a past client of mine that I might try out. It's at the Methodist church and is a bereavement group especially for mothers. I think they may know more intimately what I've been going through—and hopefully," I said, taking a deep breath, "help me move on. Not get over it—to live a new life with the experience, but without it paralyzing me every day."

"Aw, Livy, I believe in you. I always have," he said, crossing the room. He pressed his forehead to mine. "I believe in us, babe."

"Me, too," I whispered.

It was the truth. But behind that truth lived my biggest fear. Something I couldn't quite reconcile yet. Because after Ryan left, walking across the yard to Brighton's house to help him with some custom cabinet installation, I needed to go back inside to the guestroom to take the edge off. I opened my sketchbook, looking at the concentration lines I'd captured on Brighton's face. The hard planes of his stomach as it veed to the top of his shorts. Only now, I knew what was under the course khaki fabric. I was intimate with every mole, every scar, every muscled ridge of his body.

I lay down to take a nap, but I knew I wouldn't be able to drift off until I released my constantly bottled-up frustration. Ryan scratched an itch that was roaring back to life stronger than it ever had been between us. But there was one spot he couldn't quite reach. And that spot was reserved solely for Brighton—something only he could satisfy. I reached my hand under the covers and began to rub myself. It wasn't cheating; I wasn't doing anything wrong. But after my body shook, and my legs trembled at the memory of Brighton's mouth on me, I drifted off into a fitful, restless sleep.

I woke only when screams ripped through my dreams, waking me—a night terror so traumatic I was shaking and clutching a pillow to my chest as I tried to figure out what was real. I nearly jumped when I noticed Ryan in the doorway, making his way over to me in record time.

"I'm right here, Livy," Ryan said, the worry in his voice piercing my fog. "Are you okay?" He knew not to reach out for me unless I asked for it. My night terrors elicited some strange feelings from me in the past—and not ones I always wanted comforting for.

I noticed Brighton standing behind Ryan for the first time.

"I'm so sorry," I said, looking back and forth between them. Tears trailed down my cheeks as I realized how scared they must've been to hear me scream. "Did you hear me all the way from next door?"

"No, we were on our way home when we heard you scream. Scared the daylights out of us," Ryan said. He still hadn't touched me yet, but I could tell he wanted nothing more than to comfort me if I'd let him.

"What do you need?" he asked, confirming my suspicions.

"Can you just hold me?" I hiccupped through my tears. "Both of you?"

Ryan nodded, sliding into bed on one side of me as Brighton slid in from the other side. I could barely talk I was crying so hard, nearly catatonic from the nightmare that had wormed its way into my subconscious, breaking my heart. It was only a dream, I told myself repeatedly.

Ryan soothed me, walking me through a grounding exercise a spiritual healer had taught me—making sure I verbally identified something I could see, hear, smell, touch, and finally taste. As I talked quietly with Ryan, Brighton rubbed my back, easing the tension from my body with his gentle compassion.

No words were needed. They'd been there for me when I needed them. Even though I was better now—my heart rate calming—I would never get the image out of my head of me burying Ryan in the same grave as our daughter.

I didn't want to dissect what that could possibly mean. I didn't want to think about it ever again. So, when I reached out for my husband, while pulling Brighton's mouth down to mine on instinct, they met me where I needed them—both helping me surrender, forget, and come back to my body without hesitation, without question. And I came back in the most cathartic way possible—while being loved on by the two amazing men in my life.

My husband, and my Brighton.

CHAPTER TWENTY-SIX

Ryan

"I'M SORRY," LIV said again as she stretched out across the guestroom bed like a satiated cat. She didn't look too sorry, though. She looked more relaxed and happier than I'd seen her in days. Since—well, since the last time the three of us had been together. We'd only talked about doing it that one time, but when Brighton and I both found Olivia curled up in a ball, screaming so hard she was crying—there wasn't anything we wouldn't have done to help her.

That's when I realized it was already about more than just sex for Kerrington. He cared about Liv, too. No words had been needed, even though it probably cost him. Without question, he gave again. Gave us a part of his heart through his body as he helped me love and comfort Olivia down from her night terror. She still wouldn't tell me what she'd dreamed, but whatever it was, we'd helped her forget about it, at least for a little while. Kerrington headed to his room to shower and change, but Liv and I still lay in bed, her heart seeming better now that she'd had a chance to physically work off some of the fear.

"There's nothing to apologize for. I'm just glad we were on our way over and heard you."

"What time is it?" she asked, noticing it was getting dark outside.

"Dinner time. You up for going to Rudi's with us? We ditched work so we could grab some fish sandwiches and salt potatoes."

"I'd love to come. Can I have five to shower?"

"Of course. You up for driving in case I have a beer or two?"

She nodded. "I'm fine now, Ryan. Really. I just napped longer than I meant to, I guess."

"No, we just loved on you for a long time," I growled, leaning in to capture my wife's lips in a deep and sensual kiss. "Do you have any idea how sexy it is to see Kerrington slide inside you?"

"Ryan!" she said, her face flushing bright red.

"What? I can't help it. It does. Your face goes all soft and serene, like when you sleep. When he's moving inside you, it's like you're not here on earth anymore. It's the most peaceful I've seen you in far too long. Uninhibited," I said, choosing the better word. "It's sexy as hell."

"It turns you on to see me with him?" she asked, genuinely surprised. "I wasn't sure it would, or if you'd be jealous when all was said and done."

I cupped her face. "Don't get me wrong. I always want to be the first and last person to make you wear that look. But in the middle, for now, I can't explain it. Nothing turns me on more than watching the two of you surrender together."

She nodded, a smile spreading over her face. A real smile this time. One that lit up her whole face and made me want to write sonnets about it. As I watched her head for the bathroom to shower, my mind couldn't help but circle back around to Brighton. He was a nice distraction—a necessary one. Whatever it took to bring more of *this* Liv back to me. We'd loved her nightmares away until there was nothing left but three connected bodies—made for loving and pleasing this unbelievable woman. She was worth it. Every damn heartache we'd probably feel when Kerrington went back to his real life.

I'd feel the loss of him, too. I knew I would. But Liv and I would love each other back to whole again this time. Because this time, Livy's heart finally felt stronger. And that was something I could never repay Kerrington for.

I owed the man my life for bringing her back to me.

CHAPTER TWENTY-SEVEN

Brighton

OLIVIA DROVE TO Rudi's, and I sat in the back of her Wrangler. I couldn't help but notice a new, easy banter between her and Ryan. It made me smile—and I felt like I was seeing the real them for the first time. Ryan was much more relaxed and open, the surly frown line between his brows gone as he laughed at something Olivia said.

His hand rested on her bare thigh—her shorts giving him plenty of skin to find. I could see his fingers run gently under the hemline. It wasn't sexual, just a casual comfort he had—being able to touch Olivia whenever he wanted.

What I wouldn't give to have that carefree access to her—not having to wait for all of us to be together to be able to touch her. To have her heart as easily as Ryan did. But she wasn't mine, and the more I gave myself to them, the harder I was falling. I promised myself before this ever started that if feelings got involved, I'd let Ryan know and take a step back.

But I was a goddamn liar.

Feelings were already involved before I ever laid a hand on her.

Now, I was too far gone—drowning in a well of my emotions for Olivia. Part of me hated myself because Ryan was not only a good guy, but a good friend. He was mine before Olivia ever was. But the other part of me wanted nothing more than to share her again. To get my hands on her while Ryan pleasured her, too, both of us learning how to make her tumble over as she reached yet another mind-blowing orgasm. There was *nothing* like watching Olivia Wells reach her pinnacle, crashing into oblivion and knowing it was from both of us.

Stitch grunted next to me in his sleep, and I couldn't help but smile. The whole damn family had won over my heart. When we got to Rudi's and ordered, Ryan sent Liv and me outside to grab a table with the puppy while he waited for our orders at the counter.

While we waited, Liv and I chatted about what was left on the punch list at my uncle's house. What she would do when Ryan went back to work in the fall. When she was starting her new bereavement group. The kind of everyday things you chatted about with a good friend. It made me feel even closer to her.

From the outside, we probably looked like a couple, lost in an intimate conversation, our heads nearly pressed together. Which is why she startled when a woman walked up to our table and interrupted us to say hello. Even to me, Olivia looked guilty as hell, even though we'd done nothing wrong.

"Olivia?" the woman said, looking back and forth between us. I couldn't help but notice how she glanced at Olivia's ring finger. "Where's Ryan?"

"Oh hey, Kimber," she said, obviously displeased over our unwanted guest. "Ryan's here somewhere—grabbing our dinner. This is Brighton Kerrington. Brighton, this is Kimber Shanahan, professor of communications at the university where Ryan works."

Kimber's eyes flared as they traveled down my chest. I'd worn a purposefully tight shirt tonight, anything to make Olivia think about me in *that* way.

"And what do you do, Mr. Kerrington?" she asked coyly, even though she had about twenty-five years on me and was wearing a rock the size of Massachusetts.

Something made me want to put her in her place for the disdainful way she'd looked at Olivia when asking about Ryan. "I'm a general contractor," I said casually. "Brighton Design and Build. Ever heard of Erickson's?"

"Of course," she said, sniffing down at me as if that was the stupidest question ever asked.

"Bright and Classic is my line."

"*Oh*," she said, interest sparkling in her dark brown eyes now. "And how do you know the Wells? Are you a friend of Ryan's?"

"Kimber," Ryan said, coming up behind the snooty, immaculately dressed woman, "are you hassling our friend?"

"Ryan! I was beginning to wonder if you really were here tonight."

The pointed statement didn't escape me, and it didn't escape Ryan either. "Here I am. Have you met our new puppy too?" he asked, patting my head.

"Screw you," I said, laughing. This made Kimber gasp, setting Ryan into a fit of laughter.

"Calm down, Kimber. I was just kidding. This," he said, pointing to the puppy, "is Stitch. Olivia and I got him a little over a month ago. And this," he said, waving in my direction, "is a good friend of ours. Olivia got a huge contract with Kerrington's company this summer. I'm really proud of her," he said, beaming at his wife.

"Oh," she said, looking upset that there wasn't more gossip to be found. "That's wonderful news, Olivia. Why didn't you just say so?"

Olivia took a deep breath but kept her composure. "I don't like to sound boastful, Kimber," she said as Ryan set our cardboard food tray onto the picnic table we'd selected.

He sat across the bench from us, and I swiveled my legs around, ready to forget Kimber and dive into the enormous plate of fried and salty food.

"Are you coming back to work any time soon?" she asked Ryan before leaving. "Has your little"—she scrunched her nose—"family situation been resolved?"

If she'd been a dude, I probably would've stood and punched her myself. My body must've tensed because Liv reached for my hand under the table, lacing her fingers through mine.

Ryan smiled up at his coworker, his eyes crinkling. "Never better. How is your husband, by the way? Does he have a new contract at the Marriot?"

Her face paled, and I could tell Ryan knew something Liv and I didn't.

"He's fine, thank you," she said stiffly. "Well, you all have a pleasant evening."

When she walked away, I burst out laughing. "Oh man, if I had to work with someone like that, I'd have taken time off too."

Ryan and Olivia chuckled, then immediately dove into their food, quickly forgetting the Wicked Witch of Western New York. Olivia groaned when she popped a salted baby potato into her mouth. Ryan and I both groaned for other reasons, then looked at each other across the table and laughed when our eyes met.

Ryan lifted his Pabst and did a salute. "Here's to three more weeks before I have to go back to work and see that woman every damn day!"

"Cheers!" I said, lifting my beer in salute, laughing. "Man, I'd be retiring early if I were you."

"Not all of us are wealthy enough to do that," he said, laughing.

"Do you really own all that?" Liv asked.

I nodded. "Brighton Estates is mine too. It's a gated community on the lake in Watertown. I just didn't want to rub too much in her face all at once."

"Impressive," she said. Olivia picked over the rest of her food, slowing down. "Guess you aren't exactly just 'the handyman' then."

"I never pretended to be anything other than who I was, Liv," I said.

I cringed when I realized what I'd done. I still couldn't get out of the habit of calling her by Ryan's pet name. "Sorry, man," I said, glancing over at him.

He surprised me when he shrugged, taking a long sip of beer. "I think you've earned the right by now. If Liv doesn't care, I don't either."

I swallowed, looking over at Olivia. This somehow felt like a rite of passage, and I was surprised Ryan was being so affable about the whole thing.

"I like it," she said quietly, running her hand over my thigh beneath the table.

I stood up quickly, then headed over to the trashcans so I could toss the rest of my food away. "I'm done," I said, looking down at Liv with a hunger in my eyes I couldn't hold back. "Ryan—"

It was a plea, a Hail Mary to have some compassion so we could all go home and be together. A prayer that maybe he'd be willing to share his wife with me one last time. I knew this couldn't last forever, but I needed every moment he would allow me to have with her.

"Let's go," he growled, looking across the table at me. "I think our baby girl needs us."

Olivia defied the laws of physics getting us home in record time. We were like a clichéd movie. The back door had barely closed when clothes started coming off. My mouth was on Olivia's before I could tug my jeans all the way down. Laughter bubbled over her lips as she unzipped them, kissing me while trying to push me back toward the bedroom. But I didn't let her. I kicked the jeans off and picked her up, throwing her over my shoulder and carrying her into the same bathroom where she'd once drawn a bath for me.

Ryan was one step ahead now, filling the soaker tub with warm water and lots of bubbles. He slipped into the tub with a sigh, leaning his head back against the porcelain and grinning wolfishly at me.

"Get her clothes off and give her to me," he said, stroking himself.

Liv whimpered as I undressed her from behind, so she could watch Ryan pleasuring himself while he waited for her. I ran my hands over her long, soft body as I removed each piece of her clothes. Then I carried her over to the tub and lowered her over the side so she could slide easily into Ryan's waiting arms.

Then, for the next few hours, we spent our evening focused on nothing more than loving on Olivia. Long after the water was cold, we moved into the guest room, where Olivia had been staying with Stitch when I first met them. A few hours later, after our bodies were tired, loved, and satisfied, we all fell asleep together again. Olivia's legs were tangled over mine, even as Ryan snuggled her body against his own. Even though Ryan and I never touched one another, there was an unspoken bond of intimacy between us now that was just as powerful as my bond with Olivia. We were all opening ourselves to a vulnerability I was scared we'd never be able to recover from, no matter how much we tried to fool ourselves.

Because one thing was already clear to me, as I watched Olivia fall into a peaceful slumber, her body relaxed and soft as if she hadn't a care in the world.

I was in love with Olivia Wells.

CHAPTER TWENTY-EIGHT

Olivia

WHEN I WOKE the next morning, Ryan and Brighton were nowhere to be found. We'd been up late again, the three of us. I stretched across the guest bed—marveling at the situation I found myself in. I rolled over onto Brighton's side of the bed, closing my eyes and pulling his scent in. Just smelling him on our pillows turned me on more than it had any right to. I'd never forget when Ryan told me he could smell Brighton on me—the thought had shot straight to my core, my body telling me what I'd been afraid to let my heart face then.

Now there was no denying it.

But even I knew this couldn't last forever. It was meant to be a one-time deal, and already we'd given in to the passion of the three of us several times. Every time I was grateful. And every time I was afraid it would be our last. I didn't know how to balance the two. Because there was no doubt that the more I surrendered to him—even with

Ryan—the further my heart slipped just a little bit. It was something I knew I needed to address with my husband, and soon.

I grabbed my coffee and headed into the backyard with nothing further from my mind than ending something that felt so deliciously wrong, and yet was the best thing that had happened to me for as long as I could remember. For once, my first waking moment wasn't consumed with the memory of burying our daughter. It wasn't filled with the pain we'd waded through those first few months on autopilot, like two coexisting zombies. And I wasn't worried about how to fake my way through yet another day, when really, nothing felt like living for anymore.

In fact, it was almost the opposite. I couldn't wait to see Ryan this morning and find out what he and Brighton were up to. I opened the back door to let Stitch out, and shivers of anticipation ran havoc over my body. When Stitch started barking excitedly, and I listened closer, I realized the guys were outside, too.

They, too, were barking at one another, calling cheap shots and grunting with exertion. I rounded the corner to see what in the world was going on when I noticed a new basketball hoop in our driveway—Ry and Brighton sweating as they pushed and shoved in a fierce round of one-on-one. Brighton lost the advantage when he noticed me, and Ryan capitalized on the distraction, pushing off him, then spinning away and catching air as he slammed the ball in the net like any fit twenty-year-old.

It was so hot.

Brighton grinned goofily at me, and Ryan shoved him good naturedly.

I could see the lust riding Brighton's green eyes, but it was Ryan who swooped over to me and wrapped his arms around my waist.

"Ew! Stop! You're sweaty!" I said, laughing.

But Ryan picked me up and spun me around, kissing me firmly on the lips. "Morning, sexy," he growled, cupping my ass. "How'd you sleep?"

I blushed. The truth was I hadn't slept great. I'd been so aroused that I'd tossed and turned fitfully—constantly wanting to reach out to one or the other one last time.

"I slept okay," I said, pulling away. "What's on the agenda today? Other than basketball?"

"I actually need to go upstate to a local antiques dealer I use from time to time. He has some period fixtures I need for the house. Thought maybe you guys might like to come with? I could use your eye, Olivia."

I looked to Ryan. Would he want to go? Would he be okay with me going alone if he had other things he wanted to do with his day? "I'd love to go. You'll come, too, won't you?"

Ryan grinned and yanked me closer. He was looking at me, but asked Brighton, "When do you want to leave?"

"Thirty?"

Ryan bit my lower lip. "Make it forty-five and you have a deal."

I shoved off him, laughing. "No way! I've already showered!"

"You can shower again," he said, nipping at my ear as he walked me back toward the house.

I could see Brighton over his shoulder and my heart ached. The line between lust and friendship had been blurred. And even though I wanted my husband, I realized in that moment that I was already equating intimacy with Ryan *and* Brighton. And when that ended, it was going to crush me. The whole idea had been to bring a fire back to me—and it had worked a little too well.

I bit my lip and turned from Brighton so I could talk to Ryan. I let him lead me into the house, playfully tugging me along. But I stopped him in the mudroom.

"Ry," I said gently, not wanting to hurt his feelings or crash his playful mood, "I really don't want to have to take a shower again. Can we take a rain check?"

He pulled back from the kisses he was trailing down my throat. "Oh. You're serious?"

I nodded. "I'm really tired after last night, and I took a long time getting ready this morning to look pretty for you."

"Liv, you're a fucking bombshell. You always look pretty."

"You know what I mean."

He gave me the once-over, his eyes lighting up further. "You *do* look amazing. The only problem is it makes me want you even more."

He sucked on the small dip of my collarbone and cupped my ass, a move that usually did me in and had me dragging him to bed.

"Rain check?" I asked again.

He pulled back and looked at me, but I was unable to read what was behind his eyes. "Sure," he said before turning and heading toward the kitchen.

"Ryan—"

"No, it's fine. If you're not in the mood, you're not in the mood. I'll go take care of myself in the shower. Be down in thirty," he said before grabbing an apple off the counter and heading toward the stairs.

"That went well," I mumbled to myself.

"You okay?" I heard Brighton say over my shoulder.

God. Had he just witnessed that?

I turned, trying to put a smile on my face. "I'll be fine. I'm looking forward to going to the antique store with you. Is it Kent and Louie's place?"

Everyone in the design and rehab business knew of Kent and Louie Brightbeck. They were a couple who curated the best antiques in all of New York, drawing customers from across the state, and many of the surrounding ones, too. They were some of my favorite people.

"Of course," he said, grinning.

A genuine smile flooded my face, excited for our adventure. I just hoped Ryan wasn't going to hold a grudge all afternoon. "Well, go get showered so we can go! We have a drive ahead of us."

I went to the living room to grab my sketchbook with storyboards for the Kerrington property, so we could refer to it when we were at Kent and Louie's store. It was kinda cute. They both were obsessed with Desi Arnaz's character, Ricky Ricardo, so they named their store Babalu Antiques. But everyone just called it Babalu's. The old barn where everything was stored had gorgeous black-and-white pictures of Lucy and Ricky, along with all kinds of antique collectibles not for sale from the show. I couldn't wait to go back.

It was the first time in a long while that I'd felt excitement about something so normal as antique shopping. I found I had a spring in my step as I grabbed the bag I carried my sketch-book and storyboards in. Before I left the room, I noticed the sunflowers Brighton had given me. I'd stuck them in here, not wanting to offend Ryan. Even though they'd wilted, they still brought a smile to my face as I thought back to our first night together. I reached out, fingering the browning petals that were now crisping around the edges.

"When did you get those?" Ryan asked from the door.

I jerked, turning quickly and accidentally knocking over the vase. "Shit!" I said, dropping the bag to the couch so I could scoop up the long-stem flowers and upright the vase. I pushed past Ryan to grab a towel from the kitchen. When I came back in, he was still standing there, his hands in his pockets, just staring at the water that spilled over the edge of the coffee table and onto our distressed, custom-made rug.

"Ryan!" I said, pushing past him.

He grabbed my arm before I had a chance to clean up the mess. "Who are they from, Liv?"

I took a deep breath. "It's not a big deal, so don't make it one," I said. I pulled my arm away and kneeled to clean up the water. "You're overreacting."

"So Kerrington's already buying you flowers?"

"It's not like that!" I said, exasperated.

"Then explain what it is like, Livy."

"God, Ryan! Don't be a jerk, okay? He was nervous the first night we were all together and just thought he should bring something. So, he bought sunflowers."

"Did that make your insides melt? Did you swoon over it, Liv?"

"Is this because I said no? Because if that's the case, then let's go. Let's go fuck so you can remember that it's only you I want, okay? Either that or drop it. Because for the first time, I was excited to go somewhere today. I was excited to feel *normal* again. Isn't that what you wanted?" I nearly shouted.

He clenched his jaw, but when he saw the tears springing to my eyes, his face softened. "I'm sorry, Liv. I don't know what's wrong with me. I just—God! I don't know. Seeing another man give you flowers . . . that's *my* thing!"

He ran his hand through his thick brown hair.

"Next time, please just believe me when I say it's nothing," I said, grabbing the vase and my bag and brushing by him.

Even though I knew they were long past fresh, I couldn't bring myself to throw them away just yet. I trimmed the stems at an angle then refilled the vase in the kitchen sink, adding some flower food and an old penny like my mom taught me to do. I decided to bring the flowers to the sunroom so I could enjoy their last few days. Ryan knew about them now, so what did it matter?

"Ready to go?" Brighton asked from the doorway, with possibly the worst timing ever.

But the hard tic to his jaw told me his timing wasn't accidental at all.

My lips lifted to a sad half-smile. "Thanks," I mouthed silently from across the room. He nodded, then returned to the kitchen.

"Mind if I drive?" he asked Ryan. "I have a trailer hitched to the pickup in case we find something we want to bring back today."

"Sure, I guess," Ryan said, clearing his throat.

I looked between the two and took a deep breath, willing myself to relax and help change the weird energy bouncing around between the three of us. I liked it much better when were all on the same page.

"Only if we can drink their watermelon slushies in your truck, because I can't go to Babalu's without getting one," I said, trying to lighten the mood.

He grinned, picking up his keys from the counter. "Only if Ryan's buying. And I want one, too," he said. "Got your storyboards?"

I tapped the bag over my shoulder, then took Ryan's hand in my own as we walked out of the house. I squeezed it hard before climbing into Brighton's Silverado.

Ryan squeezed my shoulder from the back seat and leaned forward. "I'm sorry, Liv. Forgive me?" he asked quietly.

I held onto his hand as it rested on my shoulder and kissed it.

"Always," I whispered back. "Forgive me?"

"Always."

Only, sometimes, we don't always know what we're agreeing to, or how karma will test us. But in that moment, things felt good again. And I smiled as we drove to Babalu's, Brighton cranking up the classic rock, and the three of us singing off key.

CHAPTER TWENTY-NINE

Brighton

W HEN WE GOT to Babalu's, we were immediately swarmed. Olivia was like a local celebrity. Kent and Louie personally came over to greet us.

"Livy!" they said, almost in unison, then laughed as they took turns hugging her. "And how do you know this dashing rogue?" they asked, giving me a hug as well. I'd known them for years.

Ryan shook their hands, then stepped off to the side as we talked business, showing them the design schematics Olivia had put together.

"We're looking for a few doors we can use on sliders for a closet. Maybe with some stained glass? We also need some sconces for the fireplace in the front room. And a new mantel for the guest bedroom fireplace. Is that all?" I asked Olivia.

"I'm sure there are a few other things we can dig up," she teased, looking up at me from under her thick, blond lashes.

"I was hoping to find an alternative to the traditional, boring bathroom towel rod."

"On that exciting note, I'm gonna go look at the books," Ryan said, excusing himself. He kissed Liv's temple before heading in the opposite direction, but he shot me a weird look before turning the corner.

I cleared my throat. "Ready?"

"I have some doors I just got in today from an old church that was torn down. They'd be magnificent in the right home," Louie said.

He took Liv's hand, and Kent and I fell into step behind them as we wove our way in and out of rows of antiques.

"How are things going with the remodel?" Kent asked.

"Can't complain," I said, in the understatement of the year.

"When is it going on the market?"

I shrugged. I'd wanted to have my hands clean of it by the end of August, but now I wasn't in such a hurry. "Whenever we get it done. I still want to restore original the tin ceiling in the library, and we have several more bedrooms to finish. The back porch off the master bedroom needs to be completely torn down and brought up to code, too. Why? You and Louie thinking of moving?"

Kent laughed. "I couldn't drag that country bumpkin from this area if I tried—and trust me. I've tried. Many times. He's a country boy through and through. I'm destined to live out my fabulousness out here where no one can appreciate it."

"I appreciate it!" Liv said over her shoulder, making Kent and Louie laugh. Her eyes were shining bright, and I could see what Ryan was constantly chasing after. When Liv's eyes came alive, it wasn't just her eyes. It was her entire soul. She took my breath away, and I nearly stumbled as we stepped up to a new level of the barn, winding our way to the back room.

"These!" Louie said dramatically.

Against the wall stood a set of double-opening doors, with the top halves nearly entirely stained glass in earthy golds, greens, and grays, a rich contrast to the dark wood. They were stunning.

"We'll take them!" Olivia said, spinning to grin up at me. "They're perfect, aren't they?"

Kent laughed. "Want to know the price first?"

I looked down into Olivia's baby blue eyes, my heart taking a punch as it extended to her even more. "Nope. If she wants them, she gets them."

"Then I have one more thing to show you," Kent said.

He riffled through a few stacks of crown molding until he found what he was looking for. He pulled out two long stained-glassed panels that were framed in the same dark wood. They were breathtaking, and I knew as soon as Liv inhaled sharply that I was in trouble.

"Oh my god," she breathed out, running her fingers over the ancient stained glass. These were much older than the doors. The panels were each marked with the year on a piece of milky yellow glass—one reading 1864, and the other 1926.

"Where are they from?"

"A church in Pennsylvania," Kent said. "They're called the king and queen, for the torch and the lily in the pattern. They're quite rare."

"I bet they are," I mumbled.

Liv picked up the small paper tag that held the price, then gently set it down. "They're gorgeous, but they're out of my budget, and I'm sure they're out of yours for a flip."

The longing that filled her eyes clenched at my heart. I suddenly had the tiniest idea of what Ryan meant when he said there wasn't anything he wouldn't do for Olivia. She was so easy to want to make happy because she wore her joy so gracefully.

"What about mantels?" she asked, moving on to where they normally stored them.

I looked over her shoulder at Kent and he nodded. "Go on without us," he said. "Louie and I will get the doors loaded and I have a few other goodies I'm going to hunt down for you."

"Sounds good," Olivia said.

We looked at several mantels on our own, but nothing was quite right. "What if Ryan built one?" Olivia asked as we stood off to the side of the main walkway. We'd been looking at antiques for over an hour and had selected several other items we could use, including a pair of sconces that were time period, but not dated.

"You think he would?" I asked, looking around. "Where did he go anyway?"

She shrugged. "Who knows. He could get lost in books and office antiques for hours. He's probably still over there."

"You okay from earlier?" I asked. I didn't mean to pry, but it was obvious that there was tension between them back at the house. "You seemed upset."

Olivia swallowed, picking at the cuticle on her thumb nail. "I'm okay. Just a misunderstanding."

"I'm not that misunderstanding, am I?"

She looked up, the faintest smile lifting her sensual lips. "Why, Brighton, don't you think highly of yourself."

I shrugged, giving her the smoldering look I usually reserved for women at bars. Liv burst out laughing, deflating my ego. "Damn, you know how to gut a guy."

She stood, laughing still, and put her arms around me in mock-comfort. "There, there," she said, petting my hair. "Does that actually work these days? It's been so long since I had to bring out my A game."

"You don't have anything to worry about in that area," I said huskily.

Her laughter died on her lips as she looked up at me, each of us lost in each other's eyes, with so much more emotion swirling behind them than either of us could express.

A throat cleared, causing us to part quickly. Louie was standing there with a doorbell, his eyes wide.

"Whatcha got there?" I asked, trying to play it off.

"A doorbell," he said, holding it out and not saying anything else.

I took it from him and smiled, but Louie didn't reciprocate. *Well, shit.*

"I'm going to go get Ryan. He found a desk he wants for his office, and I needed to grab the price for him," he said, looking at Olivia.

"Oh, where is he? We've been looking all over for him?"

"I could tell," he said, turning to leave.

Olivia started to say something, and I shook my head, telling her not to. I ran a hand through my hair and cursed. I didn't care what Kent or Louie thought of me at the end of the day, but I wouldn't have them think bad of Olivia.

"You go find Ryan. I'll go talk to Louie."

"What exactly are you going to say?"

"That it's not what it looks like," I said, sighing.

"Isn't it though?" she asked, biting the corner of her lip. "He's not stupid. And every time you look at me, you look like you want to have your dirty way with me. That didn't escape Louie, trust me."

I moved toward her again, walking us both back until we were out of sight from the main floor, nestled behind a row of old, wooden doors. I pressed her up against the rough surface of the barn and lifted her hands above her head, holding her in place. Our pulses raced, and I could feel the thump of our hearts with each rise of her chest against mine.

"Brighton—"

I never let her finish. I crashed my hungry mouth down onto hers and stole, devoured. My tongue lashed at her mouth, begging her lips to part for me. Her hips arched off the wall and pressed into mine, and finally, finally, she conceded, parting her lips and letting me in. I hovered over her, taking more and more from her with each stroke of my tongue. It was animalistic, something dark and dangerous that we'd not shared before. It was a stolen moment in time that we might regret later, but while we were melded together, we consumed as if it were our last breath.

I finally pulled away, resting my forehead against hers while we came down from the high we were chasing. Our breaths mingled as we panted, my hands still gripping hers above her head against the wall. "I will never apologize for wanting you," I told her. "But you are going to be my undoing, Liv."

She closed her eyes, and I wanted to kick my own ass for taking so much from her. I knew the guilt would weigh heavy on her heart and Ryan would eventually find out. But in that moment, I didn't care. I just wanted more of her. And the worst part? I wanted her to myself the next time.

"You're already mine," she whispered before sliding out from under me and going to find her husband.

CHAPTER THIRTY

Ryan

'D OBSERVED THEM several times during the day, Kerrington and Liv never the wiser. Even a casual outsider would be able to feel the current of electricity that pulsed between them. I tamped my jealously, though, because Olivia was my wife. And no matter how great the sex was between the three of us, he would never have her alone. So, I gave them their space, because I knew they needed to find certain pieces for Kerrington's house. I lost track of time looking through the antique book collection they had. Kent usually always held at least one gem aside for me, and today was no different.

He handed me the brown-clothed hardcover book, *The Scarlet Letter* written in gilt on its spine. My hands shook as I opened the cover and peered inside.

"It's a first edition, second printing," Kent explained. "Made in 1850. In surprisingly good shape, all things considered."

"Where did you find this?"

"Estate sale. Little old lady had a massive library. I tried to curate the entire thing, but her relatives wanted most of the books to go to libraries and museums. I managed to get this one and a few others I'm saving for you."

"How much?" I asked, already knowing I'd buy it no matter the cost. Kent did, too, and he never took advantage of that fact because he knew he had a consistent customer in me.

"Twelve hundred. And that's a steal."

I nodded. "How much does the first printing go for?" I asked, knowing Kent would have the answer off the top of his head. He was as much of a book junkie as I was.

"About sixteen thousand."

I whistled.

"Doesn't mean someone will pay that. Just means that's what they're asking."

"I'm glad you didn't find that printing, then. Liv would have my head on a silver platter."

Kent laughed. "Speaking of Liv . . . how are things going? I know she was in a place the last time you guys visited. She looks much happier now. Whatever you're doing seems to be working. What's your secret?"

If he only knew.

"Must be my witty personality and dashing good looks," I joked.

Just then Liv walked over, out of breath. Her cheeks were flushed from the exertion. "I've been looking for you everywhere."

I loped an arm over her shoulder and kissed her temple. "Sorry, babe. I got sidetracked back here."

She laughed. "You always do."

"Where's Kerrington?"

"Uh," she said, looking around as if she hadn't a clue, "I think he went to find Louie. He grabbed a few more items for the house, and I think they're loading everything in the trailer."

"Will there be enough room for a desk?"

"You really found one you want?" she asked, surprised.

The one currently in my office was passed down from the professor before me, and the professor before that. And while I appreciated the legacy, it was just plain ugly.

"Yep," I said unapologetically. I couldn't wait to get rid of the Beast, as I'd affectionately named it. "You'll love the new one, I promise."

She leaned over and whispered into my ear. "I kinda had a fondness for the old one."

I groaned. "We can always make new memories."

We loaded up the desk and a few items Liv found for her own warehouse stash she kept stocked for clients and staging homes. Then we met Brighton by the truck. He was holding two watermelon slushies in his hands for us, and Louie was standing there with their signature popcorn tube filled with steaming hot nuts. I wish I were kidding. They were the best, though, if you liked hot, candied pecans. Which Liv went nuts over every time.

She stood on her tiptoes and kissed Louie goodbye on the cheek, then she climbed into the cab. I saw Louie pull Brighton aside and say something, clapping him on the back after they'd chatted a few minutes. He looked into the cab directly at me.

"Keep on keeping that lady of yours happy, Wells. She looks mighty pretty smiling again."

Liv blushed, and I nodded. I wish I could take all the credit for that smile, but considering I wasn't with her for most of the trip, I'm quite sure Louie had just witnessed the Brighton Effect. I tried not to let it eat me alive as Kerrington drove us home, he and Liv singing along to Tom Petty in the front of the cab. Somehow, hearing a song about free-falling when my wife and I were sharing a bed with another man wasn't in any way comforting. I tuned them out, thumbing gently through the delicate pages of my book. A passage caught my eye, and I nearly sobbed.

> *Love, whether newly born or aroused from a death-like slumber, must always create sunshine, filling the heart so full of radiance, that it overflows upon the outward world.*

It was as if Nathaniel Hawthorne was whispering from his grave. If Brighton was the new love, ours was the one aroused from slumber. Either way, the result was the same: Livy overflowed with happiness again, her heart creating sunshine everywhere she went. Louie and Kent had both seen it. I saw it every damn day. While it gutted me that I alone wasn't the reason, I couldn't be mad at Kerrington for being part of the solution I'd asked him to help with.

"We going straight home?" I asked them. Two sets of eyes found mine through the rearview mirror. Then they found each other's. Something silent passed between them that I really, really didn't want to know the answer to today.

All I wanted was to wrap my arms around my wife again, with Brighton enveloping her, and lose ourselves in a world where no words were needed, but every sentence our bodies uttered spoke of an undeniable, inner-woven connection that was beyond comprehension. Beyond our control. I knew in my bones we were teetering on destruction, and that we needed to nip this in the bud, soon. But I also felt the warmth today after basking in the sunlight that was Olivia when she was happy.

And I would do damn near anything to hold onto that for just one more day.

CHAPTER THIRTY-ONE

Olivia

PICKED UP MY husband's copy of *The Scarlet Letter*. It was nearly two in the morning, but I didn't dare take Stitch outside tonight. It had been a week since the last time the three of us had been together, and every time I was around Brighton, I was like a lit fuse. I didn't trust myself these days.

Why had Ryan left this out in the sunroom? Was it purposefully for me to see? Or maybe that was my own guilty conscious speaking. I still hadn't told Ryan about the kiss I'd shared with Brighton alone. I knew I had to, but the thought turned my stomach. I'd had no excuse for what I'd done.

So, why then couldn't I stop thinking about the way his lips seared mine when we were alone? I lifted my fingers and touched my bottom lip as if I could still feel his mouth consuming mine. It was utter annihilation, that kiss.

"You daydreaming?" Ryan asked from the doorway.

I dropped the book to the floor and gasped, scared I'd ruined it. But the spine was still intact, and the book had landed perfectly on its back, staring up at me. *Don't you look at me like that!* I hissed silently to the book.

Ryan bent over and picked it up.

"I forgot to show you this last week when we got home," he said. "We got a little distracted."

Had we ever.

The sex that night had been explosive. There was no other word for it.

I couldn't shake the feeling that we were all holding secrets beneath the layers of passion we were sharing, though. The energy had been so magnetic; we were so desperate to hold on to one another, as if we were all afraid that this was the last time.

And it had been.

A week had passed, and we'd hardly seen Brighton. I was scheduled to go over later this morning for the installation of the tin ceiling. He was working with the contractors, but I was laying out the design and directing the install to make sure everything looked beautiful, given the age and inconsistent wear of the tiles.

"We need to talk," Ryan said simply, staring down at the book.

"What's up?"

Stitch bounded up, hopping onto the porch swing to sit beside me, his head folding over onto my lap with a contented sigh. It gave my worried hands something to focus on as Ryan sat down beside me.

"We haven't really processed everything together."

I nodded. I knew it was only a matter of time. But somehow, I'd lived in my own little dream world these past few weeks, not wanting to desecrate the perfect little bubble I was in—getting to have my cake and eat it too. Truth be told, there was nothing in this world that would make it okay if the tables were turned. I wasn't sure how Ryan was able to compartmentalize everything. I was certainly struggling.

"Let's talk then."

The way Ryan was staring back at me—completely vulnerable and raw—made me realize I was fooling myself if I thought for a minute that he was successful at compartmentalizing any of this. "You okay?"

"Yeah," he answered automatically. Then he laughed when he saw my face. "Okay, no. Maybe? I don't know, Liv. I just feel like we need to talk about this like adults and be honest. This isn't something you can just sweep under the rug and act like it never happened. We chose this path for a reason."

"I agree. I just don't know what to say."

"Me either," he said. He lifted my hand, then kissed the back of it. "It's been amazing, though. I never knew I could find even more reasons to love you. But I feel like you're more open now since we started this. It's like I'm getting to see all these new sides of you."

I smiled. "You always had a way with words."

"I mean it. Even Louie and Kent could see it."

My heart sank. They'd seen it all right. I just hoped they'd kept it to themselves.

"You *are* happier, right?"

I thought about what he was asking. I was happier lately. It didn't negate my losses, or how often I thought about our babies. But I was happier. Was it because of what we'd done? Had it really been the catalyst I needed?

"I am," I admitted quietly. "I don't know if it's all because of what we did. But I think it's a big part of it. I think you trusting me so fully and being willing to expose yourself like that—that takes so much vulnerability, Ryan. All so I could be happy." I looked down at my hands, unsure how to say what was really on my heart. "That's unheard of. I'm so grateful to have you. And that you didn't give up on me."

"I'd never give up on you," he said, pushing the hair away from my face. I leaned into his open palm, not wanting to rock the boat. "Was it what you imagined?"

I bit my lip and nodded. "More."

"I want to put it all behind us, Liv. But the truth is, I can't stop thinking about it," he said, his voice low and heated.

"At least you'll never run out of fantasy fuel, right?" I teased.

He growled, leaning forward and biting my lower lip. He set the book onto the coffee table and moved Stitch off the large porch swing. Then he turned the overhead light off and pressed me back into the mound of pillows.

"Ryan, I thought you wanted to talk," I whispered.

"I do. But I want to be with you even more right now. I don't know why, but Kerrington makes me blind with jealousy somedays. Then other days, I'm so grateful for him—because he brought you back to me. And I can't get the images of the way you look when you're lying there, giving and receiving from both of us, out of my head. You're seriously the hottest woman I've ever known. The way you can handle both of us. Jesus, Livy."

He pressed my hand between his legs so I could feel what the thought did to him. "I want you so bad, baby."

"Out here?" I asked. The lights were out, but I had no idea if Brighton was asleep or if he was waiting in the yard like he still did some nights for our "Insomniacs' Club" meetings, where we ended up talking for hours about everything and nothing.

"It's our house, we can fuck anywhere we want," he said, running his hand under my nightgown. He parted my thighs and I couldn't stop the sigh as my eyes fluttered closed. "Besides, it's not like its anything he hasn't seen before."

He dropped his sleep pants and lay down beside me in the pitch dark. His lips closed over mine to absorb my moans as he pressed deep inside of me. No matter how torn I was feeling these days, I couldn't deny my love or attraction for my husband. And it *had* increased because of Brighton. The only problem was it also increased *for* Brighton.

"Tell me what turns you on, Liv," he said, pulling his hips back and thrusting inside of me. "When he touches you. What makes you hot?"

"You don't really want to know this, Ryan. Just make love to me. Give me *you* tonight. Just you. You're all I've ever needed."

"You'll always be mine," he growled. I wrapped my legs around his waist as he increased his pace and gave up trying to think of anything but the two of them. As my orgasm climbed, I had to bite his shoulder so I didn't scream out and wake up the whole neighborhood. He lifted my hips and pressed deeper inside of me for a few last thrusts. Until a low, guttural moan ripped through him, Ryan's body arching with his release. He dropped his weight and fell against me, sweaty and spent. I lay there, stroking his hair as he embraced me, as if he never wanted to let me go.

"Do you wish you could have him all to yourself?" he asked suddenly.

"No," I whispered, kissing his temple.

His lips found mine and kissed me more tenderly this time. "I only wanted to make you happy."

"And you have."

"Good. Then it's over, Liv. I can't share you anymore. It's just you and me from now on. Okay?"

I nodded, my insides shaking. I wanted to yell, *No! Just one last time.* But how could I? I had a feeling our marriage hinged on my answer, and I'd told Ryan what he wanted to hear.

As he took my hand and led me upstairs, instead of feeling happy, my heart was shattering. I thought of Brighton sleeping alone downstairs, his thoughts on me and when he could touch me again. Worst of all, after we showered and Ryan took me back to bed to make love to me again before we fell asleep, it was only Brighton I was imagining this time.

He might've been out of our bed physically, but the truth was, he'd never be out of it again.

CHAPTER THIRTY-TWO

Brighton

DAMN I WAS a sucker for punishment. Last night I'd heard Olivia get up, but she never let Stitch outside. Instead, she sat on the porch swing in the sunroom, looking sad and thoughtful. Then Ryan came out to join her. They talked for a while, then the lights eventually went out. I could just barely make out their outlines as he made love to her.

I didn't wait for them to finish. Instead, I went inside and took care of my loneliness and frustration. It had been over a week since I'd been with Olivia, and she was all I could think about. Now I was not only surrounded by her at their house, but at my uncle's place, too. Her design touch was everywhere, from the paint colors, to the cabinets, to the appliances. She was like a ghost who took up residence, haunting me night and day.

I tossed and turned until I couldn't take it anymore. As soon as the sun rose, I pulled on my work shorts and T-shirt, then took off for my uncle's house. I needed to beat the shit out of something, and the garage would do. It hadn't officially been on the docket to rehab before we sold. But now it was. I got out a sledgehammer and started slamming it into everything in sight. Dry wall went flying, and there were wires everywhere. I was going to strip it down to the bones.

I was in mid-swing when I saw Ryan from my peripheral vision, standing in the doorway staring at me. I pulled off my goggles and set the hammer down, my muscles flexing from the weight of it.

"Jesus, Kerrington."

"What do you want?" I growled, not in the mood today.

Something had shifted, and I knew exactly what it was. Our time together was up. I knew it was coming—I just hadn't wanted to face the sad reality of our situation: I was expendable to them.

"The same thing you do, probably. To release some of my demons. Can I join you?"

I grunted. "Just stay out of my way. I'm swinging to destroy, not to take this thing down pretty."

"Just what I need," he said, sliding goggles over his eyes and lifting his own sledgehammer he'd brought. "You woke the whole damn neighborhood. Figured we probably had the same demons to kill this morning."

I cranked the music up, slid my goggles back down, and started smashing. Yeah, it was immature. And probably going to be costly. But I couldn't stop. Everything I'd been feeling for the past six weeks boiled over.

The sight of Liv. The desire. At first, I thought it was one-sided, then she let me see into her soul, her eyes giving away the reciprocity of my feelings. But she was his. Always would be. And I hated it. Not because of who he was, but because of who I could never be to her.

I slammed the hammer down onto the workbench, loving the splintered, fragmented wood that shot out like quills across the garage. Ryan was beating down a rickety set of shelves, triumph washing over his face as it crumbled. I couldn't help but smile. Demo day was one of my favorite things to do on a flip. Yeah, I mostly stuck to new builds, but that often involved tearing down what was already there. Building something new.

I was good at that.

The destruction was what I was good at.

We slammed our sledgehammers over and over again until there was hardly a single bit of the garage left standing, except the exterior frame. Everything inside was in splinters. We were drenched with sweat, and still, I didn't feel much better.

Ryan yanked his goggles off, lifting his shirt up to wipe the sweat away. "Damn, I needed that."

"Never got that punching bag?" I snickered.

"Not sure one would last if this is what I need to work through."

"Ever think of going to see a therapist of your own?"

"Why? You think I need one?"

I raised a brow at him, then looked around.

"Touché," he said. "But wouldn't that mean you need one too?"

"Who says I don't already have one?"

Ryan nodded. "We gonna be okay, Kerrington?"

I knew what he was asking. We'd been friends first, before I ever touched Olivia. I just didn't know where my loyalty lived anymore. "Remember, it wasn't me who asked for this. I told you that from the start."

"Yeah, but we agreed to be honest, just like Liv and me. You ready to speak the truth?" he asked, challenging me with his dark brown eyes.

I lifted my chin. "I'm the one who asked for that, douchebag. I'll be honest if you will."

"You first."

"Fine," I said, dropping my sledgehammer to the floor and ripping off my gloves. "Is it over? Completely?"

Ryan pursed his lips, then nodded slowly. "I think it needs to be."

I balled my fists, my jaw clenching. It wasn't Ryan's fault. Hell, I never expected more than one night. The problem was, I got so much more than that. And now, I wanted even more. I didn't want this to end. Not with Liv. Not with any of us. I knew that was fucked up. It wasn't something that could last forever. But it didn't make me want it any less.

"Did you fall in love?" he asked.

He had to go there.

I crossed my arms over my chest. When I finally lifted my eyes to meet his, I didn't need to say anything. He could read me like a book. "What made you ask?"

"I'm not stupid, Kerrington. Neither is Louie. He knew right away, for god's sake."

"I'm sorry," I said, running my fingers through my wet hair. "I didn't—"

"Save it." He turned to leave.

"That's it?"

"What else do you want? You can't have her. She's mine."

"Trust me, I'm all too aware. You don't have to shove it in my face even more, Ryan."

"What's that supposed to mean?"

"It was just a coincidence then that you fucked Liv on the porch last night, so anyone could see? So I could *hear* you?"

Ryan shrugged, a half-grin lifting his lips.

"Dick," I said, crossing the garage.

"What? You gonna hit me now?" he asked, his chest puffing out as he took a step forward.

"You're better than this. You wanted her light back? It's back. Take it and leave."

His chest deflated, and Ryan ran a hand over his face. "It's harder than I thought it would be," he admitted. "And I know none of this has been fair for you."

"I never went into this thinking it would be fair."

"Then why'd you agree to do it?"

"Because you asked me to, Ryan."

"But you said you wouldn't risk your heart to save hers," he said, looking just as broken as I felt.

"Yeah, well, things changed."

Ryan grimaced.

"Do you want me to fire her? Ask her not to come back over to help?"

"No!" he sputtered. "Just because I'm a jealous ass doesn't mean that should affect Liv. She's happier, Brighton. It pisses me off that it's because of you. But she is happier."

"It's not just because of me, Ryan. You know that as well as I do. She's happier because of *us*."

"Well, she's going to have to learn how to stay happy with just me. I don't want to keep hurting you—it's not fair now that feelings are involved. And you're not the only one who has them," he said.

"What does that mean?" Had she told him about the kiss? Wouldn't she have warned me?

Ryan pulled a piece of paper out of his pocket and unfolded it several times. Then he tossed it to me before turning to leave.

"This is why, Kerrington."

I looked down at the paper and saw a lifelike image of myself working on the bamboo kitchen countertop, shirtless and sweaty. I was engrossed in the task, but Liv had somehow managed to capture so much in these simple lines.

That's when I realized, she saw all of *me*.

I looked up to say something to Ryan, but he was gone, leaving me alone with nothing but the evidence of Olivia's feelings and absolutely nothing to do with them.

CHAPTER THIRTY-THREE

Ryan

STORMED INTO THE kitchen, grabbing a Bubba canister and filling it with ice cold water, drinking the entire thirty-two ounces in one take. I needed to find Liv and tell her I was going into the office today. Movers were delivering my new desk, and I needed to go through some emails and catch up on paperwork before the new semester. I couldn't believe school was starting again so soon.

My breath hitched as Liv rounded the corner. She was wearing a pair of jean shorts with the bottoms frayed. The white T-shirt she was wearing was slouchy, but tied into a knot front and center, drawing my eyes there and making me remember every naughty thing I'd done to her the night before.

Her baseball cap was pink and matched the dusty pink suede Adidas she was wearing. The V of her T-shirt neckline slouched low, and I couldn't help but sneak a peek of her swelling bustline, wishing we were spending the day together instead.

"You going to Kerrington's like that?" I asked, hating the way my accusation sounded, even to myself. She had a right to dress any way she wanted. I knew it didn't drive her fidelity in any way. Still . . . she looked too damn cute.

"Yeah. What's wrong with it?" she asked, looking disappointed as she glanced down.

Shit. That wasn't my intention. "Nothing. You just look— hot. Too hot to be stuck inside installing a boring old tile ceiling today. Want to play hooky again? Go to our park or something?"

Her face relaxed, and I felt guilty knowing it was just my jealousy driving me.

"I wish I could. But you know this is one of the biggest installs left that I have a hand in before we stage the house."

"He's really that close to finishing?"

"I don't think so. But the rest of the stuff he has on his punch list is more interior items that he doesn't need my help with. By the way," she said, pulling out a sample-sized can of paint from the bag she was carrying, "did you see what we picked for the outside of the house? We're fairly sure this is the one we're going with, but I want to try it out today. Let it dry and see how we like it. What do you think?"

She showed me the can of paint, her face alight with excitement. I didn't mean to rain on her parade, but it was just a dark gray. "Gray?"

"It's not just *gray*," she said, as if that was so base of me. "It's Roycroft Pewter."

"Of course, it is. So silly of me," I teased.

"And the best part is the front door." She pulled another pint of paint from her bag and handed it to me. "Plum Suede. It's going to be stunning!"

I scrunched my nose at the untraditional color. She could call it whatever she wanted, but it just looked like a dark purple to me. "Please tell me our front door is never going to be that color."

"Not if our neighbor's is," she said. "Besides, the rich tones of this plum will look way better with the gray. It wouldn't look as cohesive against white."

"Thank god for small favors," I teased because I loved the midnight black Liv painted ours when we first moved in. "So, you're going to test the paint and install the tiled ceiling? That all?"

"Yep," she said, not catching my tone. "Then I have a bereavement meeting tonight at the church around seven, if we're done by then and I'm not too sweaty."

"That's ten hours away, Liv. I'm sure you can make time."

"You're right. It's just that Brighton really wanted to finish up the library today."

"Library?"

"Oh, I forgot he hasn't shown it to you yet. He's not renovating it, except to reinstall the original tile ceiling. He has all the original tin in his garage."

"No, he doesn't," I said, knowing damn well the garage was empty this morning. "We demoed it this morning."

"That explains why you're so sweaty," she said, wrinkling her nose. "I meant that's where he found it. I'm sure it's been cleaned and is in the library by now. You ought to pop by sometime and look at it. You'd love it, Mr. Professor."

"I'd love to, but I'll be out most of the day. Guess I'll see you after you get home?"

"Sure," she said, pecking my cheek on her way out. "Have fun setting up your new desk."

"Thanks. Have fun yourself," I said. Then I added, "But not too much fun," before she slipped out the back door.

Kerrington better stick to his damn word, or the garage wouldn't be all I'd be demoing.

CHAPTER THIRTY-FOUR
Olivia

BRIGHTON WAS NOWHERE to be found when I arrived, but his truck was in the driveway. It didn't mean he was there, but at least I knew he'd get his tush over sooner or later. In the meantime, I painted a large, square patch on the front door with the dark plum I'd selected. I loved the rich, bold choice and hoped Brighton would too. He told me to go crazy and choose whatever complementary door color I wanted. Plum Suede it was.

Then I painted a similar-sized patch next to the door on the Hardie board siding with the "gray" paint, as Ryan called it.

"Roycroft Pewter. Great choice."

I turned toward the sound of Brighton's voice and grinned. He was standing on the front lawn in nothing more than his running shorts and the most magnificent set of abs ever. I forced myself to look away and finish painting the small patch.

"It should look beautiful together, especially with the black shutters," I said.

"It's already beautiful," he answered. "You ready to do this thing?"

I wet my lips, pulling the bottom one in and biting it for a minute so I could collect myself. I was nervous to be alone with him again after the incident at Babalu's. I took a deep breath and turned, smiling at him. "Ready as I'll ever be."

"Let me just take a quick shower and change. Everything's up there, and the crew should be, too. Why don't you head up and get a jump start since you're the mastermind anyway?"

"Yes, sir," I said, playfully.

Brighton grabbed my wrist before I headed into the house. "Be careful, Liv," he warned, his eyes smoky and unsettling. "I like the way you said that a little too much."

"What? Sir?"

Brighton growled, and I wanted to laugh, but I knew this was torture for him. If it had been Ryan, I would've teased him further with the suggestive banter.

"I'm really sorry," I said instead. "I know this can't be easy on you."

"You don't know at all what it's like for me," he said, his eyes going from playful to serious just like that.

"Then tell me. Talk to me. We were friends first, weren't we? That was real."

"Are you saying everything else wasn't?"

"No! That's not what I'm saying at all. I just mean—our friendship doesn't have to change, just because of what happened."

"Because of what happened? You mean how you let me slide between your legs, Liv?" he said, his breath warm and close, sending goose bumps over my entire body. "Or how I tasted you? Touched you? Learned every inch of your body like my only job was to study its topography? Because of that? Is that what you meant?"

"Brighton—"

"Don't. Just don't. You have no clue what it's like to wake up and smell you in your house. Then hear you and Ryan joking around in the kitchen, your laughter pulling me forward like a siren. But I can't have you anymore. You're right there," he said, his voice raspy and thick, "but I can't touch you anymore. I can't taste you again. It's torture.

"I promised Ryan I would tell him if my feelings ever got in the way. And you know what? They're in the fucking way. He was smart to cut this thing off—whatever it was between the three of us. Because you're under my skin, Olivia. And the only thing stopping me from fucking you so hard you never want to let go is the fact that we were friends first. I know you'd instantly regret it. And I won't be anyone's mistake. I won't."

My lip was trembling, and I was on the verge of crying. Because he was right. I *didn't* know what it was doing to him—I'd been worried about my own feelings toward him and how to navigate it all with Ryan. "I didn't know you felt that strongly."

"Bullshit!" he said. "You've felt it too. Every time I've stared into your soul. When I drove myself deep inside of you—your nails digging into my back for more. When I was finally able to kiss you alone. That—that's what's going to hold me over after all of this is behind me. Because I *know* damn well, whether you can ever say it or not, that you feel it too. That's my only consolation."

He moved in even closer and pulled me flush against his chest. "I know you feel it, Liv. *Say it*."

I shook my head, looking away. I stared at the new oil-rubbed, bronze planters stuffed full of cheery, purple tulips on the front porch, trying to hold the tears in. I wished I could tell him that he was right. Of course he was right. But I was married, and I could never say those words back.

Or worse, give him false hope.

His eyes followed mine to the graceful flowers. Then he lifted my chin, so I was forced to face him. But I kept my eyes down, unable to meet his. Because he was right. I couldn't help what my heart wanted. And it wanted Brighton. The only problem was it wanted Ryan, too. And I couldn't live without him. But I was starting to worry I wouldn't be able to live without Brighton either.

"Look at me, Liv. Please."

It gutted me. I owed him this, no matter how much it broke me.

I dragged my gaze up to finally meet his soft green eyes, only they weren't so soft, they were searing with heat as if he were trying to brand me. "If you feel this, too, if I was *ever* anything more than just a plaything for you and Ryan—you need to tell me. I need to know this wasn't for nothing."

"I can't," I whispered.

His jaw clenched and he released my chin, swearing.

"Brighton—"

"I can't do this, Liv. I can't sit here and watch you and Ryan be so happy without me. I thought I could. Hell," he said, running his fingers through his hair, "all I've ever wanted was to make you happy. It's why I agreed to this to begin with. But somewhere along the way, I fell. Okay? I fucking fell for you."

Brighton shook his head, then put his hands on his hips as he looked at me. I bit my lip, the tears now silently spilling over onto my cheeks.

"If you ever felt it too, just give me something. Because I love you so goddamn hard. I haven't said those words to a woman in years. I never meant for this to happen. Trust me. I know you can never be mine. But I love you, Olivia North, and I *need* something. Anything."

I closed my eyes and whispered, "Tulips."

"Huh?"

"I love tulips. Love them with my entire heart and soul. I wish I could surround myself with tulips every damn day, okay? I just love them. I can't explain it. I can't deny it. Everyone thinks my favorite flower is a peony. But you know what? Tulips suit me better. And if I could smell a bouquet of tulips every day of my life, I would be so happy."

"Tulips," he whispered.

"Tulips."

He reached out and squeezed my arm. "I never knew you liked them so much," he said, finally grinning.

"I don't like them," I said.

"You love them."

"Looks like I do."

I walked over the threshold, feeling a million pounds lighter for having released the heavy burden that had settled on my heart since the moment I walked up to the Kerrington estate that first day and laid eyes on Brighton.

I'd known then that he was going to spell trouble for me. I just never imagined it would be this liberating and heartbreaking all at once. He was my captor, my savior, and my downfall—all rolled into one.

"By the way, the color of the door is definitely staying," he said from behind me.

It was the first time I laughed honestly all day. I glanced back at the overflowing planters with flowers nearly as dark and elegant as the front door. "I hope the tulips are too," I said.

"Always."

CHAPTER THIRTY-FIVE

Ryan

THE MOVERS BROUGHT my new desk up to the office and helped me arrange the space since I'd also changed out the aged leather sofa. I upgraded it with a brand-new Chesterfield in Vintage Cocoa from Pottery Barn. It suited me better. I put my hands on my hips, surveying the room with pride, when a light knock drew my attention to the door.

"Kimber," I said unenthusiastically, "I didn't know you'd be here today."

She laughed, stepping into my office without an invitation. "Oh, you know me. I'm here every day."

If the gossip about her husband were true, I could understand why.

"Are you officially back?" she asked, her gaze sweeping over the office with approval. She looked back at me, her eyes raking over me as well.

I saw the interest there, and quite frankly, it made me nauseated. Even if I weren't married, and she didn't have a good fifteen years on me, I still wouldn't punt that one. Her insides were as black as her artificial hair.

"Nope, just getting my office ready," I said as I turned my back to her and started unpacking the books I'd boxed up while the office was being painted over the summer. It was now a soothing dusky blue, called De Nimes—and of course Liv had been right. It was perfect.

"It's so you," she said, stepping closer. She went to pull a book from the box and accidentally brushed my hand. "Can I help with anything?"

I took a deep breath. "Nope. Thanks though. Just want to get these unpacked so I can get home for dinner."

"Is Liv working today?" she asked. "You know, with that man you introduced me to. What was his name? Bart? Burton?"

"Brighton," I ground out between clenched teeth. I was losing my patience with the woman.

"Oh, right!" she said gaily. "Brighton Kerrington. I looked up his line on Erickson's, you know."

Of course, she did.

"Hope you found something you liked," I said, not taking the bait.

She wrinkled her nose. Clearly, she was fishing for something, but I wasn't biting.

"Sorry to rush you, Kimber, but I really need to get this done today. I'm officially still off and want to enjoy the rest of my summer with my wife. So, if you'll excuse me."

"Oh, of course," she said, fingering her long, pearl necklace. "Did you know he just launched a new bedroom suite for his Bright and Classic line?"

I hadn't known that, but I wasn't giving Kimber the satisfaction.

"Yeah, I heard it's pretty amazing."

She smirked. "Oh, it's amazing all right. You should check it out. In case you want to switch things up at home, too."

I froze, not daring to give her the satisfaction of turning to look at her. "Thanks, Kimber. I'll keep it in mind. Have a nice evening," I said, dismissing her.

I waited until the clack of her heels faded down the hall before I opened the browser on my laptop. My stomach sank when I saw a gorgeous bedroom set pop up on my screen. It was a large, masculine four-poster bed the color of oak that's gone through several stages of distressing. It reminded me of a grayish brown driftwood, the woodwork was so fine. The ensemble also included a fourteen-drawer master chest of drawers that was both classic and stunning. Its nickel drawer pulls were the perfect choice, and I knew Liv would approve of the design aesthetic if she saw it. The last piece was a hope chest at the foot of the bed, made of the same beautiful wood, the sides inlaid with the same paneling as the tall, oversized dresser. I wondered where the end tables were or a mirrored dresser you were used to seeing in a bedroom suite.

It was a stunning collection, but I couldn't, for the life of me, figure out why Kimber would care whether I saw Kerrington's new line. I was about to close my browser when my eyes fell on its name.

The Northern Wells Bedroom Trio.

CHAPTER THIRTY-SIX

Brighton

LIV AND I were having beers on the patio, the firepit crackling, when Ryan finally pulled into the driveway. We'd been talking about her bereavement group and how that went. The short answer was—far better than she imagined it would. The more complicated answer was about all the feelings it dredged back up. I thought Liv was going to push me away and not share anything from the meeting. She surprised me when she grabbed some cold beers and asked if I wanted to join her outside.

"Hey, man!" I called out as Ryan headed over to us. He put his hands on Liv's shoulders, and she rolled her head to the side, relaxing into his touch. The intimacy was a punch to the gut. I had to figure out a way to get over it. At least until I was able to finish the house.

Ryan squeezed Liv's shoulders, then sat down in one of the chairs, running his hand over his face.

"Long day?" Olivia asked, handing him her beer. We were on number three. We should've stopped two beers ago, but we were having fun chatting as the sun set and fireflies came out, signaling their mating calls for all the world to see.

"You could say that. I ran into Kimber today."

"Oh," was all Olivia said. "She still being Kimber?"

Ryan chuckled, pulling from the beer. "Yeah. The office looks good though, Liv. The color you picked is amazing."

"Thanks," she said. "We're actually using it in the master bedroom at Brighton's place, too. It's a great neutral for a blue."

"Speaking of bedrooms," he said, turning his attention to me.

Shit. That look told me one thing, and I wasn't sure I was ready to talk about it yet.

"Mind telling us why you named your new bedroom line what you did? Does Liv know?" he asked, turning toward his wife.

"Know what?" she asked.

I closed my eyes, running a hand along the thigh of my jeans. How could I explain why I did what I did at the last minute? My marketing team had nearly killed me, making the last-minute change and having to update all our advertising and marketing materials at the eleventh hour. But I knew the minute I saw the set in production that it needed its new name. I couldn't articulate it—which was about to be an issue—it was just a feeling. A way to keep them and this special time with me always. To prove it was real. Eventually, they'd be in my rearview, nothing but a memory.

"About that," I started, looking at Ryan.

"What?!" Liv asked. "You guys are freaking me out a little."

I wet my lips. "Erickson's just released my newest collection. It was special for me because I created it originally by hand for my own home. I'm guessing you've seen it?" I said, looking at Ryan.

He nodded. I pulled up my phone to a marketing image I had of the set and handed it to Liv. Her eyes lit up when she saw it.

"Brighton! This is gorgeous! Congrats! Why didn't you say anything?"

I shrugged, waiting for her to see the name of the collection. She was too busy zooming in on each piece, looking at it with her design eye. "I release new furniture all the time in my Bright and Classic line, to keep it fresh and current, even though the pieces are meant to be timeless," I said, sounding like a sales pitch. I had to just spit it out. "This line was getting ready to drop, and my marketing team sent me the finals for approval a few weeks ago, right after the first few times we were—"

I paused. What did I call what we'd done?

"Intimate?" Liv suggested, her eyes rounding. I guess she'd gotten to the name of the collection. She looked up at me. "The Northern Wells Bedroom Trio? Really, Brighton?" She burst out laughing.

The weight on my chest lifted, and I felt like I could finally breathe.

"Glad someone's amused," Ryan said, sounding surly.

"Oh for god's sake, Ryan. What's the big deal? I think it's pretty cool." She handed the phone back to me. "It's a gorgeous *trio*," she said, looking pointedly at Ryan. "You built this originally for your own home?"

I nodded, happy to move on to the design side of things, and not stay fixated on its sentimental name. I hadn't done it to be a dick. I'd done it because my time with them would forever be etched into my heart. It was a way to permanently mark our time together. There was another reason, too.

"A few years ago, I needed a change. I was in a rut after college, and I was having a hard time getting over the loss of my son. So, in my spare time, I started creating a bedroom set in my personal workshop. I didn't know I was going to keep it for myself at the time, or that it would be a protype for a future line. I just needed to work off some of my pain. Then I started thinking about what I liked and needed. Looked at my own room. All I needed was a new bed frame, a manly chest of drawers, and a storage chest."

"What was the storage chest for?" Liv asked. "That's not a standard addition to a bedroom set."

"No, it's not." Of course Liv would pick up on that. "Remember how I told you both about my college girlfriend, Caroline? She was the mother of my son," I said, clearing my throat. I took a swig of beer, gripping my thigh with my other hand. "She died from a rare and aggressive form of cancer. When her parents finally got through the business of going through her things, they found a box of baby items that she'd kept. It gutted me to go through them. The things we'd bought for him with so much hope and excitement."

My leg was bouncing, and Liv leaned over, placing a hand on it to help calm me. "It's okay, Brighton. You don't have to tell us if you don't want to. But you *know* we understand what you're going through. We have small boxes for our babies, too."

I nodded, glancing at Ryan. I expected him to still be grumpy, but his dark brown eyes were full of compassion.

He nodded, letting me know things were okay after all. I breathed a sigh of relief, then kept going.

"I ended up keeping each of the pieces for my own bedroom because I loved them so much. But I happened to share them with my Erickson rep one day, who fell in love with them, too. They wanted me to make more for the set, but I refused. It always just felt like a trio. Not everyone needs or wants the matching end tables and two exactly matching dressers. And in a weird way, I wanted to keep everything exactly as it was because of the storage chest. I wanted it to be a sentimental line. And it is for me. Which is why the name just never seemed to be quite right, to capture all these *big* feelings I had when I created it.

"So, a couple weeks ago they ran all the files by me for final approval—and I just kept looking at the chest. Thinking about the *trio* part of it. You guys kept coming to my mind. Maybe because you know what I've been through. Maybe because the three of us will always be the only trio close to my heart. Hell, I don't know. It was a way for me to make you permanent in my life, I guess."

"Brighton!" Olivia said, squeezing my knee. "You're a permanent part of our lives, regardless. Do you really think we could go through something like this with just anyone? That after everything we've shared with you—how vulnerable we were—that we'd just cast you aside and not stay in touch?"

I shrugged, looking to Ryan. Maybe because it had all been in his court, and he was the one who'd wanted to stop it. I would've given myself over and over again to them, regardless the damage it was doing to my heart. Because I was having a hard time walking away, even though they needed me to.

"Kerrington," Ryan said, drawing my attention his way. He stood up and walked over to me, grabbing my hand and yanking me up from the Adirondack chair. He pulled me in for a dude hug with the other arm, patting me on the back a few times. "You're not getting rid of us, asshole."

I grinned. There was the Ryan I knew and loved. And, yes, I realized I loved him, too. Only it was more platonic, like a brother or a best friend. But to Olivia's point, what we'd shared had been so emotionally vulnerable. It was hard not to let my guard down with them both.

"Thanks for understanding," I said.

Ryan laughed finally. "A freaking *bedroom* set though? Really subtle. Don't think Kimber's radar wasn't going off all over the place."

Olivia covered her mouth, stifling her laughter.

"Oh man, sorry about that. There was no reason for anyone to ever draw a connection. And if they did, well, you both were central in rehabbing my uncle Isaiah's place. It was just a tribute to that help."

"I'm not worried," Ryan said, laughing. "Let the old bat stew and go crazy trying to figure things out. I was already involved in one scandal with this one over here," he said, tossing his thumb over his shoulder at Liv. "What's one more?"

We all settled back into our chairs and finished our beers before calling it a night. Liv and I needed to finish the installation over the weekend, and I couldn't wait to show Ryan once it was finished. Now that I knew how much he loved books, I wanted to share my uncle's library with him. And I had a special book I found that I wanted to give to him.

As close as we were all feeling, and as tipsy as we were, I was kinda hoping they'd invite me to join them again. Just one last time. It was pathetic, I knew that. But I was always hoping for just *one more time* with Liv. Especially after what she'd told me earlier. It was something I'd carry with me forever and was far more special than if she'd just come out and said the damn words.

So, while they slept, I couldn't stop my mind from spinning in a million different directions. About them. Our lost babies. Our intimate and special connection. About the whole experience this summer. It would be something I'd never forget, and I never wanted them to either.

I pulled out my phone and started doing some research, excited when my idea started coming to light. A few quick texts later, and I was finally able to lay my heart to rest.

CHAPTER THIRTY-SEVEN

Olivia

WE'D FINISHED THE ceiling installation in the library and were waiting on a few larger items to be delivered—including the chandelier I'd sourced to replace the existing two-story one. With the original tiles back in, the new chandelier would better compliment their rich, dusky hues of plum, green, and gold.

It wouldn't be long now till the entire house needed to be staged and finally put on the market. My heart ached at the thought of having anyone other than Brighton living next door. I knew it wasn't reasonable to daydream about him staying, but my mind couldn't wrap itself around the idea of having new neighbors. Or not seeing Brighton come bounding down the front steps in nothing more than his work shorts and bare chest, his blond hair damp from a hard day's work.

I *had* to stop imagining that.

Ryan and I were doing so much better. Between that and the bereavement group, I had to admit, I was feeling more connected and present in my life again. Not healed, not by a long shot. But the extreme loneliness and deep emptiness in my heart was starting to ebb, leaving me with a healing I wasn't fully ready for—even if I was grateful for it.

Since we'd gone back to just Ryan and me in the intimacy department, things had really heated up—and I kept quiet about missing Brighton. It was like being given a treat you never knew you loved, and it soon became your favorite. It filled you, satiated you with so much delight. Then the chef took it off the menu permanently, and everything else tasted bland in comparison.

It was like we had to expand our repertoire and get more creative to fill the void and high that Brighton left. Even if it was an unspoken understanding, I knew Ryan felt it, too. But he stopped asking me to talk dirty to him about our shared time together. At first, it turned him on to hear me describe our nights together, telling him what I'd loved, what made me climax the fastest, and what turned me on the most. It was like an aphrodisiac, making us both hungry and carefree as we explored our connection even deeper to fill that void. But everything—at least for me—seemed to pale in comparison.

Lately, I found excuses to have some alone time, trying to sort through all the feelings in my heart so I could process everything that had happened over the summer. We weren't talking about it together, but I was working through the loss of Brighton on my own. Now that I was able to start facing the loss of our babies, it was easier to process the hole he was creating, too.

Even though I saw him most days, Brighton was being respectful and keeping his distance. Part of me dreamed of him pushing me up against one of the walls at the house just like he'd done at Babalu's. But I knew it wasn't healthy and would lead to no good. So even though he fueled many of my fantasies, that's all it was these days.

The night before the chandelier was to be delivered, as we climbed into bed, Ryan let me know that he was expected at work the next afternoon for an all-hands planning session and reception with the returning professors, faculty, the provost, vice chancellor, and chancellor of the SUNY school system. Unfortunately, spouses weren't invited because it was just for school employees.

"That's okay," I said, curling against Ryan's chest. "We're installing the chandelier late tomorrow afternoon. It's the last thing we're completing on his punch list for the day because we'll need his foreman, Rob, for it, and he's coming over after his last job. The thing is massive. I can't wait for you to see the library this weekend when it's completed!"

"You're really excited about this, aren't you?" He kissed my forehead, rubbing my shoulder with the hand that was wrapped around me as I snuggled into him. "I can't tell you how happy it's made me to see you like this, Liv. I wasn't sure if you were going to be able to stick the job out."

"Like what?" I asked, tracing his chest with my finger, drawing circles through the sprinkle of dark brown hair there.

"Full of life," he said quietly. "Do you realize you haven't stayed in bed all day for weeks? I think it was after the accident—that was the last time. That damn Brighton Effect," he said drolly.

"It's more than that," I said. "Yeah, that helped. I was skeptical at first about that, but you were right. The trust that required, and the vulnerability to be so free, it changed me. It made me open again in a way I'd not let myself in a long time. I'm sorry about that. About all the time I wasted grieving when we could have been living. I think that's what we should take from their losses. Instead of wanting to die because they didn't make it, I'm finally ready to live, to honor their memory. I think I've realized how precious life is *because* of them."

Ryan rolled over to face me. "Liv, this is huge."

"I know. I mean it too. I can't go back to the darkness, Ry. After I'm done with Brighton's job, I'm thinking of going back to work full time. I hope that's okay."

Ryan dipped his head, kissing my lips softly. He teased the lower lip with his teeth, desire tugging at my body. He pressed his tongue forward, a soft, slow sweep that was sexy as hell. I reached up, lacing my fingers through his hair and pulling slowly. His kiss deepened, widening his mouth so he could take everything I was willing to give. And I gave it all. I surrendered to my husband in a way I hadn't in a long time—letting him take the lead, dominating every inch of my body until my thighs were trembling from exhaustion and my heart was racing from the intense pace of it all.

We fell asleep wrapped together like we did in the good old days—during the before. We were naked and sweaty, and I couldn't care less. My heart and my body were overflowing and grateful. And for the first time, Brighton wasn't the last thing on my mind as I drifted off to sleep.

WE ENJOYED A lazy morning in bed reading and catching up on news before we finally got up to eat. I checked Brighton's room, but he must've headed over to the house already. His work boots were by the backdoor, though, and they were covered in mud. I could've sworn they weren't when I swapped out the laundry last night before we crashed. I glanced out the window and saw a lot of foot traffic over at Kerrington's place. Things were really hopping now. There was scaffolding set up around the perimeter of the house, and men were dangling at various heights, spraying the Hardie board with the paint color Brighton approved.

"Looks like they're busy today," Ryan said, coming up behind me and kissing my neck. I nuzzled into him.

"You heading over after breakfast?" he asked.

I nodded. "I need to show Brighton some ideas in my inventory for staging. I might take him over to the warehouse soon so he can see a few things in person. Let him decide on a couple pieces I'm torn on. By the way—what's going on with the garage? I thought he wasn't redoing it?"

Ryan chuckled. "Yeah, we kind of beat the crap out of it a couple weeks ago. Demoed the whole inside in one morning. Not sure what his plan is with the space. I thought he'd loop you into whatever he was planning over there. The color looks nice though."

It really did. He'd already repainted the exterior of the garage, and it looked so much nicer now with the fresh coat of Roycroft Pewter, bright white trim, and Tricorn Black shutters. I'd have to ask him what his plans were for the inside. Even though I wasn't a landscape architect, he'd asked for my help with designing and decorating the outdoor living space, as well. He wanted a similar setup as Ryan and I had, only he wanted a hot tub installed under a trellis thick with vines. I told him we could certainly plant a climbing vine, but they'd take time to fill in. Once they did, it would offer some much-needed privacy, since we could see into one another's backyards, despite our driveways separating the two homes.

Ryan and I chatted some more about our day and kenneled Stitch, as we were both going to be gone for so long. I'd have to run over and let him out at least once. He really was the best puppy though. I set his favorite blanket in with him, and he was out like a light before we even locked the back door.

Ryan stopped short on the back steps and I nearly collided into him, knocking him over.

"Why'd you stop?" I asked, placing my hand on his back. He stepped aside and I gasped.

Sometime overnight, Brighton had planted hundreds and hundreds of tulips lining the entire interior perimeter of our white picket fence. A thick sea of romantic, deep-purple flowers stared back at me. My heart constricted with both the tenderness of his gesture and the pain of what it represented, and what we'd never have. The tears swelling in my eyes didn't escape Ryan's attention as he turned to look at me.

"Was this Kerrington's doing?"

I bit the corner of my lip and nodded. "I think so. I mean, who else would do this for us?"

"For us? Or for you?" he snarled.

"I don't know, Ry. Okay? I'm assuming it's for us since it is *our* house."

Ryan picked up his phone and called Brighton, leaving him on speaker phone.

"What's with the explosion of tulips, Kerrington?" he asked, the second Brighton answered.

Brighton chuckled. How he could be so blasé about it, knowing the significance, was beyond me. He said easily,

"Just a little way to say thank you for all the free labor I got this summer. I'm paying Liv, but you put in a lot of sweat equity into this place, too. I can't thank you guys enough."

Ryan nodded, appeased. "A case of beer would've been fine, but thanks. I guess. Liv is on her way over."

"Cool. You coming, too?"

"Not today. Have a work event this afternoon, then a reception to schmooze with the chancellor later."

Brighton laughed. "All right. Maybe tomorrow then? I could use some help with a custom build I'm doing in the small office off the front room. My little pet project."

"Sounds good," Ryan said.

I rolled my eyes when he hung up. "Satisfied?"

He looped me in by the waist and kissed me firmly on the lips. "Nowhere close. Maybe you can help with that later," he said suggestively.

I swatted at his arm, laughing. "Good luck today."

I kissed him one last time before heading across the yards, my housewarming gift for Brighton in my hands. The house wasn't done yet, but I thought it'd be a good time to give it to him since it wasn't as labor intensive today.

He pulled me into a hug when I entered the kitchen, and I froze for a moment before finally relaxing into his embrace. My barometer lately was—would this make Ryan jealous? I hated that it'd come to that between us when Brighton knew every inch of me as intimately as my husband did. He'd touched, caressed, kissed, or made love to every single part of my body during our brief time together. Nothing had been off limits when the three of us collided.

Now, everything was off limits.

And yet, tulips.

He'd planted my entire backyard as a reminder of our unspoken love. I felt guilty as hell that Ryan had no clue. If he suspected anything, I'd probably come home to the Great Tulip Massacre. Now that sharing was over, it was *over* in Ryan's mind.

Only my heart hadn't gotten the memo, and it was hard to turn off all the emotions that were rooted in my heart and taking over the needs of my body.

"Brighton," I said, tears flowing over. I hugged him closer, tighter. I was afraid to let go and meet his eyes. I was afraid I'd cave if I did. I'd underestimated the impact of seeing him after such a grand gesture.

He ran his hand from my scalp down my back, comforting me as I cried against him. "Shh . . . Liv, you're killing me. It was meant to be sweet. I didn't mean to upset you."

I finally pulled back, glancing up into his eyes and seeing straight into his soul: all the pain, all the pleasure, all the laughter, all the love we'd shared. There was heartache there, too, and I hated that I was the cause.

"It. Was. So. Sweet," I said between sobs. "Completely wrong, you jerk. But Brighton, my god," I said, my heart aching just as badly.

He dipped his head, about to brush his lips against mine, when we heard a truck rumble into the driveway. I jumped back, putting distance between us.

"The guys must be back from lunch," he grumbled.

"That's okay. We need to get to work anyway. But thank you. I will think of you every time I see them."

"That was kind of the point."

The crew came back in, nodding as they passed through to the back of the house. They were doing the final coats of the interior painting downstairs today.

"I almost forgot! Here," I said, handing him the bag I was carrying.

"What's this?" he asked with outstretched hands, grinning like it was Christmas morning.

"I always get my clients a housewarming gift, and I saw these at the farmer's market several weeks ago and immediately thought of you."

He pulled out the small house plant first, his eyebrows scrunching. "You bought me a pot plant?"

I laughed hard. It *did* have similarly shaped leaves. Not that I'd know or anything. "It's a pachira money tree," I explained. "We need to plant it by the front porch to attract wealth and prosperity in selling the house."

"Gotcha!" he said, grinning. "At least we don't have a homeowner's association here. They might not believe me if I told them it was really just a money tree."

"It's not *that* bad!" I said, quirking my eyebrow at him.

He winked, then dug into the bag and pulled out a green candle. It was from a local herbalist and reiki master. She made her own candles and said she infused them with good energy, whatever that meant. This one was called "Abundance."

"I'm sensing a theme," he said, laughing.

"There's a jade crystal somewhere inside. Burn the candle at showings. It smells heavenly and the jade represents wealth, luck, and prosperity."

"Thanks, Liv."

I grinned. "Keep going."

He dug in the large gift bag again and pulled out the miniature St. Joseph Statue and full-out belly laughed. "Are you *trying* to get rid of me fast or something? I can take a hint, you know."

"I just thought since you're selling this for your family, you probably wouldn't want to sit on a lease for too long. Anything we can do to bring in luck is worth a shot, don't you think?"

"I thought you said the secret room was enough of a draw to sell it fast."

"Oh, it is. But you can't take a chance in this market."

"No, we wouldn't want that," he said solemnly. "Thank you for everything, Liv. This was so thoughtful of you."

"We have to go bury the Saint Joseph statue next to the back door," I told him, reaching into the bag myself. I pulled out the plastic gardening spade. "We're going to do that together as soon as you open the last gift."

"There's more?" he said incredulously. "You didn't need to do all this, Liv."

"And you didn't need to plant a zillion tulips in my back-yard, but you did. It's what we do when we care about someone."

The twitch of his jaw didn't escape me. "Yeah, *care* about someone."

I handed him the last gift, a small rectangular box I'd wrapped in silver. He opened it, setting the paper and box cover onto the kitchen island. "What is this?" he asked, looking at the inscription on the small pewter plaque.

It read: "May God's blessing rest upon this house and all who dwell within! May all who enter this house also be blessed!"

"It's a mezuzah," I explained. "I know you're not Jewish, and we're not either. This is just a housewarming one, but the idea's the same. It's a blessing you normally attach near your front door. I've always loved the tradition after learning about it from my best friend's family when I was a kid. Ever since then, I've always hung one anywhere I lived. We have the same one in our house."

"This is thoughtful, Liv. I really appreciate everything."

"It's nothing," I said. "This home has a special place in my heart. I just pray whoever winds up here loves the home as much as we do, and that they make many happy memories here."

"I don't deserve you," he said, picking up Saint Joseph. "All right. Let's go bury a saint."

CHAPTER THIRTY-EIGHT

Brighton

WE BURIED POOR Saint Joseph upside down outside by the back porch as directed by the little hand-scripted card included with the good luck talisman. Then we spent the afternoon going through the punch list for the project, and Liv's own punch list for her design plan. She showed me the look and feel she was going for with staging, and I loved it. It was every bit as warm, inviting, and classic as the Wells's own home. It complimented the historic home but wasn't stuffy. In fact, it was bright and inviting, with lots of plants and clean lines. The rooms spoke for themselves with their ornate woodwork. This allowed potential buyers to not focus too much on the furniture and pay attention to the details that would sell it.

She was a smart woman. Not that I didn't know that before. But she was in her element when she was discussing design. And it was sexy as hell. A couple times I found myself brushing away a stray hair off her face or touching her arm while we were laughing. I couldn't help it. She was like a magnet, and I couldn't fight the pull no matter how hard I resisted.

Luckily, Rob got there before I could do anything stupid, but the tension had been building all day. I was finding reasons to brush against her, or accidentally touch her hand. The electricity between us hadn't died just because Ryan said it was over. How come he got to decide anyway? Shouldn't Olivia have a say, too?

Rob brought a team of six men with him and together, using the balconies as leverage for a pully system, along with a thirty-foot scissor lift, they managed to remove the old chandelier and install the new one.

We closed the blinds and flipped on the lights, and I was blown away.

"Brighton!" Olivia squealed. The guys all smiled at her reaction.

"I have to admit, I was skeptical when you told me you picked out an antler chandelier."

She laughed. "This isn't your average antler chandelier for sure," she said, her eyes raking over the giant light fixture.

The bottom was a circle, the hoop measuring about four feet across. It gradually tapered as it went up the full five feet to the top, branching out a little at its peak. It looked more like artfully arranged driftwood than it did antlers, but I'm sure that was the point. It was upscale rustic elegance.

"Where in the world did you find this thing?" Rob asked, tilting his head back to take it all in. The small naked bulbs cast a warm glow, making the massive library feel cozier, just as Liv wanted. It was a stark contrast from the cold crystal chandelier that was there before.

"It used to be in a restaurant in New York City," she said. "A famous chef I shall not name owned it. He decided to fold when the market crashed, and I've been saving it for the right project. This is a showstopper and needed the perfect space for it. None of my other projects felt right before. This," she said reverently, "is the perfect home for it."

"Kinda sucks that I have to sell the place. It's growing on me," I said, looking up at the manly, yet elegant, light fixture. Ryan would have my balls for even joking about that. But it was going to be hard to walk away from this house. It had grown beyond just a flip, or even a passion project. It wasn't just Liv who had my heart; these walls did, too.

"If I ever find another one-of-a-kind Grand Teton antler chandelier, you'll be the first to know," she joked, bumping my hip.

Rob laughed, then shook Olivia's hand. "Good to see you again. Hope Kerrington here hires you for his next project. I can already see the improvement in his choices for this house."

"Gee, thanks," I said. "I'm right here, you know."

"Yeah, yeah," Rob said. "Catch ya later, boss."

Rob and his crew pulled the lift from the room and into the hallway, parking it on the landing at the top of the stairs before pushing and shoving their way down to get off for the night. It was a Friday, so they'd probably be headed out to Rudi's.

"Well, I should probably get going, too. It's been a long day and Stitch needs to go for a walk," Olivia said, glancing back up at the chandelier one last time.

"Mind if I join you? I could use a good stretch myself."

"Sure. Let me just get changed, and I'll see you at home," she said.

Home.

Why did the Wells's house suddenly feel like home to me? I couldn't explain it. When I'd gone back up to Watertown, I'd had no interest in making the rounds with my regular friends or hanging out at the Wet Bar—aptly named because of its waterside location. Instead, all I thought of was getting back home to Liv. Well, truthfully, Liv and Ryan.

It wasn't exactly like I had sexual feelings for the guy. I just didn't swing that way. But you can't share something as deeply intimate and vulnerable with someone and not feel *something* stronger than normal. I now equated Ryan to passion, connection, and love, just as I did Olivia. The two of us shared many good talks over the summer, sometimes with Olivia, sometimes without. He'd quickly become one of my closest confidants. The kind of friend you kept for a lifetime. The kind of man I'd ask to be my best man someday.

Not the kind of man you stole a wife from.

Why, then, couldn't I stop desiring Olivia? Stop myself from actively seeking her out? Spending as much time with her as I could? *Wanting* her in every way imaginable?

I was screwed. Certifiably, irreversibly screwed.

And yet, I still loved her. I'd been working on something I wanted to give her. Tonight seemed like as good of time as any with Ryan gone for the evening. It's not that I was hiding it or wanted her to. But it was a special gift for a special woman, and I craved the connection that privacy would offer us.

Yeah, I know. I was being a selfish SOB.

I just prayed Sir Isaac Newton's Third Law wouldn't apply in this case. I didn't need the opposite and equal reaction to come back and bite me in the ass from this gesture when it came solely from a place of love.

CHAPTER THIRTY-NINE

Olivia

WE TOOK STITCH for a long walk, heading all the way up to the dog park to let him run around with some other dogs for once. He still wasn't that big yet, so it was fun watching him gently approach the other dogs in search of a new friend. I waved at the woman across the park who seemed to be the owner of the Husky who was now happily trotting around playing tag with Stitch. It was a dog match made in heaven.

Brighton and I sat on a bench as we watched the dogs play. It didn't go unnoticed how he accidentally brushed my hand a few times with his own. He even reached out and squeezed it for a moment, so I squeezed back, though I was grateful when he let my hand go. The last thing I needed was for a student of Ryan's or a client of mine to see us.

"So, when does Ryan officially go back?" Brighton asked, watching as Stitch discovered his reflection in a puddle.

"Next week. But he's already been going in a little to get things set up and ready before the students are back on campus," I said, frowning. I wasn't ready for summer to be over. I had gotten so used to having Ryan home all the time. Our relationship had grown so much stronger for it, and I was afraid of slipping back into bad habits once the stress of our normal schedules sank back in. "Did I tell you I've decided to go back to work full time?"

Brighton turned on the bench to face me. "That's wonderful!" he said, beaming. "How do you feel after making such a big decision?"

I let out a shaky breath. How *did* I feel? Ryan hadn't even asked me that, though I knew he cared. "Scared. I know it's all in my head, but I feel like I'm betraying Laelynn by moving on, going back to the way life was before. It's not the same, Brighton. I'm not the same."

"No, you're not. You know what you are?"

"What?"

"Stronger. More healed. You're *ready*. That's not a betrayal. That's a commitment to life. I'm certain she'd want that for you. Parents and children—no matter how young—share an inexplicable, inextricable bond at a soul level that can never be severed or replaced. Even if you have kids in the future, it doesn't alter or affect the specific and exact way your heart loves Laelynn. Likewise, her little soul up there somewhere," he said, pointing to the sky, "will never *not remember* your DNA. Your heart. Who knows—maybe you'll meet her again in another lifetime."

I bit back my tears, clutching the edge of the bench. "I hope so. Because I'm not sure I'll ever get pregnant again in this one. My body hates me."

A single tear fell from my eye, tracing a hot trail down my cheek. Brighton wiped it for me, then pulled me in close for a hug.

"I am right. And I can't wait to see Sam again, either. Maybe he and Laelynn are up in heaven together. I'll tell him to watch over her, like a big brother."

I pulled back, wiping my eyes. "You talk to him?"

"Yeah," he said, as if it were the silliest question in the world. "Don't you?"

I backed up, giving myself some space. "No, actually. I haven't. I don't know why, but it hadn't occurred to me."

"Just because she's not with you down here doesn't mean she's not with you here," he explained, placing his hand over my heart. "I didn't get therapy right away. But after Caroline died, and I got Sam's things, it broke me. Absolutely broke me to see his tiny booties and hold his fetal death certificate. The little blue cap the hospital put on him before handing him to Caroline to hold was in there. And a picture of Caroline while she was holding him, tears and all," he said, his eyes glassy. He looked away, trying to compose himself.

"Once I started seeing someone about my grief, they recommended a couple of exercises. They might be good for you. Do you want to hear them?"

Was I ready to?

I watched Stitch play happily with his new friend. Took in the bright copper sky as the sun set over Lake Ontario. Breathed in the fresh lake air. The fact was, I was still living. I owed it to Laelynn to be stronger than this. To make my life count, since hers was over way too soon.

"I would. Let's walk and talk and head home before it gets dark."

Much to the disgust of Stitch's new friend, I leashed him up and we headed out. On the walk home, I listened to Brighton's own path of healing. It made me realize how much Ryan must be holding in. He'd had to be so strong for me all this time. I'd forgotten how to be there for him, too. Instead of turning to another woman for comfort—his priority was making me happier.

I was certain I didn't deserve Ryan.

"I think I'll try writing her a letter, like you suggested," I told Brighton when we got home. I let Stitch off his leash in the backyard and closed the gate behind us. "It's still nice out. I may just curl up out here with a journal and try some of the exercises you shared. I really appreciate it."

"Appreciate what?" he asked, searching my eyes as if trying to memorize every fleck of blue.

"Being brave enough to open up about your grief. I don't know a lot of men who could do that. For continuing to give to me, even though I haven't given you nearly as much in return. For the tulips," I said, smiling at the explosion of color all around me.

"I have four sisters, Olivia. I know how to get in touch with my feelings."

I laughed. "How did I not know this?"

"We were too busy learning each other in other ways." Brighton pulled me closer to him, so our hips were almost touching. Our lips were only a breath apart.

"I finally understand why Ryan did what he did," he said. "There's not a damn thing I wouldn't do to keep that smile on your face. *Nothing.*"

His hand was in my hair before I could stop it, his mouth crashing down onto mine. I dropped the leash and wrapped my hands around his head, pulling him even closer as I sank into that kiss. He lifted me up, and I wrapped my legs around his waist as he deepened the pressure—owning me in a way I'd never experienced. It was as if he could read every single one of my deepest, darkest secrets with that kiss. Drawing them out and asking for more. For total surrender.

He slammed my back up against the house and kissed my neck, my collarbone, my ears, before capturing my mouth again on a moan. Stitch barked happily at our feet, thinking it was a game. Laughter bubbled over as he jumped up on Brighton's legs, trying to get to me.

I rested my head back against the house, my chest rising with the passion that was bubbling over. Thank god for Stitch because I was *this close* to losing any common sense that was left after that kiss.

Brighton slowly lowered me to the ground but pulled me close in a fierce embrace as he kissed me one last time. "By the way, I have something for you."

I bit my lip. I wasn't sure I could handle one more thing that would bring me even closer to him. But I nodded. If he'd gone out of his way to think about my heart, the least I could do was accept his gift. I followed him into the house, making our way to the guestroom where I'd slept with Stitch. He placed his hand over my eyes, bringing back memories from the first day I'd met him. Here we were all over again. I inhaled sharply, afraid to open my eyes. I knew whatever I saw was going to sink me even further. And the truth was, I wasn't sure I was prepared.

"Open your eyes," he whispered in my ear.

There was a storage chest, much like the one at the foot of the bed in his collection for Erickson's. Only this one was whitewashed, with a bouquet of tulips mixed with delicate sprigs of lily of the valley painted on the top.

"What is this?" I asked, walking over and kneeling next to it.

"It's a memory box," he said, shoving his hands into the pockets of his shorts. "I figured you might have a few things you've set aside from Laelynn that are special to you."

I ran my hand along the top of the wooden chest. "This is beautiful. Where'd you get it?"

"I made it for you," he said, squatting down next to me, resting on his heels. "I started it after one of our first conversations in the backyard at night—when you opened up about your losses. I like having all of Sam's stuff in one place. Sometimes I write him Christmas cards, or birthday letters, and put those in there. I just thought you might like to do the same. That it might be therapeutic for you."

"I love it," I said, opening the lid. Inside there was a smaller box. "What's this?"

"It's for the really important things," Brighton said.

I knew exactly what things he was talking about. Laelynn's hospital bracelet. Her little lock of hair. The fetal death certificate. I later found out that was also the only proof of our daughter's birth—still or not. I had a little pink hat with a bow sewn onto the front, and a blanket someone made by hand and donated to the hospital for the babies who didn't go home. They wrapped her in it before handing her to us after her birth.

"Thank you," I whispered. Tears were streaming down my cheeks as the weight of his gift sank in. He'd started this before we were ever even intimate together. "I don't have words for how much this means to me. I know Ryan will love it, too."

Brighton pushed my hair aside, then wiped the tears from my cheeks. "I didn't mean to make you cry," he said, helping me up to a stand.

"You said you wrote through your grief. Did you journal? Write letters? What helped?"

"For me, it was being able to process my guilt for not being able to protect him—save him."

"Brighton—" I said, my heart breaking in a million pieces that he blamed himself in any way.

"I know it's stupid. There was nothing I could've done, nothing Caroline did, to affect the outcome. But the first thing I did was write an apology to Sam for not being able to change things. Then I wrote a letter telling him all the things I'd hoped for in his life. And how he'd changed mine for the better. How even though his loss was the single most devastating thing to ever happen to me—his life, for even that brief time he was inside Caroline—was the best part of me. I wrote letter after letter until my heart had bled all over the pages. It was the only way to get everything out of me—the guilt, the anger, the jealousy I felt when I saw other families. The depression. I've been where you are Liv. Maybe not the same way since I didn't carry him. But I'd have traded my life with his in a second if god offered me a chance."

I wrapped my arms around his waist and rested my head against his chest. I knew exactly what he meant. "I'm not sure I'm brave enough to write something like that."

"You're braver than you give yourself credit for. But you can journal instead if it helps. For me, it helped to have someone to write to. Otherwise, it would've just been a bunch of entries of me going off on god."

"How did you stop?" I asked quietly.

"I started living. I started trusting that, for whatever reason, god has bigger plans for me than I could even begin to comprehend. I can't control life like a puppet master, so I decided to go with the flow more. Trust that something better was coming after all that grief. I had to start believing and honoring the fact that Sam's short life and death meant something."

"And that worked? Sheer will?"

Brighton shrugged. "It did for me. Well, that and a lot of therapy."

I hugged his waist tighter, then looked up at him. "You're my therapy, Brighton."

He bent down, brushing his lips so softly against mine I almost questioned whether it really happened. It didn't matter though. No matter what happened in my life, I knew I would never be able to erase the ghostlike imprint of the feel of Brighton's lips on mine. He'd seared his mark on my heart and my body forever, no matter how hard I'd tried not to let it happen.

"And you're my tulip," he said, pressing his lips more possessively against mine this time, making sure there was no mistaking where I stood in his life and what he wanted.

Only I had no clue what to do about it.

CHAPTER FORTY

Ryan

SAT IN THE darkness of my Jeep, watching as Brighton left the guest bedroom off the sunroom—the room where Liv had slept with the dog. She was back to sleeping in our bedroom though, so I wasn't sure why they would be in there alone together. All I knew is my inner Hulk was about to come out, and I needed to get it under control fast before I said or did something I'd regret. I gripped the steering wheel so tight my knuckles turned white. I didn't want to think about what it meant that they were in there this late. Or what the betrayal of their solitary kiss meant. As far as I knew, Olivia had never kissed him when I wasn't there with them.

If we were dating, it would be one thing. But she was my *wife*. And, yeah, it had been my bright idea to share her with him in the first place. But that wasn't what troubled me. What I wished I had control over was Olivia's feelings *now*.

Through the darkness, I watched as her hands went to her lips. I noticed how she didn't move from her spot, watching where he'd walked out of the room long after he'd left. What was going through her heart right now? The entire time I was gone today, all I could focus on was getting home to Livy. While I loved my job, a room full of stuffy academics held nothing to the light that radiated from her these days. I couldn't seem to get enough.

Apparently, Kerrington couldn't either.

Man-to-man, we'd be discussing that in the morning. For now, all I wanted to do was wipe the memory of Brighton's kiss from my wife's lips. Still white knuckling the steering wheel, I took several rounds of deep breaths, willing myself to calm down before I went in there. I gathered my laptop and the small gift bag the school had given me to celebrate my fifteenth year of teaching. I couldn't wait to show Liv the theatre tickets inside, so I focused on that instead of the jealousy burning through my veins like a bad high.

I could ask Olivia point blank what had happened, and she would tell me. But I didn't want to know tonight. Tonight, I just wanted to make sure I was the one on her mind as she fell asleep. By the time I got inside, Olivia had already gone upstairs to our bedroom. I took Stitch out to the bathroom one last time for the night so she wouldn't have an excuse for one of the late-night outdoor chat sessions she seemed to be so fond of with Kerrington.

We trotted up the stairs together, and I saw Liv curled up in our bed, a book by one of her favorite rom-com authors in her hand.

"Hey," I said, walking over to the bed.

She set the book down, a big smile on her face as she looked up at me.

"Hey, yourself, handsome. How did the event go?"

"You know how it is. Nothing to write home about," I said, leaning over to kiss her. I couldn't taste Brighton on her—he'd been replaced by the familiar aftertaste of her Crest toothpaste. I nipped at her lower lip. "Sorry I got home so late."

"That's okay," she said, pulling my head down to deepen the kiss. Maybe I was reading more into the situation than what had really happened. Either that or she was feeling guilty.

Either way, I was going to erase Brighton from her mind tonight until he was just a distant memory. There wasn't enough space for the two of us in her heart or on her body anymore. Olivia was mine, and I intended to make sure she never forgot.

THE NEXT MORNING, I bumped into Kerrington in the kitchen as he was getting his coffee. His blond hair was tousled, and he had nothing on but his running shorts. It was hard to wipe him from her heart when the guy was parading around our house half naked, looking like a Greek god.

"Hey, man," he said. "Want a cup?"

"Sure." I was on my way to the store to pick up the punching bag I'd ordered. I needed to get it set up in the garage and get some of this energy out. Especially after last night. "You guys have a successful day yesterday?"

"Yeah. You should see that thing. It's massive. Olivia knocked it out of the park. You should come by later and check it out."

"I'd love to. She's something else, isn't she?"

Brighton looked at me funny, and I couldn't blame the poor guy. I knew I was baiting him, but I couldn't help myself.

"You two have any more plans today?" I asked, taking a sip of my coffee as I looked over the mug at him.

He grabbed the sprouted nine-grain bread he and Livy favored and popped it in the toaster. We'd invited him to eat at our place, too, because I'd gotten a peek inside the fridge at his uncle's house and it looked worse than a college frat house.

"Yeah, she's taking me over to the warehouse so we can finalize the staging. She has a few pieces she wants to show me in person."

"You're ready for staging?" I asked, surprised.

The outside had been painted a stately dark gray, the front door an elegant, rich plum—much like the tall, bronze planters full of tulips that sat on his front porch. Yesterday a land-scaping crew came out and worked their magic, cleaning up the overgrown backyard. Nothing was cut down, just shaped into submission with bright pops of color added. The front flowerbeds were larger and lusher, looking like something out of a design magazine.

"Yep," he said, looking proud. "We have a few more things on the punch list, but the end is getting closer in sight."

For some reason, it didn't make me as happy as I thought it would to hear he was almost done over there. In just a few short months, we'd grown close. And not just because of what we'd shared with Olivia. I considered him a real friend now.

"The summer's flown by," I said, shaking my head. Maybe I just needed to shoot straight with him about my concerns from the night before. "Hey, I need to ask you something."

"Sure, what's up?" Kerrington buttered his bread with the ghee Olivia used too. They were both health nuts.

"I saw you and Olivia in the guestroom last night when I got home. What were you doing in there?"

Brighton stopped buttering, his knife paused midair. "Maybe you should ask Olivia."

"I'm asking you."

"I just gave her a little gift, okay? That's all. Have her to show it to you later. I know she was planning to today. I've got to get over to the house."

"Was the kiss just a little gift, too?" I asked. I couldn't help myself.

He set the knife down, then shoved his breakfast in the trash can. "Look—"

I stood, squaring off with him. "No, you look. You *promised* me, Kerrington."

"You think I fucked her? In your house?" He looked incredulous and disappointed all at once, and I knew immediately I'd guessed wrong. Maybe it really was just a simple kiss.

I raised both hands. "You can't blame me for asking. I *saw* you kiss her before you left the room."

"It was a simple peck. We'd had an emotional talk yesterday about Sam and Laelynn. It was nothing more than a friend would do."

"Yeah, but she hasn't fucked any of her other friends," I pointed out.

"God, dude, listen to yourself. This is your *wife* you're talking about. In case you forgot, *you* were the one who instigated this whole thing. The only time I've been inside your wife was when you gave me permission, asshole."

Ouch.

"Stop kissing her behind my back then, capisce?"

"I hear you loud and clear, *friend*." With that, Brighton dropped his coffee into the sink and turned to leave.

I didn't know what was wrong with me. He wasn't wrong. Still, the sting of jealousy was just too much to bear—a casualty I never really considered since Liv and I were so damn tight. But the longer Kerrington was in the picture, the harder it was for us to move on. I loved the guy. I truly did.

But my days of sharing were over.

CHAPTER FORTY-ONE

Olivia

I HEARD THE TAIL end of Ryan's conversation with Brighton, and my stomach knotted with anxiety. I didn't want to walk in the kitchen and face him, knowing he'd seen us kiss the night before. God! I'd been so careless.

"Liv?" he called out.

Damn squeaky stairs.

I rounded the corner, staging a smile on my face that I just didn't feel this morning. "Morning, babe," I said, leaning in for a quick kiss. "You smell nice. You going somewhere?"

"Just running to Outdoor Joe's to grab a punching bag for the garage. Want to come?"

"I'd love to, but Brighton and I are headed to the warehouse today to go through some of my inventory for the staging."

"You can't do that alone?" he asked casually, though the edge in his tone told me something different. "Ever bring other clients with you to the warehouse for personal opinions, Liv?"

I bit my lip, not sure whether to laugh or cry at the way Ryan was acting. I poured my coffee into a to-go mug. "Are you upset about something, hon?"

"What did Brighton give you last night? Other than that kiss?"

I gasped. "Were you spying on me or something?"

"No. Should I be?"

"No. You don't have any reason to, Ryan. So why were you?"

He sighed, looking tired. He ran a hand over his beard, his jaw tensing. "I didn't have to spy. The blinds were raised, and I could see you kissing him clear as day when I pulled into the driveway last night. Which means anyone walking by could've too."

"It was just a quick peck goodnight, Ryan. It wasn't like we were making out or anything."

"Just a quick peck. Sounds like you two got your stories down pat."

"Fuck you," I spat. "I didn't do anything wrong. Yeah, he kissed me. So what? You let him *fuck me*, Ryan. This was a simple, sympathetic kiss for the shitty day I had yesterday. Have you asked me how my day went? No. You didn't. So, before you judge, how about you stop being a jerk, okay?"

I shoved off the kitchen island and stalked toward the mudroom to grab my keys. Ryan blocked the door before I could leave. We were both angry and not in the best place. Emotions had escalated quickly, and I wasn't sure why he was acting like this now. We'd just made love for hours last night. He never once said anything about me kissing Brighton.

"I have plans today, and I need to get my day started," I said tersely.

"Show me what he gave you first, Olivia. Show me what you were doing in the guestroom together when I wasn't home."

I turned to face him, anger drawing my brows down in frustration and impatience. "You really want to see what he gave me? Fine. But just know that you're making a huge ass of yourself right now, Ryan."

I spun on my heel and marched toward the guestroom. I could feel Ryan's looming presence as he trailed right behind me. I would leave from the sunroom when we were done and put some distance between us today. I needed it after the wonderful start to my day.

I pointed to the beautiful memory chest now sitting at the end of the guest bed. I wasn't lying when I told Ryan *that* kiss had only been a peck. Though I did feel guilty about not disclosing the kiss earlier in the evening; but now certainly wasn't the time for that.

"He wanted to give us a gift, so we had somewhere special to store Laelynn's things. Because he knows how much I've been hurting this summer, and the seven months before that. When he lost Sam, he liked having all his son's things stored in one place, along with all the letters he wrote to him over the years. He thought it might be helpful if I did the same."

Instead of Ryan cooling off, he looked more upset.

"He made you a fucking memory box? Is the guy in love with your or something?"

I gaped at him. "Are you even hearing yourself? I just said, he made this for *us*."

Ryan went over to the box, looking down at the serene flower bouquet hand-painted on top. "The guy sure has a thing for tulips, doesn't he?"

He glared at me, as if willing me to admit something I wasn't ready to talk about and didn't know how in the hell to define anyway. I didn't *know* how I was feeling about everything. Ever since Ryan opened the floodgates with this whole unusual situation, the more confused I became. One minute he wanted Brighton in our bed, encouraging me to freely give myself and do the unimaginable things I'd done. Telling me how turned on he was by everything. How he *loved* watching me be with Brighton right in front of him.

The next, he was an anger ball, his jealousy erupting over the top of his carefully erected walls.

"Don't be a jerk," I seethed. "He has a thing for us. That's what he has. It's called a friendship. And in case you missed the memo, it's with *us*. You were the only one who pushed for it to be more. Then you were the one who got to say when it was over. So blame yourself, Ryan. You're orchestrating the whole damn show."

Ryan shoved his hands through his hair. "Fuck!" he yelled, turning from me. "The guy doesn't just get to give you gifts whenever the hell he wants, Liv. You're still *my* wife."

"You're right, I am. But I'm *his* friend. And I'm not sitting here while you make more of this than it is. You still haven't asked me why yesterday was so hard. So you know what? Screw you, Ryan Wells. Screw you."

I turned on my heels and slammed out into the sunroom, ready to lose myself in work.

"Liv, we're not done. We *need* to talk about this."

"No, Ryan. We don't. I didn't do anything wrong. I let him comfort me with a peck goodnight. That's it. It's not like we fucked or anything."

Right before I slammed out of the house, I heard him say quietly, "Truth, Liv?"

"I'm not really in the mood right now," I said, pausing.

"Truth?" It came out as a sad-sounding plea.

I didn't want to hear what his deepest fear was, though I sensed what was coming. And I was right.

"Do you love him?"

I turned to my husband, a lone tear now running down my cheek.

"Ryan, don't. Let's talk when we've both cooled down. This is only going to hurt us if you push like this when we're both mad."

"Mad? I'm not mad, Liv. I'm fucking devastated. Gutted. Because I can *see* it on your face."

He walked over to me, backing me up against the French doors leading outside. I could see Brighton's house from the windows, but he was nowhere to be seen.

Ryan's jaw tensed again, anger and pain blurring behind his glassy, tear-filled eyes. "Tell me the truth, Livy. Do you love him? Have you fallen for Brighton?"

I turned my head, another tear falling down my cheek. We didn't lie. But I didn't want to admit to the complicated feelings that were racing under the surface of my skin, ready to erupt.

He hit the glass next to my head with his palm, making me jump. "Answer me!"

I closed my eyes, my heart bracing for the worst—knowing my world was about to unravel. But after everything we'd been through, I knew I owed him the god's honest truth. "Yes."

Ryan slammed his hand against the door again. Only this time, his palm shattered the small glass windowpane next to my head.

"Jesus Christ, Ryan!"

He glowered at me for the longest moment, then shoved past me and out the door without saying another word. I watched as he got into his SUV and peeled out of the driveway, his tires leaving the smell of burning rubber against the asphalt of our quiet street.

It felt eerily like an omen as I clutched my stomach and sank to the floor of the sunroom, our marriage slowly spiraling into a crash and burn around us.

CHAPTER FORTY-TWO

Brighton

THE SOUND OF tires squealing in front of the house had me glancing out the window toward the street. When I saw it was Ryan's SUV and not some stupid kid, worry flooded over me. I reached for my phone and called Olivia. When she didn't answer, I got even more worried, so I texted her, asking if she was okay.

I got no response. I decided to wait two more minutes, then I'd text her one last time. If I still didn't hear from her, I was storming back over there to check on her in person. Just when things were getting better with her healing progress, too. What a selfish prick Ryan was being.

> **BRIGHTON:** I need to know you're okay. Text me back or I'm coming over.
>
> **OLIVIA:** . . .

The three dots came and left several times. I slid my sneakers on. Something was wrong.

> **OLIVIA:** Ryan and I got in a fight. I'm okay, just shaken. Be right there.
> **BRIGHTON:** We don't have to go today. You can take some time if you need.
> **OLIVIA:** No. I'm not going back to that. To the Liv who hides.
> **BRIGHTON:** I'll be waiting for you then.

When Olivia finally showed up, her eyes were red and puffy. It didn't take a genius to figure out the fight had been bad.

"Want to talk about it?"

Her jaw tensed, and I watched as she bit her lower lip. Then she started crying. *Aw, shit.*

I scooped her hand into mine and led her upstairs to the library, which was the only room where we could have any privacy since we had a full house. The punch-list crew was busy today. What was worse—my time here was now limited. There was such little left to do, even with the last-minute garage add. The truth was, I had an efficient crew, and my reasons for stalling the flip were running thin. Even Rob was asking why we'd had so much scope creep and last-minute changes. It was because I couldn't bear to leave Olivia. And I didn't have a clue what to do with that. There was nothing worse than falling in love with an unattainable married woman. Unless that woman also happened to be your best friend's wife.

But the connection with Olivia was unspoken and powerful. Every time we were together, it was as if our bodies were being pulled together. And not just in a sexual way. I *needed* to be close to her. To be in her presence. To bask in the light that was Olivia when her soul was happy. And it had been lately.

I held her in my lap now on the large, oversized sofa. It was leather, but dozens of throw pillows kept it from feeling cold. My back was to the arm of the couch, so I stretched my legs out straight, letting her curl against my chest as she cried.

"I'm not sure he's ever been so mad before," she said quietly.

"Is it because of me?" If I was a betting man . . .

She nodded. "He loves you, you know. As a friend. I've not seen him get close to a guy in a long time. I was afraid this was going to happen eventually. The jealousy."

"He has nothing to be jealous of. You're his. And we all stopped."

"That's not what he's jealous about."

"What is he jealous of then?"

Liv looked up at me with her wet, blue eyes, pleading with me to understand. "That I still think about making love to you," she admitted, her voice soft and low. "That I've thought about being alone, just the two of us."

"But it's not like you've acted on it."

"No, but it doesn't mean the longing isn't there. That he can't *feel* that betrayal."

"Liv—"

Her eyes were glued to mine, full of pain and need. I knew if I bridged the gap between us, it would be over. There would be nothing that could stop me from taking her—selfish, hot, fast, completely.

"You've gotta stop looking at me that way."

"I can't," she said. "I love him so much. But I love—tulips, too. I don't know what to do with that. But I know I can't be happy without you."

I gripped her hips, pulling her closer against my body. "We shouldn't do this alone, though, Liv. We can't take it back once we do."

"Just hold me then."

I nodded into her hair, inhaling the fresh scent of summer and sunshine. She nodded off for about thirty minutes, so I held her in my arms and comforted her as she slept. Her face was much softer and more serene than when she'd first come over. She didn't look as haunted when she slept. She looked peaceful, even though I knew the war that was being waged in her heart when she was awake.

A loud noise from somewhere below startled her and she sat straight up, laughing when she slid off my lap and onto the floor. She rubbed her backside. "Wow. That was graceful."

I lifted her to a stand. "Well, you were sleeping peacefully until that happened."

"How long was I out?"

"About thirty minutes or so."

"I'm so sorry, Brighton. I know you don't need to get in the middle of our issues."

"There's no helping that, Liv. I'm exactly in the middle of your issues. In fact, I *am* your issues."

"Not all of them. Ryan internalizes things. He always has. Ever since we started trying to have kids, I'm realizing he's stuffed down even more in a misguided attempt to keep me happy. To help me heal. All this time, he was hurting just as badly. He was simply better at hiding it."

"Grief does funny things to us."

"I'll say," she said, waving her hand back and forth in the space between us.

"We didn't do this out of grief, though. We did this to heal. To bring back your light. There's a big difference."

"Well, you brought it back all right," she teased. "Maybe a little too well."

She bit her lower lip again and looked up at me. I know it wasn't a come on, but hell if it didn't stir things in me even more. I quickly changed the subject, looping it back to Ryan.

"Hey, so I found this book I think Ryan might like. I noticed he picked up a first-edition book at Babalu's, so it got me thinking, since this library is full of them. I found one I think he might appreciate."

"Ryan is obsessed with old books. I'm sure whatever it is, he'll love it."

"Come here. I want to show it to you," I said, grabbing her hand like we had the first time we'd met.

We headed for the secret stairs, only this time, I let Olivia press the magic button. The shelf swung open and we entered. I'd stashed the book in here so there was no chance of it walking off with a crew member. It was worth about eighteen hundred dollars and was autographed by W. Somerset Maugham, and I really wanted Ryan to have it.

The room was tiny, but my uncle kept some of his most treasured books in here—probably because of their value and the lack of sunlight to cause damage. Behind the small open-slatted staircase was a cozy reading nook with cashmere blankets and throw pillows. Floor-to-ceiling bookcases flanked the stairs, and a huge watercolor painting of the house filled the wall space on the backside of the "magic" door into the room. I suspected Olivia was right that it would be a selling point.

I grabbed the book off the shelf then joined Olivia on the bench of the reading nook, handing it to her before I sat down. She ran her hand over the textured red cover reverently. "This is too much."

"He's a good friend," I said, shrugging. "I don't have the same sentiment toward old books, so why not pass it on to someone who does?"

"Maybe because it has to cost a small fortune?" she teased.

"It's just money."

Her eyes grew soft and she set the book down onto the nearest shelf. "Would you do me a favor? I'm not ready to go home yet, and my heart's not on work today."

I nodded my head. I'd move heaven and earth for the woman.

She turned on the small sconces that were nestled among the books, then closed the magic door. Intimacy shrouded us as she fingered the book spines on the nearest shelf. One caught her eye and lit her face with joy. She pulled it down and joined me on the bench again, reclining across the small surface and resting her head in my lap.

"Read this to me?" she asked, looking up at me.

I ran my fingers through her soft, blond hair that flowed over the sides of my leg and onto the cushion. I fluffed out one of the cashmere blankets over Olivia and gently stroked the side of her face, lost in those dazzling blue eyes of hers.

"You are going to be the death of me."

"I'd rather be what brings you life," she said, her pulse jumping in her throat.

I had to tread carefully because Liv and me in this tiny, intimate space would only spell disaster if I weren't careful. It was too cozy. Too *private*. It was as if we'd shut out the outside world and descended into a magical fairy tale where only the feelings between us pulsed through the air and nothing else existed.

I flipped open the book to a random spot and started reading *Little Women* as Olivia curled onto her side and listened. I read that way for about twenty minutes, until a certain passage caught her attention and she sat up, transfixed.

"'Upon my word, I was so tumbled up in my mind, at one time, that I didn't know which I loved best, you or Amy, and tried to love you both alike. But I couldn't, and—'"

Her eyes were wide, and her breathing was shallow. I saw the dilation of her pupils and the way she licked her lips as she stared at the words coming from my mouth. I paused and set the book down.

"Olivia—"

"I've made mistakes too," she said, her eyes hot with longing. "I've not been listening to my heart or telling Ryan how I really feel."

"And how do you really feel?" I asked, my voice thick and husky from the way she was staring at me.

"I feel like I wasn't ready for our time together to stop. Even though Ryan started it all, it wasn't just his to finish or tell me when we were done. It was so much more than just our bodies, Brighton. I never meant for my heart to become so invested, but how could it not? Especially when it was with you?"

She moved closer on the bench, her hand cupping my jaw. She looked like she wanted to say more, so I didn't respond, I just held the depth and space she needed to work out what was racing though her heart.

"I need to know, Brighton. I need to know if what we have has taken a part of my heart forever, or even all of it."

"Liv—you don't mean that."

"I need you to make love to me. I need to know if you see me, and if you want me, for just me. Or if it's only when the three of us are together. I need you to get clear on that, and I need that, too."

"Liv—"

She lifted her lips to meet mine, brushing her tongue over my mouth to part it. I wish I could say I did the honorable thing and said no—that we needed to figure this out another way. But her lips were too soft, and my heart was too far gone.

And Ryan was the last thing on my mind as I cupped Olivia's head and deepened the kiss. One way or another, this was about to change everything. And I had no willpower to stop it.

CHAPTER FORTY-THREE

Olivia

I LOST EVERY OUNCE of willpower and common sense as I deepened the kiss with Brighton. My skin was burning for his touch, and I could do nothing to stop it. It was as if, all this time, it was leading to this. It had been my deepest fear and my most secret desire. One way or another, after today, I would know. I would know if Brighton had stolen all of my heart, or if it was still shared—torn between the two men in my life.

I sat all the way up, letting Brighton pull me onto his lap as I straddled him, our hands unable to pull clothes off fast enough. It was as if the fire was racing up both our forms and we needed to feel him inside of me before we were all the way consumed—scorched by the very passion that was driving us.

The first thrust in was heaven, my body aching around his and surrendering completely. *Holy hell*. It was as if we were the ones married, our bodies knowing every need, every desire, every response before it happened. He gave as much as he took, my body arching, pressing, needing him deeper and more fully than we'd ever gone. I reached up, gripping the back of the staircase as I rode him, Brighton worshiping my breasts as I came the first time.

Then he gripped my hips and held me still, thrusting deep inside of me, his hips bucking off the bench so he could fill me, drowning me in his desire. Our bodies were hot and sweaty when we finally came down from our high together. I wrapped my arms around his neck, felt his lips lick the salt from my collarbone.

I ran my hands through the sweaty hair on his neckline, pressed my bottom deeper down onto his lap as I purred from the contented bliss of a full-body, full-soul orgasm. It had never been like this with us before, because we'd always held back a small part of ourselves in front of Ryan. But this—this was the glorious loving my body needed, *craved* to feel fully alive again.

But I didn't have even a moment to enjoy the sensation.

Footsteps echoed on the hardwood floor of the library. Then, our world was fractured, destroyed by two simple words.

"Olivia? Brighton?"

It was Ryan.

He was on the other side of the wall—the only thing that separated us from the library. I held my breath and my body still. Brighton lifted his finger to his lips. Neither of us moved as guilt washed over me like poison.

Oh my god. What had we done?

"Liv? Brighton? You guys in here?"

We could hear him pacing the room, as if searching. "Huh." His hand brushed the outer wall; he was so close we could hear his fingers running along the books. I was terrified my heartrate would give us away, and I felt like I was going to black out from the shame.

Then his footsteps fell away, and my phone buzzed from the pocket of my shorts that were crumbled on the floor. Thank god the phone was on Do Not Disturb and hadn't rung.

When we heard the click of the library door, and no further movement, I slid off Brighton's lap. He handed me his T-shirt to clean up before I slid back into my clothes. I gripped the phone in my pocket, afraid to look.

Brighton cupped my chin, lifting my face so I could meet his eyes. Tears were streaming down my cheeks as I looked up at him. "What did I do?"

"What did *we* do, you mean. You aren't facing this alone, Olivia. This was both of us—and I won't regret it," he said, his mouth crashing onto mine possessively. I whimpered into his kiss, but drew strength from his warm, thick tongue as it captured mine. We were entwined in so many ways now, it was hard to separate myself from him as he comforted me.

"I will face this with you, Liv," he said after we broke apart. He rested his forehead onto mine, his hand still cradling my head.

"It's not yours to face," I said quietly. "Ryan's my husband. I'm the one with the scarlet letter here, not you."

"It's not that simple, and you know it," he said. "Don't do this to yourself. Don't you dare take this on alone and act like you did everything wrong. If Ryan was that concerned over the possibility of losing you, he should never have shared you with another man to begin with. Fuck, Liv. If our situations were reversed, I *never* would have let another man touch you."

I backed up for a second, putting some much-needed space between us. I couldn't think when I could still smell the sex on his skin. Which meant if I could, Ryan would.

I knew it was bad when my mind started spinning, trying to figure out how to get home and take a shower without raising any suspicion. I was already spiraling from my deceit. The realization that I'd broken our wedding vows crashing over me like a giant tsunami.

My hands shook as I buttoned my jean shorts all the way, running a hand over my hair. "He's going to smell you on me," I whispered.

"Take a shower here then."

"In front of all these workers? And come home with wet hair? No way. That will look even worse. And I'm not ready to face Ryan yet with this. I'm not. I can't."

Brighton wrapped me in his arms one last time, hugging me as tightly as he could as if to transfer all his bravery to me for what I might face when I went home.

"If you need anything—anything at all—you text me. I mean it. I'll stay over here for the rest of the day to give you some breathing space and to work anything out if it comes up. But Liv?"

"Yeah," I said, glancing up into the eyes I'd grown to know as closely and deeply as my husband's.

"I love you. I loved you before, and I love you even more now. Do not deny what just happened between us. That wasn't just physical. That was you getting my entire heart. Just be careful what you do with it, okay?"

I nodded, torn even worse than before.

But there was one thing I wasn't torn about, and did know even clearer now, no matter what happened in the days ahead with Ryan and me.

"I don't just love tulips, Brighton."

"I know," he whispered, brushing my lips with his.

"But I need you to hear it."

"You don't have to do this right now, Liv. I know you're hurt and confused."

"But I'm not confused about this. Because you're right. There's no denying the depth and complexity of what just happened. I have no clue what it means for any of us going forward, but I know for certain that I love you, Brighton— even more than I love tulips."

A small smile played on his lips, lighting his eyes even more. But no matter how much I longed to stay and savor the moment, I had to get home and face Ryan and the fallout of our earlier fight. I opened the hidden door, praying Ryan was truly gone. The library was empty, but every step echoed loudly, as if the room now held our secrets. I knew in my heart I wasn't ready to tell Ryan about what had happened yet. Because I knew it would absolutely crush him, and selfishly, I wasn't sure if it would end our marriage.

I needed time to think.

As I left Brighton's house and headed home, I prayed that our transgressions stayed buried between the pages of the books that were shelved around the secret of our deceit.

CHAPTER FORTY-FOUR

Ryan

I HEARD LIV COME home through the sunroom, then the water running through the creaky old pipes as she snuck into the shower. Tears ran down my cheeks into my beard as I pet Stitch on the living room sofa. I looked up at the oversized picture of Olivia and me heading back down the aisle after saying our wedding vows. Olivia's blond hair was captured in flight as the soft breeze came rolling off the lake, lifting it in beautiful repose. Her eyes shone bright as they looked at *me*. Before this summer, her eyes had only ever shone like that for me.

I'd pushed her away, though, with my stupid plan.

I loved Liv with all my heart, but if what my gut was telling me was true, I would be the one broken beyond repair. Because not a single person in this world mattered to me more than her—not even our babies. I knew that was harsh, but I hadn't had time to love them, to know them as intimately as Olivia had, carrying them inside her body.

But I had over eight years to love the woman who was my entire world. Nothing mattered without her. I knew she felt the same way—but dangling Brighton in front of her had been a huge mistake I'd have to live with for the rest of my life. Even so, I wasn't sure I could ever forgive her if she ever chose him over me.

"Ryan?" Olivia was walking around the house, calling out my name as I sat in the dark. It was still light out, but I'd drawn the drapes in our formal living room, needing the privacy and seclusion.

She rounded the corner, wearing a pair of thin cotton pants and a wrap top that hugged her body. All I could see when I looked at her was Brighton's hands on her. Only this time, it didn't turn me on. This time, it made me want to cry.

"What are you doing in here all alone?" she asked, sitting next to me on the couch. At least she didn't smell like him. I would've lost it if she had. She smelled of fresh tangerines and basil from the body wash she favored. It used to turn me on, but now it only covered the deceit I *knew* had happened.

"I came home to apologize, Liv." I looked down at my hands in my lap, twisting my wedding band.

"Ryan, you don't need to. The argument was my fault, too."

"Yeah, but you've done nothing to break my trust, so I shouldn't have accused you of anything."

"I understand though, Ryan. Things have gotten so—complicated, lately. I wish we could turn back time."

I took her hands, noticing the slight shake. "Where would you turn the clock back to if you could? Before Brighton? Or before our first miscarriage?"

Olivia inhaled sharply.

"Because I think I might turn it all the way back to the before. Back when we were Liv and Ry. I miss those crazy kids."

Tears were falling down Olivia's face now, and I reached over and wiped one away.

"Why the tears?"

"Because we can't go back to the way we were, Ryan. That was never the goal. I wish to god things had turned out differently. But I would never give up the short amount of time we had with Laelynn. God just needed our babies in heaven more than we needed them here on earth, I guess."

I squeezed her hand.

"Our relationship was born in grief, Ryan. From the moment my parents died, you were the one there to comfort me. But our love grew out of those ashes, stronger than ever. Taking root in the soil of my pain. When we lost our first baby, grief was a little too comfortable for me. It was easy to go back there and dwell in that space. Then it was one loss after another, making it impossible for me to crawl out of that misery. Grief changed us. There's no denying that. I hate where I was a few months ago.

"But I'm different now, and you are too. There's no magic machine that would take us back to the Liv and Ry we once were. Those people don't exist anymore. My grief and your anger have changed us. Brighton changed us," she whispered.

"So, you wouldn't take any of it back then?"

Olivia shook her head. "As weird as it sounds—no, I wouldn't. I've loved our babies. I love you, and—"

"You love Brighton," I finished for her.

I watched the pain ride across her face, but she didn't deny it. Fresh tears slipped down her cheeks as she bit her bottom lip. "I never asked for this, Ryan."

"No, I was the idiot who got us here."

"Out of love," she said, meeting my eyes. "I know how much you love me. What you did was the bravest thing I could ever imagine to save our marriage."

"Did it work?"

She grew quiet. "I guess we'll see. I do feel happier now."

"You look it," I said sarcastically.

She smiled, placing a hand over her mouth as a nearly hysterical bubble of laughter spilled over.

"Where were you?" I asked quietly. "When I came back to apologize, you were nowhere to be found. Brighton's crew said they thought you were upstairs in the library, but I couldn't find you anywhere."

The nearly inaudible gasp would've slipped by me if I hadn't been looking for it. If I wasn't so good at reading people after so many years of teaching them.

"We—we were supposed to go to the warehouse today, but I was pretty upset after our argument. So, we did go up to the library to talk, and to get something he wanted me to give you—though I accidentally left it at the house," she said, switching gears.

"Then where were you?" I pressed. "Your cars were both still in the driveway, but you weren't here, and I couldn't find you anywhere over there."

She picked at the skin of her cuticles, not meeting my eyes. Then she took a deep breath and finally answered, "We went for a walk. I needed to clear my head, and I couldn't focus on work."

"So you *walked*? With Brighton?"

"Yes. What is this, Ryan? An inquisition?"

"I don't know, Liv. Do you need one? How come you won't meet my eyes?"

"Ryan!" Olivia said and stood up, Stitch bouncing off my lap and following her from the room.

Before she got to the door, I stopped her though, with five simple words.

"Did you sleep with him?"

She placed her hand on the doorframe, pausing before turning back to look at me. Her body was rigid, but I saw the rise and fall of her shoulders.

"Truth, Liv. Did you fuck Kerrington behind my back without me?"

This time, I heard the gasp as loudly as if I'd just struck her.

She turned slowly, her eyes finally meeting mine. They were full of tears, and something else that I couldn't read. Fatigue? Despair? Anger?

The room was deathly silent.

I would wait for her answer.

The truth was the only thing we could always count on between us at the end of the day. She took a deep breath, then squared her shoulders as she met my eyes.

"No, Ryan. I didn't. Are you happy now?"

No.

She actually said no.

I closed my eyes as my heart slowly strangled itself.

"Yeah, Liv. I'm happy now. I finally have the clarity I need."

CHAPTER FORTY-FIVE

Olivia

THEY SAY PAIN ebbs and flows over time, until one day, you find yourself accidentally living in joy again. Then each step from there is a little bit easier. The end goal? Being back to normal, I suppose. Though, in retrospect, what even is normal? Maybe we're all just living lies that no one else is privy to. Someone looking in from the outside at my and Ryan's perfect life—with the white picket fence, the Cavapoo puppy, and the historic home in the city—would only see what we wanted them to.

What they wouldn't see is the layers of secrets we'd started to create in a misguided effort to find joy again. You know how the saying goes—the truth shall set you free.

Here's what I say: SCREW THAT SHIT.

I mean, seriously. Just when I was starting to bloom again, when I *thought* I was finally starting to feel joy—we landed in a bigger pile of manure than we'd started with.

And it all started with the fucking truth.

If Ryan had just left things alone—hadn't *pushed* to know whether I found Brighton attractive, or whether I would've slept with him if we weren't married—maybe our lives would be on a different trajectory.

Instead, the truth hadn't set us free.

It had buried us even deeper until I could no longer see the light of day. Until telling the truth terrified me—because once the truth came to light, I was in jeopardy of losing the last part of my past, and the only thing at the end of the day that still meant something to me.

Myself.

The me I could look at in the mirror with a sure heart, knowing I was trying my hardest, doing my best, and living as closely as I could to love.

These are the thoughts that race through my head at three in the morning. Or when I'm in the shower, the scalding water never hot enough to burn all the memories away. But when I'm in my therapist's office?

That's when they finally come out.

All of them.

All the dirty secrets I'd kept locked inside over the summer.

Ryan doesn't ask me for the truth anymore. In fact, we'd gotten rather good at going back to the way things were during *the before*. Only this time, the before is Brighton.

This time, the only truth pact I have is with my therapist, Dr. Paul.

And, yes, it's the same man Ryan tried to get me to see months ago. He'd been right about so many things. The only thing that kept me from truly healing before were the secrets of my heart that I'd been too afraid to share. Now, after everything we'd been through, I had nothing left to lose.

They say the only way around suffering is to go straight through it.

Well, here I was . . . ready to march right in. Because I knew my joy was just on the other side of it. So, when my therapist asked me why the change of heart, I just smiled and gave him the truth.

"It all started with the Brighton Effect."

If you fell head over heels for Olivia, Ryan, and Brighton's complicated love story, and want to find out what happens next, *flip the page to read the Prologue for The Brighton Effect.*

THE
BRIGHTON
EFFECT

PROLOGUE
Olivia

THE FUNNY THING about a lie is that instead of making you feel better, the truth starts to eat at your soul, demanding you look in the mirror and face it. Until you do, everything in your life, and I mean everything, becomes centered around that lie—and what made you speak the poisonous words to begin with.

For me? It was nothing less than bone-splintering fear.

The lie? One simple word: *No.*

Before that, our eight-year marriage was built on love, respect, and most of all—honesty. When your relationship was born out of grief and slides even deeper into the darkness loss after loss, the only thing that *can* set you free is the truth. It's your lifeline. Your only ray of hope.

Which was why we'd created a truth pact, Ryan and me. It was as sacred as our wedding vows, and maybe even more so because it came after the loss of our first miscarriage. How do you bear such grief? How do you go on? We naively thought if we were one hundred percent honest with one another, that would be enough. That would solve all our misery, like a crutch through the thick pain and muck of heartbreak.

It worked for a while—through another miscarriage. Until, finally, that fragile, false hope we'd shackled around honesty shattered after the loss of our daughter. Stillborn. The truth was, no words, no matter how honest, could bridge the hollow, gaping hole where my heart used to be. The loss of Laelynn obliterated me, until I became so broken, my husband was desperate in his attempts to reach me. To save me. To restore me to the woman he'd fallen in love with. Even if it meant sharing me. But when Brighton Kerrington entered our lives, the truth suddenly became a whole lot more complicated.

"And you fell in love with him?" Dr. Paul asked, reviewing my chart.

"I did," I answered honestly. Because after that one lie burned hot across my tongue, I knew the only way out, was through. Through the darkness that caused me to lie to begin with, betraying myself and all our marriage stood for.

"And do you still love him?"

"I've never stopped."

"How does Ryan feel about this?"

I lifted an eyebrow and glanced at my therapist. "How would Mrs. Paul feel if you fell in love with another woman?"

"Touché," he said. "However, *Mr. O'Brien* would be pretty shocked if I fell in love with a woman, I have to say."

His warm smile helped me relax. "Point taken."

"Why don't we stick to *your* marriage?"

I nodded, picking at the cuticle by my thumb. It was a nasty habit I found myself leaning on when I was uncomfortable. Which was often these days.

"Back to my question. How is Ryan handling all of this?"

"As well as you could expect. He went back to work and is finding excuses to be away from home more."

"Do you think he's avoiding you because he knows you lied?"

"I don't think he knows," I said quietly. "Not for sure."

"Really, Olivia? You don't think he suspects at all?"

I thought back to the subtle ways he'd changed over the last several weeks. How distant he felt, and how our lovemaking had gone from the best it'd ever been to almost nonexistent. It felt as if all the progress we'd made over the summer was disappearing just as quickly as the warm temperature that would soon give way to the bitter cold of winter.

"What would be the worst thing that would happen if you told him the truth?"

Dr. Paul was Ryan's idea to begin with. Four months ago, I'd wanted nothing to do with him. Now, he was my biggest ally and staunchest supporter to heal and get things right this time. I'd failed so epically in handling my grief after losing my babies. In fact, I still had work to do there. But we were tackling one fissure at a time. Because you can't address the foundation when the upper floor is on fire.

My job was to put out the fire and pray that the damage wasn't irreparable. Then address the unstable foundation my life was built on these days. I felt like at any moment, everything would come crashing down again, plunging me back into darkness.

"That he would leave me. That he would stop loving me."

The words crawled over my skin like death itself. For all our troubles, Ryan was my soulmate. There was no two ways about it. Losing Ryan would be like cutting off my oxygen. I wouldn't make it long without him. I wouldn't *want* to.

The only problem was—Brighton was now wedged into my heart, too. It was so strong and palpable that I no longer felt complete without them *both*.

I know "they" say you should be complete all on your own. Here's what I say: SCREW THAT SHIT.

Am I a complete and happy human being without a man? Well, sure. But who really wants to be alone? Not me. The only problem? Now that I've felt the warmth of Brighton being in my life, it was impossible not to want them both. That's not something I've been able to share in those exact words with Ryan. Partly because he's been stuffing down his own pain for so long, that I was afraid one more "truth" might send him overboard. But mostly, it was because I highly doubted his idea of happiness involved having an open marriage. The term itself left an icky taste in my mouth, but at the end of the day, that's all it would boil down to. And Ryan deserved better.

Brighton did, too.

"You need to tell him the truth, Olivia. Your real healing won't begin until you do. Though, I have to say, I'm proud of how much you've opened up since we first started working together."

"Yeah, sorry about that. I was in a place."

"Oh, I remember," he said and chuckled. "While I don't agree with Ryan's methodologies, you do seem happier and more capable of handling whatever comes your way. Including telling Ryan the truth and dealing with the fallout from that, Olivia. You're stronger than you give yourself credit for."

Was I? I wish I had the confidence in myself that Dr. Paul now had. They say the truth shall set you free. I guess we were about to find out.

AFTERWORD

Dear Readers,

Please don't be upset with this cliffhanger! When I was orig-inally plotting out *The Truth Pact*, I had a certain outcome I wanted in my head, and these three kept changing things up on me, keeping me on my toes. Their grief and love were so deeply interwoven in their relationship, making it so much stronger than a "traditional" open relationship. This was never meant to be a ménage story. That's not what *The Truth Pact* is about, other than the shared intimacy that arises from the three of them choosing to try to heal in this way together—and the fallout as a result.

I can't say more about the future of their relationship, just that I'm sorry for having to split their story in two. But I couldn't do it justice trying to rush the ending and cram-ming it into this first book. Too much healing still needed to happen. And as it turns out—everything I thought I knew about their story as the author was nothing at all like what was about to happen.

You see, Ryan, Olivia, and Brighton are so special to me because of how much they pushed me to step out of my comfort zone to tell *their* story the way *they* wanted it told—not how I'd originally planned, or how you might like to see it end. Theirs is a love story that will live on forever, and hopefully they'll hold a piece of your heart too, as they have mine.

I hope you fall in love even harder after reading book two of *The Truth About Love* duet—*The Brighton Effect*. As always, reviews and recommendations are the best way to show a writer how much you enjoyed their book. They help more than you can imagine.

Mad love to each of you!

XOXO, Colleen

ACKNOWLEDGMENTS

There are so many people to thank when it comes to putting a book together. I'd like to give a special shout-out to my longtime editor, Erin Servais, of Dot and Dash, LLC, who has moved from getting her name lopped off over the course of two pages to my numero uno spot—it's kind of the equivalent of getting a chair named after you!

I also couldn't do what I do without the help of my amazing cover designer, Marisa Wesley of Cover Me Darling, LLC, my graphics designer, Kate Farlow of Y'all. That Graphic., my paperback formatter, Stephanie Anderson from Alt 19 Creative, and my proofreader, Denise McGhee. I was also honored to work with Grey's Promotions for this duet—and it was a dream come true! Thanks to all the amazing ladies there for your hard work and support.

An extra special shout-out goes to all my readers, beta readers, my ARC team, my Colleen's Angels VIP Readers' Circle, all the bloggers and bookstagrammers who have shown me their love and support, and all the other authors who support, champion, lift, and inspire me daily to be my best, to grow, and to keep writing!

I would also like to thank a few special people who filled an important role for me with this emotional story. The first is my friend Erin, who acted as my sensitivity reader because of her personal experience with her own stillbirth. She was able to help me better understand the little things someone who has gone through this unimaginable loss *might* think, face, feel, or do. Though every grief process is different, she made it easier for me to hopefully paint a more realistic scenario surrounding Olivia's grief. I truly hope I did her proud, and that I've shed a light on the topic for others.

I also want to thank Erin, Heather, Jackie, and Rorie for being my first ever alpha readers! Woot! I love you ladies so much and appreciate the earliest read-through. I know this book is better and the characters are stronger because of your first reactions and feedback. Thank you for helping me to become a better writer.

Additional thanks also go to Jackie James, my unofficial ARC Angel Supreme (you're way better than a soft taco supreme!). Sometimes it takes a village, and Jackie is one of the founding members of mine.

I'm also forever grateful to now work with Carolina León, who is my personal assistant extraordinaire. While originally finishing edits for *The Truth Pact*, I was also releasing two other books and could hardly keep my head on straight. I don't know what I would've done without you!

Thank you to my ride or dies—Deena, Erin, Heather, Jacque, Jen, and Sheila. Your friendships all mean something different and special to me. But one thing is the same—I will love each of you through the end of time and beyond. I see and know your souls and am so grateful to share this lifetime with you!

An extra special heap of love to Heather, who sat and listened to me bleed my heart out about Ryan and Olivia and the crazy ideas I had about how to end their love story. After a big brainstorming sesh—and a lot of excited encouragement and understanding—she helped me realize one book just wouldn't do the story the justice it deserved. That's how *The Truth Pact* became a duet, and *The Brighton Effect* was born. I adore your heart, brain, creativity, passion, kindness, and friendship. Thank you for being my ear, a rock in my life, and a positive inspiration. (Not to mention the hours you agonized over cover ideas with me!)

I also want to thank my kids, who are beyond understanding when mommy goes into her "writing cave" with her earphones on—lost in a world of make-believe. Especially when I was supposed to be "off" this fall, but Liv and Ry's story wouldn't let me rest until I got it down. I wouldn't be the woman I am today without my two "babies." I'm so grateful you both made me a mother and helped grow my heart three sizes bigger. Keep being the awesome individuals you are. I hope someday you chase your own dreams just as hard.

I always save the best for last—my rock, D. We don't need a truth pact to know there is no one else for us than what we find in each other. I got lucky that I found my soulmate in you. But even if I hadn't, I would wait lifetimes until I found you and we were reunited once again. Thank you for holding me when the depth and heaviness of this book got too much for me to bear. For understanding that my characters are just as real for me as my living, breathing friends, so when their hearts are getting raked over the coals, mine is too. Thanks for always giving me a safe place to land, and for encouraging me to face my fears and write it anyway. I don't know what I did to deserve you, but you're my proof that there is a god—and that she's probably a woman with the biggest heart I could ever imagine. She keeps bringing me you, after all.

A SPECIAL SUPPORT
MESSAGE FOR READERS

Dear Readers,

As you can imagine, *The Truth Pact* was difficult for me to write because it's so different from any of my other books. It's all about THE FEELS, on every single page. My author tagline is "sexy and flirty, sweet and dirty" for a reason. But *The Truth Pact* has a whole different layer of complexity to unravel and was unlike anything I'd ever tackled. It was often gut wrenching for me to crawl into it every day—even as I couldn't stay away from it—because Olivia and Ryan's story was *that* compelling for me to write. I literally lived and breathed their pain and growth every time I dove deeper into their story.

That said, I knew I needed extra help to make sure I captured even a fraction of the grief someone may experience when they live through the losses that Olivia has. Luckily, my dear friend Erin offered to help me through some of the harder details that accompany the loss of a child due to stillbirth. Though I wasn't friends with her at the time when she delivered her daughter, Kailey, I met her soon after while she was working through her grief and leaning on KinderMourn to help her through the worst of it. She was kind and brave enough to share some of the little, important details that parents suffering this type of loss might experience. Things that make Olivia's experience even more real, and that I couldn't have dreamed up on my own. For that, and her friendship in general, I am forever grateful.

If you are in Charlotte, North Carolina, KinderMourn is an amazing resource to reach out to if you have experienced the loss of a child. They can be found at:

kindermourn.org.

Additionally, they share a list of resources if you are a parent dealing with grief at:

kindermourn.org/copy-of-grieving-parents.

Just know there are many national organizations that can help so you don't have to suffer alone.

I'd like to leave you with this special quote for all parents who have experienced the heartache of a precious, angelic stillborn baby. My heart holds yours in your loss with deepest love.

XOXO, Colleen

"You were born silent.

Perfect and beautiful.

Still loved.

Still missed.

Still remembered.

Every day.

Stillborn.

But *still* born."

—Michelle Salisbury

BOOKS BY C.M. ALBERT

ARDEN'S GLEN ROMANCE SERIES
Faith in Love
Proof of Love
Visions of Love

LOVE IN LA QUARTET
Book 1: *The Stars in Her Eyes*

CONSUMED SERIES
Book 1: *Consumed by Love*

STAND-ALONE BOOKS
Last Night in Laguna
The White Room

COCKY HERO CLUB
Mister Stand-In

THE TRUTH ABOUT LOVE DUET
The Truth Pact
The Brighton Effect

ABOUT THE AUTHOR

USA Today bestselling author C.M. Albert writes heartwarming romances that are "sexy and flirty, sweet and dirty!" Her writing infuses a healthy blend of humor, high-heat romance, and most of all—hope. When not writing, or kid-wrangling with her handsome hubby, she's either meditating, kayaking, reading, hugging a tree, or asleep. But first, coffee. #TonyStarkForever

JOIN C.M. ALBERT ONLINE AT:

WEBSITE: colleenalbert.com
FACEBOOK: facebook.com/cmalbertwrites
READER GROUP: facebook.com/groups/ColleensAngels
INSTAGRAM: instagram.com/cmalbertwrites
TWITTER: twitter.com/colleenmalbert
TIKTOK: vm.tiktok.com/ZMJpyfT6C
GOODREADS: goodreads.com/cmalbert
BOOKBUB: bookbub.com/profile/c-m-albert
PINTEREST: pinterest.com/cmalbertwrites
NEWSLETTER: subscribepage.com/w5x4p1

www.ingramcontent.com/pod-product-compliance
Lightning Source LLC
Chambersburg PA
CBHW031619100726
47898CB00006B/1859